Hey

MW00962617

A Novel

Stephen Williams

Hey Kid

With exception of historical facts, the names, characters and incidents are a product of the author's imagination and are used fictitiously. Any resemblance to any person living or deceased is entirely coincidental.

ISBN-13: 978-1976181238
ISBN-10: 1976181232

Dedication

This book is dedicated to my wonderful wife Janet who has always been there to support me and to my Son Mark, my Daughter Victoria, and my Daughter-in-Law Shawna. No man could be blessed with a more incredible family. I love you all very much

Prologue

Hey Kid is a story of a young boy born in the wartime East End of London. It's a story of his experiences, and those of his family, during and after WWII and continuing in to the late 1950's.
It was a time when society was starting to radically change and "Baby Boomers" were being born. Their impact on society would be massive in years to come.

The previous generation had been locked in the Edwardian era but two World Wars in three decades changed all that. They were a generation who lost their youth and provided us with the freedom we still enjoy today, for which history shall remember them and we shall be eternally grateful.
Social changes were happening, such as workplace equity, which was in its infancy and immigration was at an all time high.

Growing up in London's East End was a journey that allowed the people living there to witness the many changing images of society from immigration of the masses to the acknowledgement of changing lifestyles, equality and labour issues and the rebuilding of one of the biggest cities in the world. It was like looking through a kaleidoscope of life.

The story of George Rudge is of one young man and his family, of loss, love, failure, and success. It's a story of many people of post war London and it is a reflection of the times and the changes of the new post-war era.

The Early Years
1939-44

1939-44

The dreary Victorian terraced row houses with their black slate roofs and red clay pot chimney's spewing out a thick, dirty grey smoke that filled the sky emanating from the coal burning fireplaces were a common site in London before the Second World War. The smoke often resulted in an ugly thick, choking smog, locally known as a "peasouper," that would blanket large areas of the city in the winter months, so thick that you could easily walk past someone less than two or three feet away and not even know they were there. In addition you could become the ungrateful owner of a cough that would sound like a steam train chugging loudly out of the station and it would leave you spewing a nasty green, spit filled residue originating from your now smoke filled lungs.

The East End of London was an industrial hub and very, very working class. It was home to the docks, industrial factories, street markets that sold everything from food to clothes at a cut price rate and the area also housed the biggest knackers yard in London.

It was the home to hundreds of small dismal, soulless Victorian terraced houses that were usually no larger than about 700 square feet. The terraced buildings were crammed together like the illegal possessions in a smugglers trunk with no room to spare but they often housed families of up to eight or even more.
Most homes had running cold water, an outside toilet and a tin bath that graced almost every back yard as it hung on an old rusty nail that had been pounded into the brick wall outside the back door.

The cold, dingy, uninviting metal container would make its entrance into the house on a Friday night or a Sunday afternoon for the weekly tradition of "family bath time."

The matriarch would be responsible for the hot water, which would be boiled on the gas cooker and emptied into the dismal metal receptacle that was already half full of cold water ready to welcome and cleanse the inhabitants.

It was usually the master of the house who got to bathe first and the water was topped up for the next in line, usually the mother, and the performance would continue until everyone was thoroughly cleansed, if using carbolic soap in dirty water can be called cleansing. After the weekly ritual was concluded they were all ready for the upcoming week.

The grungy dirty water was tipped out into the back yard where it would make its way like a polluted river meandering to the outside drain, leaving a messy soap stained trail that would often remain until the rain came and washed it away.

The gas and electricity supply to the houses were metered but the residents couldn't be trusted to meet a monthly or quarterly financial obligation so a pay-as-you-go method was initiated. Utilities were paid for by putting a shilling a time in the meter whenever it ran out. It wasn't unusual to go without one or even both utilities a day or two before payday, which meant living by candlelight and eating jam or spam sandwiches until there was money to feed the meter monster once again.

The meters would be emptied several times a year and that was the job of the "Meter Man," the Gas Board or Electricity Board employee who had the key to the meters "money box." That was a time that was welcomed by the children as well as the adults. There was often a small refund after the meter was read, as much as four or five shillings sometimes, and if the children were lucky, very lucky, they may get a penny liquorice or some equally enticing treat bought for them.

The meters were housed in a small cupboard in the front room of the house, a room that was usually kept as a "best room" regardless of the appalling lack of space in the rest of the house. The front room was kept in prestigious condition, so much so that a ritzy West Ender would have been proud to have been welcomed by it.

It was the room that often housed a nice sofa and chair, accompanied by a small table that would be decorated with ornaments, such as a vase, family memorabilia and old photographs. It was really a futile attempt to move up in class and show everyone that the space meant nothing and its contents were a show of an imagined, or desired wealth and a direct link to the to the Victorian era of yesteryear. Of course it didn't really matter what was in there as the room was rarely, if ever, used!

Nick and Doris Rudge lived in such a terraced house on Wightman Street in Canning Town close to the Royal Docks. Both of their families had lived in the area for generations and they had lived at number 24 since they were married almost 11 years earlier.

Doris had given birth to their three children there as well. Louise 9, Joe 8, and Rose 6 all shared the two-bedroomed house that Nick had cleverly converted to a three-bedroomed abode, three very small bedrooms.
The largest of the rooms was the master bedroom, which contained a bed, a wardrobe and dressing table with a cracked mirror hanging on the wall above it.
Next was the girl's room, which had two small beds, a chest of drawers and a small rope that ran the length of the room and supported several coat hangers which held a mixture of dresses and "Sunday best" clothes.
Joe's room was the smallest. One bed, no window and a door-less wardrobe complete with mismatched shelves that were home to all his worldly belongings.

It was the same in most of the houses in the area.
People were poor but always willing to work and they supported each other in times of need. It was a tough hard working life but it was all they had ever known.

Hey Kid

It was September 3rd, 1939, on a sunny warm morning when the Rudge family, including Nick's parents Harriet and Tom, and Doris' parents Fred and Rachelle, were sitting huddled around the old arch shaped wooden Marconi radio eagerly awaiting the Prime Ministers message. That day almost everyone in Britain was waiting in trepidation to hear the broadcast.

The Prime Minister, Neville Chamberlain, was to make an announcement about what was happening in Europe. The Germans had invaded Czechoslovakia a few days earlier and now they were in Poland. Everyone was talking about it and acknowledging that there were problems brewing in Europe yet again, though it's doubtful anyone could have imagined how big those problems would become in the next few years. An anxious uneasy tension filled the air with everyone wondering what would happen next. Neville Chamberlain and his government had issued an ultimatum to the German Chancellor and now the response was due.

At precisely 11.15 a.m. the Prime Minister interrupted the regular broadcast with a message that would go down in history forever:

"This morning the British Ambassador in Berlin handed the German Government a final note stating that, unless we heard from them by 11 o'clock that they were prepared at once to withdraw their troops from Poland, a state of war would exist between us.

I have to tell you now that no such undertaking has been received, and that consequently this country is at war with Germany."

Some 12 minutes later air raid sirens unleashed their loud eerie alarm that sounded like it had whined its way down a tunnel and spewed noisily out of the exit. Unlike the many tests that had been sounded before this one was different. This time the sirens announced to everyone that Britain, for the second time in just 25 years was at war with Germany. There had been so many tests of the warning system before but this time it was finally for real.

Workers started protecting important buildings with sandbags that had been prepared just in case war would become a reality. Gas masks quickly became a requirement for everyone and within a very short time thousands of children were to be evacuated from London and other major cities. The government had put their plans in place for evacuating children from major cities and "Operation Pied Piper" went into affect on September 9th.

Nick and Doris Rudge had made arrangements for their children a few weeks earlier, fearing the worse, with Nick's uncle Bob who was an Estate Warden for a wealthy family in Oxfordshire. As much as they didn't want to split the family up they knew what they had to do. Nick took a rare day off work to take his children to Paddington station with Doris on the following Monday morning.

Together as a family they boarded one of the busses on Victoria Dock Road and after a couple of changes they would eventually end up at Paddington station where the children would board the train going to Banbury, Oxfordshire.

The crowds at Paddington station were not nearly as bad as expected. A lot of children had been evacuated in the preceding two days and within less than two hours the Rudge children were sporting labels attached to their duffle coats with their name and destination on them and they were loaded on the Banbury bound train.

Hey Kid

Tears and indescribable feelings of loss and sadness were the norm for both parents and children but knowing London was Hitler's major target most families reluctantly sent their offspring to a safer place and sadly, for some children it would be the last memory of one or both of their parents.

With the children safe and away from the bombings Nick now had a decision to make. Should he join up now or should he wait and see wait happened?

Nick's younger brother Tommy had joined the Royal Marines about six months earlier. He knew that at 24 years of age and single he would be amongst the first to get called up anyway if war did break out. He didn't have what could be considered a good job as a factory labourer so he decided to join the Marines. He thought that it may even be a good career for him. Doris' younger brother, Harry had also joined up several months ago and he was now in the Royal Navy.

London wasn't being bombed that September though the German planes started bombing runs shortly after and within a year the Dock's became a major target for Hitler's Luftwaffe.

For now the evacuation of the children from major cities had gone as planned and the British Expeditionary Forces were mobilised to protect the borders around France and Belgium. Many were saying the war would be over by Christmas and the Germans would pull back their army but it wasn't to be.

The children were still in Oxfordshire over the holidays so the childless Christmas celebrated was very different from previous years. Doris' parents, Rachelle and Fred and Nick's parents, Harriet and Tom were the only ones sitting around the table with Doris and Nick. That Christmas was very different day and none of them knew when they would all be together as a family again.

Hey Kid

Nick made his decision and waited until the New Year to enlist. In January he signed up and he was soon off to Chatham for training with the Royal Navy.

He returned home twice before he was shipped out and on his second return Doris greeted him with a huge, unexpected surprise. She was pregnant but now they had no idea where Nick would be when the baby was born.

It was later in January 1940 when Doris was eventually able to get time and visit the children in Banbury. Of course they all wanted to come home, but the decision was made for them and they would stay in Oxfordshire until it was clear what was happening.

Doris told them that their dad had joined the navy to help with the war and he wouldn't be home for a while either. Although they didn't fully understand the dangers of war they were very proud of Nick for joining up and Joe said that with his dad, uncle Tommy and uncle Harry fighting, the Germans didn't stand a chance!

Doris returned to London and carried on working. She was close to both sets of parents and they would often all be together to listen to the news broadcasts and they all hoped that the war would soon end.

George Nicholas Rudge made his entrance into the East End of war torn London in the early hours one morning in July 1940. Doris's mum Rachelle had been staying overnight for a few days and was waiting in the living room, ready with the hot water and towels. Old Mrs Ketchum, the matriarch grandmother of the street was also there, keeping her company.

At about 5.30 they heard the wailing noise of a new born baby and the Midwife came out an announced, "It's a boy, and a blooming big one with lots of hair too." There were of course smiles all around as Rachelle and Mrs Ketchum went in to take over the dowager duties as the smiles and the congratulations continued as visitors came by over the next day or two.

Doris was holding on to her new son and smiled as she said, "George, I'm going to call him George after the King and Nicholas after his dad."

With both sets of grandparents living close by Doris had lots of help but she was still missing the children and now she wondered if she should evacuate to Oxford to be with them. After a lot of thought she decided to stay and at least she wouldn't be alone. It was a close family with Nick's dad Tom and Doris' dad Fred served in the Essex Regiment together in WWI and they had been friends for years. They were also both part time Air Raid Wardens, a job they took seriously but always seemed to wind up with a pint in the local pub unless they were on shift work.

Tom worked at the Iron Foundry and had been there since he was a boy, except for the break of last war. Fred, like Tom, had also worked most of his life for one company as well, the local glass factory, Canning Town Glass Works. No matter how the shifts worked out here was never a week that went by when they didn't share a pint in one of the pubs.

With George being looked after by both sets of Grandparent's while she was working Doris was able to take different shifts at work. She had worked at Tate & Lyle up until she had the George but now there had been a huge evacuation of the Expeditionary Forces from Dunkirk. It meant that the war was picking up speed and an invasion was now imminent. The biggest need now was for the war effort so she took a job in a factory that made parts for military vehicles.

Hey Kid

Doris heard very little from Nick during the year and any letter she did receive was usually censored so she had no idea where he was or what he was doing.

It was the same with Tommy and Harry, though they did know that Harry was now somewhere in the Pacific region so for sure he wouldn't be coming home any time soon.

In the summer of 1940 the Luftwaffe started to send fighter planes over Britain and the Battle of Britain began. Dog -fights in the air became a daily event and on one occasion when a German plane was shot down the pilot parachuted into a Farmer's field in Banbury. The children watched as the local men captured him and marched him through the town where the Army took over. After a couple of months the war in the air seemed to ease off but then the bombings started.

On September 7th that year the bombings over London started in full force they and became a nightly event with thousands made homeless and the Dock's, as predicted became the main target for the German bombers. There was no way now that the children could come home but George was there in the care of one set or another of grandparents much of the time. No one really wanted a baby there when bombs were falling and Fred tried to convince his daughter to join the children in Banbury, but she stayed and continued to work at the factory.

There were many near misses, but Doris, George and his grandparents seemed to have luck on their side as their homes were missed by the bombs, though not by much. Sadly old Mrs Willoughby's house behind Tom and Harriet's received a direct hit and everyone inside was killed instantly. By December the bombings had lessened a little and Doris was making plans to go and see the children.

She desperately wanted to go and see them at Christmas but it didn't work out so the second childless Christmas, with the exception of George, sadly and quietly came and quietly went.

Hey Kid

With so many people affected she couldn't get time off very easily but she eventually did get to take George to meet his brother and sisters in January.

Doris took George on the train to Banbury and stayed three days. Louise and Rose made a big fuss about holding their new brother and feeding him but Joe wasn't quite as sure about babies and all he said was "He don't 'alf 'av a pair of lungs on him making all that racket!"

That would be Doris' last visit until the school year was over and at the end of term she would have the children return to London. There were still bombings but they had subsided a bit and quite a few parents were bringing their children home.

The children came back in July and Doris was at Paddington with both grandmothers and George to meet them. All three of the children were really happy to be back after so long away from home. As much as Banbury was a nice place and Uncle Bob took good care of them it still wasn't home.

Joe was soon off with his mates and he was as happy as a pig in mud when his lifetime best buddy had come back to London as well. Joe and Alfie (Tubby) Henderson were only three days apart in age and had been best mates since they could talk. Up until the evacuation they had been in every class at school together and had never missed a birthday party for each other until the evacuation separated them.

In September it was back to school. All three of the children attended Ravenscroft Junior School on Denmark Street. The school that they went to before, St. John's was gone, destroyed in the first month of the bombings.

The bombs had somehow missed Ravenscroft but the houses opposite from Croft Road right up to the old Blacksmith's were now just a pile of rubble, fenced off with wire and warning signs about the danger of unexploded bombs.

Hey Kid

The classes in the school had children of varying ages and they also had drills twice a week on how to put on a gas mask and where to get to if there was an air raid.

Louise, the oldest, and Joe, a year younger, were in the same class. Rose was the youngest and she was in Miss Weir's class. She didn't mind at all being separated from her older brother and sister, she enjoyed not being told what to do all the time by both of them.
There were continuing air raids and the sound of fire engines and ambulances were an everyday occurrence but school went on as normal as it could in the circumstances.
The kids carried their gas masks to and from school but if they went out to play somewhere they always "forgot" them.

A Christmas card came in December that had been so censored all Doris could read was "Miss you and the kids, Love you all N."
They had even blacked out his whole name.
This Christmas would be different. The children would be home for it for the first time since the war started.

George was now walking with great success and he quickly became the centre of attention, especially with Louise who treated him like he was a live figure of her dolls! Rose pulled her weight as well but Joe always seemed to be off somewhere with Tubby and they were often found with Granddad Fred. Fred also had a small allotment and he grew quite a few vegetables to share with the family and it seemed to be a great meeting place for the kids as well.

Food was rationed and in short supply but somehow, Fred always seemed to have a good cache of fresh eggs and other food items from somewhere. He would say they were "surplus to requirements." Probably best not to ask! At least they didn't go hungry surplus food seemed to always be handy!.

Hey Kid

Even war seemed to have its routine.

The war carried on through the year and seemed like it would never end, never knowing when or where the next bomber would distribute its deadly load amongst the populous.

The children still went to school on a regular basis and attended classes that had varying age groups but Louise still managed to get into Grammar school and Joe eventually went to a Secondary Technical School hoping he could at least learn a trade.

Letters from Nick were as rare as ever but in 1943 Tommy came home. He had been wounded and had a couple of operations before arriving back in England. Tom and Harriet threw a party for their youngest son and gave him a real hero's welcome.

Unfortunately, Tommy's injuries were more serious than anyone realised at first. He had survived an explosion but it was a serious head injury. He would never be the same or be able to work again.
He started to experience a lot of problems, like having fits and suffering from insomnia, often followed by some very serious headaches. It had been almost a year since he was injured and eventually he was sent to a Military hospital in Birmingham for treatment.

It was a traumatic time for Harriet and Tom as they could think of nothing but the worst as their lives seemed to be one of unfair and incomprehensible misery. They would catch the train and visit Tommy as often as they could but they feared he would never be the same again.

Their fears unfortunately would come true and Tommy never returned from Birmingham. Eight months and several more operations later he passed away quietly in his sleep.

Hey Kid

George was of course too young to know what was happening but he could sense the sadness that engulfed the family and the grandchildren saw their granddad Tom cry for the first time.

George didn't know at the time but Tom and Harriet had lost four brothers between them in WWI and also a daughter who died when she was only four years old. Now all they had left was Nick and no one even knew where he was.

It was a sad time but the family rallied around and life went on, but it was never the same for Harriet and Tom. George would say later in life that his first memory was of that time and seeing, or more likely feeling a painful sadness in the family.

As the year grew on Doris would hang her head and fight back the tears as the postman failed to deliver a letter from Nick. It had been almost three months and there had been nothing. It would be a few more months before the odd letter would come but at least when they did finally come Doris knew Nick was still alive.

Life for families at home everywhere was hard, even devastating at times. The resilience of the human spirit was often tested but never broken in those war torn times.

Fred and Tom were working and Doris was still helping to churn out "war parts" at the factory. The children were being looked after by Harriet, or Rachelle much of the time and they were also becoming quite independent, sometimes cleaning, cooking for themselves and helping out around the house.

Joe was still off with his mates, especially on a Saturday morning when they could go to watch the pictures at the Odeon. It cost three pence on a Saturday morning but only one of them would pay. Once inside the designated payer would make their way to a pre-arranged emergency exit location inside and let the others in for free. They had to be quick and were almost caught a couple of times but as soon as they mingled with the rest of the audience the game was over and they had won. Free movies!

The war had become the norm in an uneasy way. Everyone knew someone who had been killed, injured, or captured and although good news was always talked about with smiles and laughter, bad news had also become a way of life.

Letters from Harry to Fred and Rachelle came about three times a year and it was obvious that he was still somewhere in the Pacific, but there was little more news than that. Like Doris, Harriet and Tom had very little correspondence from Nick and even though Tommy had been gone for more than a year the loss was still felt very heavily and the fear of losing their only remaining child was a heavy load on both of them.

October 1944

George was four years old in October 1944 when there was a rather loud "rat-tat-tat" at the front door.

A strong knock on a Saturday morning gave rise to the thought that someone was delivering a telegram and Harriet, who was visiting, looked at Doris nervously and went to answer it. Her stomach was churning like a small puddle was trying to become lake and she was praying it wouldn't be a telegram. The thoughts running through her mind were all about what she would say to Doris if it was a telegram and she was shaking so much she could hardly turn the door knob.

Hey Kid

Harriet paused for a second then reluctantly opened the door. Her eyes grew to the size of a couple of saucers, accompanied with a mouth that opened so wide she could have stuffed a Granny Smith apple in and still had room for more. In front of her stood Nick with his finger up to his smiling lips to tell her to hold her silence. All she could do was nod, smile, cry a little, and shake like a leaf as put her arms around him.

A voice came from the kitchen "Who is it Mum?"
Harriet gargled a reply in a mumbling, blubbering fashion "You, you better come here Doris." She stammered.

Doris felt her knees weaken and almost buckle as the thought of bad news rushed through her mind like a storm ripping through a bed of flowers. It was a telegram she thought. She knew it was. She got up smartly but quickly so as not to arouse any fear or worry in the children that something could be wrong and she was shaking like a soaking wet dog that had come in from a thunderstorm.

As she entered the hallway she saw Nick standing there with a grin as big as the proverbial Cheshire cat and she started to shake even more. She laughed, cried and as she ran towards him she yelled out to the children "It's dad, it's your dad" and she leapt forward and flung her arms around him, holding him so tight she could have got on the professional wrestling circuit with that strong Bear Hug.

The tears of joy were flowing down her face and the intelligible words were spluttering out of her mouth in such a rambling manner that the language could easily have been taken as Chinese or double Dutch if anyone had heard her. The three eldest kids run out screaming "Dad, dad," and it was a homecoming that would be the best memory for all of them for the rest of their lives.

After a minute or so the screaming quietened down along with the hugs and laughter and Nick looked along the passage to see a somewhat confused and almost forgotten little boy standing with a look of wonderment on his face.

George had only ever seen the pictures of Nick that Doris showed him so many times and heard the stories about him from everyone else. But to him "Dad" was still an almost fictional character who only existed in photographs and tales. He had never actually thought of his dad as being real.

The kids all parted as Nick got down on one knee and held his arms out towards the son he had never seen. He smiled at George, who was coaxed by Louise, and George cautiously and slowly, wearing an unsure look on his face, slowly moved forward.

"Come here George," said Nick in a voice that was deep but soft and loving and also trembling as he fought back his own tears of happiness. "Come here George, I'm your Dad."

As George got close enough Nick picked him up and George instinctively put his arms around his father's neck for the first time. It was a scene that brought tears and smiles to everyone and that second the bond between father and son was sealed right there and then.

Nick was on leave and back on home soil for the first time in almost four years. He told the kids all kinds of stories, naturally with some amazing Rudge embellishment, and made it all sound like the war was a minor incident that was going on out there and laughed as he said, "We're kicking Adolph's arse so hard every day he has to stand up when he poop's."

Within no time the homecoming celebration was really taking place. Nick was to stay home until almost the end of November and because he would be leaving again they celebrated an early Christmas that year. Fred, not unsurprisingly, "found" a huge turkey, some beer, several bottles of wine, and a Christmas cake!

Rachelle, Fred, Harriet, and Tom were there for the whole day though for Harriet and Tom it was a mixture of happiness and sadness. Two sons had gone to war and only one returned but at least they were still able to share this Christmas with Nick and celebrate the memory of Tom.

George and the other kids looked on at Grandmother Rachelle as she light all the candles in her funny candlestick holder, the one she always kept in the front room on the fireplace and everyone had to be quite for a minute while she said a blessing but when that was done there was nothing but smiles and lots of chatter as the food hit the table.

It may have been November but it was one of the best Christmas days in history.

1945

The war was coming to an end but Nick had only made two visits home by February and then he was gone again and Doris had no idea where to. This time though she knew in her heart that he would return safe. She told herself that so much it just had to happen!

Both Granddads Fred and Tom were still doing night patrols in the Home Guard but most of the checks they were doing were taking place in the Trossachs pub on Barking Road or the Queen Victoria on Star Lane.

Louise was to stay on at school taking extra classes to become a nursing student but Joe, who had learned a lot at the technical school, was unable to get a part time job in any trade and would pick up a few hours each week delivering parcels for the Post Office for a short time. Rose was 12 years old and still had three or four years left in her education.
George was five years old this year and though he had spent most days with Harriet or Rachelle while Doris was working every day things would change in September when he started school.

In May the war in Europe was over and huge celebrations were held all over the country. Within weeks some of the men who were friends and neighbours before the war had returned home but for others their return home was much longer. And some never came home at all.

The war was still going on in the Pacific but that wouldn't last much longer either. They had heard from Harry and the news reports were that the allies were winning the battles against Japan and victory was not that far away.

Everyone had a story to tell and now it was as if the bad times were fading quickly into the past. One of the consequences of war was soldier's coming to experience emotions that ranged from happiness to grief. Men were returning every day and some families were being reunited whilst others had been destroyed and there was no family to come home to.

Nick was in Scotland and hadn't been demobbed. He was hoping to be home for George's first day of school but that wasn't to be either. Unfortunately the wheels of Naval bureaucracy turned as slow as a sloth wearing ankle weights.

George started at the Creedon Road Infant School in September. It was a strange day for him and he didn't know a soul in his class. He really felt out of place. He didn't like his teacher very much either, Miss Casey. She was short and stout with black curly hair and a mole on her face with hairs growing out of it. George's first impression of her was that she was a witch in disguise who had been sent by some foul organisation to steal children!

Everything went reasonably well for the first two or three days but then George soon started to get bored and he would pretend to fall asleep at his desk. He was given a book to test his reading skills but they weren't very good, despite his sisters trying to teach him over the last year. Rose had tried but Louise was softer and would often read the books to him more than try to teach him to read for himself.

Rather than admit he couldn't read the words like most of the other kids did he decided to look at the pictures in the book and make up his own story. When the teacher wasn't impressed and gave him a telling off he looked up at her and calmly said, "I don't like you."
That really set the tone for George's first year at school!

By the end of the first term George had the dubious honour of being dubbed the class clown. Notes were often sent home on a regular basis about his mischievous behaviour and his lack of attention in class. Doris was far from happy with what she was hearing.

Louise would make excuses for her little brother and offered to help him learn to read better and to become more appropriate at school. She persevered with him but it was a task much harder than she ever imagined.

Nick was eventually given extended leave in early December and would be demobbed in the new-year and it was no surprise that Fred came up with another magnificent feast for Christmas Day once again. Christmas celebrations were held as a family in peacetime for the first time in George's life, and just like before the war everyone huddled around the radio and listened to the Kings Christmas day message.

There was no Tommy or Harry present but glasses were raised, several times, in memory of Tommy and to the time Harry would return safely home as well.

For Harriet and Tom it was a sombre time as their loss continued to haunt them but they knew that Christmas was a special time for the family and they too celebrated with the kids the best they could. Gifts may have been sparse but the company, like the food was as good as ever.

The war was over, times had changed and next year would be the beginning of a new era with a whole new future to build.

The Post War years

1946

As the New Year started so too did the news for the Rudge family. Harry had written to say he was remaining in Australia as an attaché at the British Consulate in Canberra for at least the next year. The war was over down there too and he was looking at staying in the Navy as a full time career. There was lots of work left to do in the Pacific theatre as well. At least that's what Harry said. Doris said she thought he had met a girl there and that's the real reason why he wanted to stay.

It was early in the New Year when Louise announced to everyone that she had a boyfriend, which came as no surprise to anyone. She had been seen with Frank Foxton on a lot of occasions recently and Granddad Tom had been teasing her for quite sometime about how cute Frank was and Louise would blush every time Frank's name was mentioned.

Joe was 15 years old this year and looking forward to leaving school. The all knowing, granddad Fred had already arranged a job for him at Lampson Paragon, the bookbinding factory, if he wanted it. Fred had some good contacts there, but then again it seemed like Fred had good contacts everywhere!

School resumed in January and both Louise, who was in Grammar school and Joe, who went to Technical school were in their last year. Joe would take up the job at Paragon in August and Louise would spend the next two years at nursing school. Rose was still at Grammar school and George was back for his incarceration at the much dreaded and much detested prison known as Creedon Road school.

Early in the year Doris, like many others, had her hours cut at work so she applied for, and got a second job at the Trebor sweet factory in Plaistow.

Hey Kid

The war was over but with so many returning soldiers there wasn't enough jobs to go round and many people found themselves without employment, taking whatever work they could get when they could get it.

Nick would take George to school some days and then he would go looking for work. He had worked at Canning Town Glass Works with Fred before the war but they had been badly damaged in the bombings and were only running at about 40% capacity. His job just wasn't there anymore. It was the same story for so many who returned but at least the docks had started to hire so Nick tried his luck there.

Both Tom and Fred had a little influence with some friends and by June Nick started as a dock labourer. They were known as "Dockers" and it was hard labour intensive work unloading ships cargo manually. But it was paying work and to Nick that was all that mattered.

Little was seen of Louise most days as she was either studying or with Frank Foxton. When she was home she would get teased with Nick asking all sorts of embarrassing questions. Louise would blush very easily and say very little but as Frank was well liked it was all taken in good humour. She still had time to spoil her baby brother and would even take George along when she was seeing Frank sometimes as well.

Joe was doing okay at Paragon but he knew it wouldn't be a job forever. He was only 15 years old but he was determined to find a real job and meaningful career, he just didn't know what yet. Rose was the quite, smart one getting on with school and doing her chores at home. In her spare time she was content just to play with a few friends or read a book.

George however, was still very mischievous and was often in trouble at school. The favourite comments from the teachers were that he talks too much, doesn't listen and doesn't pay attention. He was however, very good at picking up things when he wanted to and he could now read very well for his age. His sense of humour was unfortunately a sore point for some of the teachers as he not only had a smart remark to make several times a day but he had a habit of laughing out loud at his own jokes as well!

The first year of school finished in July and everyone had somehow managed to survive George's pranks and warped sense of humour, as well as his smart arsed attitude. There was no doubt that Miss Casey was happy to see the last of him in her class.

There were six weeks of summer holiday but there was to be no more than a couple of days here and there for going away anywhere, unlike some families who managed to go away for a whole week or even two. A day at Southend-on-Sea or at Clacton was about all any of the family would get that year.

September meant the same school once again for George but luckily a different teacher. The wicked witch was no longer and now a very young Miss Hart would be the homeroom teacher. She was far more patient than George's last teacher and he couldn't get under her skin at all, though not for the lack of trying. Miss Hart took everything George could throw at her with a pinch of salt. Even when she made George stand silently in the corner she never raised her voice at all. On the plus side she would often laugh at some of George's silly jokes, which is something that never happened in his last class. It was a minor miracle but not one note was sent home the whole term.

For George school was more a punishment than a privilege as he suffered his unfairly imposed sentence. He would walk sadly to his daily unjust mistreatment like the Hebrew slaves toiling the heavy rocks across the desert to build the Pyramids. Every day was a new sentence to him, which was a cruel injustice and unwarranted but not one adult would ever listen to his pleas of abuse and he was destined to get an education.

Hey Kid

It was Christmas time again, "Right on time, just like last year." as Fred would say.
Christmas day was an almost identical repeat of past years, except that right after dinner this year Louise was gone, abandoning George and her family to spend time with Frank.

There were presents for everyone but only one gift each and there were no gifts exchanged beyond the smiles and hugs between Nick and Doris. Money was tight, but thanks once again to Fred, the food was plentiful.

Just before the New Year made its entrance Nick and Doris received a letter from the Council housing department. They were to be relocated as some new temporary Nissen huts that had been built and the Council were moving many of the local residents into them.
A lot of houses were being demolished to make way for new structures and their house was to be one of them. The whole of Wightman Street was going to be razed to the ground, along with the streets either side, and new homes built. Tom said he heard that they were even putting inside toilets in the new homes when they were built.

Nick had lived on that street or close by all his life and now the Rudge family had spent the last Christmas in the house where all the kids were born and where Nick and Doris had lived in since they got married.

The Docklands were menagerie of races, religions, and colours and at one time there was work and housing for them all but the war had changed that for everyone. For Nick and Doris and for all their neighbours their one time poor but happy streets were to make room for a new development. Later, they were to witness the demolition of the houses they had spent much of their lives in and though they knew it was for the best it was still a heart breaking experience. The black slate roofs and the red chimneypots, along with the crumbling, old, sandy

Hey Kid

bricks were smashed into smithereens as the cacophony of huge, loud bulldozers rumbled through the once full of life streets indiscriminately demolishing everything in their path. Now the one-time residents were left with nothing but memories, good and bad and the final sad memory was to be one of a pile of rubble, an unsightly, ugly debris made up of the broken bricks of their demolished homes.

1947

Nick and Doris were given the keys to their new residence that was located less than a mile away on Edward Street, in March. The new temporary Nissen hut was a half round pre-fabricated asbestos and tin building that looked like an Anderson air raid shelter only above ground. It had two full bedrooms, a small storage room and one larger room that housed the kitchenette and living area and a fireplace that was more like a small, square cast iron box with a chimney that went straight up through the curved roof to the outside.

The outside toilet was a wooden and asbestos shack attached to a coalbunker and Nick painted it blue. He had managed to purloin a couple of gallon cans of miscoloured paint and he thought it might brighten up what he called "Temple of Poop."

Doris would be forever sprinkling talcum powder or cleaning the "Temple" with pine-sol, a cleaner with a fragrance of pine trees. In the summer the stench was so bad at times that Nick would say "It smells like someone grew a Christmas tree in a pile of shit and set fire to it."

The kids laughed when he made his wise cracks but all of them would try to avoid exposing their bodily functions to the timber and asbestos lodge if they could and instead wait until they got to school and find relief there.

Having two bedrooms was a real problem because there were four children. Nick moved one of the interior asbestos wall's enough to create a third small bedroom at the cost of turning the storage room into little more than a cupboard. He built bunk beds in for George and Joe and it wasn't really a bedroom it was more like a large closet with a place to sleep against one wall. It also housed Joe's old, ugly door-less wardrobe and there was just enough room to climb into bed.

The Nissen hut was to be temporary accommodation while the rebuilding was going on and families that occupied them were to be re-housed in "a short period of time." Temporary dragged into almost four years before the next move happened.

There were 12 Nissen huts on Edward Street all in a row, all built on a concrete slab foundation and all exactly the same. They were built on land that had been cleared when the streets had been bombed during the war and there were a lot of those streets in the East End.

The Rudge's lived at number 4 and next door at number 6 lived the ever grumpy, Mr Watson. He was old and miserable but Doris told the kids they had to be respectful of him and to mind their manner's as he was a widower and a soldier from the First World War. Of course they were all respectful, well at least when there was an adult around. Joe was the worst when it came to playing pranks on Mr Watson, like putting Vaseline on the doorknob or knocking on the door and running away.

Sadly Mr Watson was truly a grumpy old man and even Nick would make comments like "I guess the Kaisers men weren't such a good shot after all, they missed old Bill Watson." Then he would follow up with "Mmm maybe they were good shots, they missed deliberately so we would have to suffer the miserable old sod."

The best prank Joe played involved Mr Watson's little vegetable patch. Everyone was encouraged to grow some vegetables to help subsidise their groceries.
Mr Watson grew carrots, rhubarb and had a cabbage patch of which he was very proud. Of course he never shared anything he grew, unlike the rest of the neighbours who would "trade," or even give away some of what they had grown.

Hey Kid

Not Mr Watson. He would go and saunter around his little garden and pick a leaf of the cabbage to examine. He would hold it up to the sky and examine it back and front, bringing it towards his nose and appreciating it like some expert sommelier sampling expensive wine before folding it, popping it in his mouth and chewing it. He usually finished with a self-satisfied grin defining how he inwardly would be congratulating himself on his success as a gardener.

Joe was hiding behind the outhouse watching Mr Watson one day and George spotted him. As George got close Joe signalled him, putting his finger to his lips and waving his other hand downward, signalling George to stay low and quietly take his place next to his brother.

They watched as Mr Watson performed his cabbage routine like an actor playing his part in a Shakespearean play for the 100th time.

George wasn't sure what was happening until Mr Watson started to chew on the cabbage. Joe broke into a fit of muffled giggles and in a broken, giggling manner said to George, "I pissed on his cabbage"

They both ruptured into laughter and with tears streaming down their face ran off with a grumpy old Watson shouting some words of abuse after them but he was totally unaware of what he had in his mouth.

On another occasion that was linked to Mr Watson in a roundabout way George, using his imagination and wit was to come to the rescue of Mrs Freeman's cat.

Old widow Freeman lived at number 8 and she had a big ginger cat called Marmalade, who was always out roaming around the streets. Every evening you would here her singing out " Here Marmalade", and making weird sounds like "coooee" that were actually slightly melodic, as if the cat understood her strange melody.

Nick was often heard to say, "There she goes, letting the neighbourhood know her pussy is loose on the street again," to which Doris would reply in a scolding tone "Nick, the kids!!" but everyone just giggled.

In the meantime Mr Watson would grumble "That smelly furry fluff brained hairball comes on my land he's going end up under it, bleedin' damned hairy ginger nuisance."
He hated Marmalade with a passion, probably even more than he hated the local kids.

One day George could see Marmalade wandering over to Mr Watson's back door, and Mr Watson was outside. It was only a matter of time before the cat would be caught but George came to the rescue.
Quick as a wink he ran over and managed to catch Marmalade. Holding the purring cat tightly he retreated to behind the outhouse. That's where he had the brilliant idea of disguising the cat so Mr Watson wouldn't be able to recognise the furry pet.
George had spotted a half used can of leftover paint from painting the Temple just sitting there under the coalbunker covering. The brush was also close by sitting soaking in some turpentine.

He proceeded to change Marmalades identity with an extraordinary camouflage and a few meows, screeches and scratches later Marmalade, and much of George, was now "mismatched blue."

George was very proud of his achievement and carried the cat in to show his mother what he had done. Instead of receiving the reception and congratulations he thought he deserved he was unexpectedly greeted by Doris a very surprised with,

Hey Kid

"Aghh oh my God George, what have you done?"

Nick walked in just then and his eyes widened three sizes in amazement, though he was also fighting back his laughter.

"You've done it this time young 'un" he said shaking his head but still finding it hard to hold back the laughter.

The decision was quickly made that they would have to tell old Mrs Freeman so Doris went off to deliver the news while Nick grabbed a towel to wrap round the struggling feline and started cutting hair off with a pair of scissors and cleaning it with some turpentine on a rag. He knew too much turpentine would burn the poor cat so he clipped as much hair as possible and decided shaving the rest and hot water was probably the only solution.

Mrs Freeman came running in totally horrified. She was in such a panic all she could do was wave her arms in the air, cry, and blubber a load of gibberish. Doris calmed her a little and called Louise to come and put the kettle on.
Louise, Joe, and Rose all looked on in utter amazement as Doris and Nick cut the hair on the cat as short as they could and then Nick lathered the cat up with soap and water. Bit by bit and with a gargantuan struggle holding on to a fighting cat wrapped tightly in a towel he slowly but surely shaved the thing inch by inch until all there could be seen was a hairless blue shaded ugly cat.

Luckily Marmalade survived the camouflage of the century though was rarely seen outside again except in the arms of Mrs Freeman in her back yard. George had probably done old Mr Watson a favour, which was far from his intention!

Nick was now working quite regularly in the docks and Doris managed to get a new full time position at Tate & Lyle, so now she could quit the part time job at the Trebor sweet factory.

Hey Kid

Louise was 17 years old and had managed to get into nursing school at St. Mary's hospital. She would spend overnight there for six days then be home for two days before returning for another six days of day shift.

The family was seeing a lot less of her between work and Frank Foxton but she was one of the happiest people ever and very dedicated to her nursing studies as well. When she was off work and at home she would spend quite a bit of time with George who was still her favourite and try to keep him well entertained, which wasn't always the easiest of tasks.

One Saturday George took his imagination along to explore the bombed Odeon that was just one street away from home. It had been badly damaged in the war and later by a fire, probably started by someone just like George.

The out of bounds fenced off building was due for demolition like so many others but in the meantime it was a marvellous place of exploration for George. He could defeat the invading Germans, be an actor on stage or even an explorer in an ancient temple.

As he was pursuing his fantasies one day he fell down an open pit, just managing to grab a metal bar that was lying across the top of what was actually a manhole. The drop below was about 10 feet and as he looked down he could see the deadly jagged rubble pointing up and waiting to impale him. It was the first time he had experienced real fear. If he let go he would almost definitely be killed on the pointed pile of rubbish below.

A couple of minutes seemed like an hour but as luck would have it Joe had been sent to look for his brother. When George heard Joe shouting he yelled back as loud as he could and Joe followed the scream of fear to its source. He couldn't believe his eyes when he saw George holding onto the metal bar for dear life.

He had been ready to give George a bollocking because Doris had made him go and look for his brother but that thought completely disappeared when he saw George hanging within seconds of possible death. He pulled him out and then gave him the bollocking plus more but when they went home Joe didn't say a word about it to Doris. Lucky George was saved once again.

Joe, just a year younger than Louise was getting bored and was looking for something meaningful to do as a career. The idea of binding books for the rest of his life was a near suicidal thought. It was a job but he had come to detest every working hour he was enslaved there.

Rose was still at school and had taken on the task of trying to keep George out of trouble from when their schools had finished until either Nick or Doris got home. Luckily for her Fred and Rachelle still only lived a short walk away so on days when there was no school or if Rose had something else to do, she could, with great relief, leave him with the grandparents.

With Nan and Granddad living close by, about half way between the old house and the new residence, it made watching George very convenient, especially for school holidays. Granddad Fred however, worked shift work at the Glassworks so at times George had to be quite, which for a fidgety, mischievous almost seven year old was a real task. At times he would stay with Tom and Harriet as well but they lived a little further away now so it was less convenient.

When granddad Fred was at home he would spend time with George telling him all kinds of stories about his own past, from fighting red Indians in the Americas to helping the Wright brothers design the first plane!

Hey Kid

Grandma Rachelle always said that Fred could tell the best whoppers in the world and should have been a politician. Fred actually did serve in the First World War in France with George's other granddad, Tom but George was more enthralled with the stories about Fred fighting the Fuzzy Wuzzy's in the Sudan and the Zulu's in the Boer War in Africa.

Of course the first Boer war was fought in 1880 and the Sudan war just a year later, which happened to be a few years before Fred was born and the only red Indian Fred had ever seen was when he had watched a cowboy movie.

He told all kinds of stories about all kinds of events and times, with more than the appropriate embellishment that seemed to be a trademark of most of the adult men in George's life. George was thoroughly convinced that Fred had been to both the North and South poles, fought in darkest Africa, rode a tiger and taught the Aborigines in Australia how to make boomerangs. No tale was too big when it came from Fred!

After listening to Fred's amazing stories George knew for sure that the war would never have been won if not for both of his incredibly brave granddads and the undercover risks they took for their country.

George was told, and believed that Fred's words to him were top secret and he was never to tell anyone but both Fred and Tom were secret agents who spied on the Germans and helped hundreds of prisoners secretly escape.
On top of all that they were special advisors to Winston Churchill!

Fred also showed George an old brass key that was wrapped up in a satin cloth, actually a blue rag and told him it was given to him by the King himself and would open the back door to Buckingham Palace if ever he needed to go and see

him. George was amazed but he would keep the story secret so as not to endanger the King,
Luckily, by saying nothing he would at least never hear the laughter of those not as gullible as he was!

They were great stories and would not only entertain George at the time but he would remember them, embellish them even more and tell them to others in years to come.

George and Fred would sing together as well with Fred taking the lead to teach George all the old war songs and a few other memorable ditties. George's favourite got him into trouble with his mum on lots of occasions but he thought it so funny it was worth the telling off he got.
It went: (first verse sung to Land of Hope & Glory other two verses to Colonel Bogey)

> Land of soap and water,
> Hitler's taking a bath.
> Churchill's looking through
> the keyhole,
> Having a jolly good laugh
> *Be..e..e..e..cause...*
>
> Hitler has only got one Ball
> Goring has two but very small
> Himmler has something similar
> But poor old Goebbels has no
> Ball's at all
>
> Hitler has only got one ball
> The others in the Albert Hall
> His mother, the dirty bugger
> Cut it off when Hitler was small

Along with a few equally tasteful other songs George became quite the showman during Music lessons at school. He only stopped, or at least stopped getting caught, after Doris put a bar of soap in his mouth after she heard him practicing his "word substitutions" to the songs and hymns the sang at school.

In August George was once again spending the day with Grandma Rachelle. She was in the kitchen preparing some food when there was a knock on the door. "Get the door George, I'll be there in a sec," Rachelle shouted from the kitchen.

George opened the door and almost wet himself. He looked up at a man dressed in a long black coat sporting a scraggly beard and wearing a black hat. The visitor's sharp brown eyes pierced down at young George who was now starting to tremble. In a deep and authoritative voice he looked at George and said, "I'm here for Rachelle."

George went white with fear, turned and ran directly into the kitchen at lightening speed and before Rachelle could ask who was at the door George spluttered out "Nan, it's the Devil, the Devil and he's here for you. Run Nan, run."

Rachelle looked at him in wonderment, as George had now turned a ghostly white and was shaking like a bowl of jelly being held by someone having an epileptic fit. Rachelle walked quickly to the door with George following her with tears rolling down his face. How was he going to explain this to everyone?

Rachelle's reaction when she got to the door was "Uncle Sol, what is it, what's happened?"

George had never seen this person before and there was his grandmother calling the Devil "uncle."

"Uncle Sol." He thought, Nan has an uncle and he's the Devil?

Rachelle invited him in but he declined just giving her some information about someone who had died. She lowered her head and looked sad. She told the man at the door that she would be there, wherever "there" was. The strange, scary man turned and left, and George was totally confused. Rachelle shut the door and walked into the living room and sat on the couch. After a minute or so of silence she looked at George and forced a smile.

"Don't worry George," she said. "It's okay, that man is an uncle of mine, my dad's youngest brother, my uncle Sol."

The first thought that went through Georges mind was how could a grandmother have an uncle? To him she was old so her uncle must been over 100 but in reality he was only a few years older than Rachelle.
George never knew that his grandmother was actually born Jewish. She had married a gentile and never continued to follow her faith, though George didn't really know about other faiths anyway. He had met her sister and her brother at some point but didn't really know all of them. Her brother Arthur was in the scrap metal business in Manchester and her sister Betty now lived in Canada.

Like many other East End Jews Rachelle was born in Whitechapel, an area bustling with small businesses, street carts and men hawking their goods in the market. There were Jews, Irish, Chinese, Greeks and hoards of others who had settled in the area. It was a true melting pot, a menagerie of human diversity and by the 1920's mixed marriages had become quite common, except for the Catholics that is, who seemed to only ever marry other Catholics.

In truth, George never really knew what a Jew was. Rachelle tried to explain a little bit to him and she told him that there were other Jews in the area that he knew, like Mr Curran the grocer and Denny Mincer the tailor.
George knew Denny Mincer made suits for everyone at his Tailor's shop on Barking Road. Nick had a suit made by him

and he called him a four by two. George thought it was because of Mr Mincer's size, he was short and had very broad shoulders so four by two made sense. He also knew of Tubby Isaacs who sold cockles, mussels, and winkles in Aldgate because his granddad played darts with him and he was a four by two as well. George thought he was short like Mr Mincer. He knew Jesus was a Jew because that's what they said in Sunday school, but he was a King and he lived in the desert somewhere in North Africa and then he became a Christian. He didn't know that a four by two was actually Cockney rhyming slang for a Jew.

George's mind was spinning for a bit but then his Nan explained it all in simple terms telling him they were all just ordinary people but they prayed in different ways and had a few different traditions. George almost understood somewhat but it was still confusing.

Rachelle's uncle Aaron, who was actually George's great, great uncle, had passed away and the funeral was tomorrow at the cemetery on Mile End Road. George didn't know uncle Aaron but tomorrow he was to attend his funeral.

The next morning George arrived at his grandparents house shortly before eight a.m. dressed in his Sunday clothes, clean shoes, pressed shorts and a blazer. He's school cap was cocked on his head with his masses of curls protruding in every direction and half of his shirttail hanging out, something quite normal for George.

After sitting at the table and eating his Weetabix, very carefully and under his grandmother's watchful eye as he was known for spilling something – anything- down his shirt, they were ready to go.

Rachelle was wearing a plain black scarf and a black overcoat. George had never seen her in a black scarf before she always wore colourful ones the times she did wear one.

They took the bus from Barking Road all the way to Mile End.

Hey Kid

When they got off the bus George looked up and saw the building in front of them with people starting to walk in. "Is that the church Nan?" he asked. Smiling she said to him quietly "Yes George, we call it a Synagogue, but it's almost the same."

Walking up to it he saw Mr Curran the grocer who delivered Nan's groceries on a Thursday. George always liked Mr Curran because he somehow always seemed to have a spare piece of chocolate or a sweet with him and a joke to go with it. He didn't look happy this time though.

George took his cap off, just as he did when they went to St Luke's church but Rachelle told him to keep it on. "That's rude," he thought to himself but lots of things were different today so for once he just obeyed.

It was a little weird for George as all the women and kids were on one side and all the men were on the other side. It all seemed strange to him and nothing like he was used to at church. He kept looking round and fidgeting. Finally his Nan turned to him and said "George keep still, what's your problem?" to which he replied "Nan, where's the Cross?" Rachelle held back her smile and as she gave him a mild cuff to the head she said "That's on Sundays, now keep quite."

For George things went on forever with some old man rambling on in a foreign language then another person singing at the speed of light sounding like he was whining to be let out from the inside an industrial washing machine. After going to the graveside for a while they went to a hall about 150 yards away and had food, much to George's delight.

Rachelle seemed to know a lot of the people there and George wondered why he had never seen any of them before, except for Mr Curran. The other boys, and men, were wearing funny little beanies which his Nan told him were called "Kippah's, but of course George thought she said kippers and started giggling as he got a visual image of men walking around with a smoked fish on their head. Rachelle saw into that one very quickly and with no words but a stern look coming his way George pointed his eyes to the ground, bit the inside of his cheeks, and said nothing.

By three o'clock they were on their way back home and in later years George would find out what Jews and Judaism was and much more but that day was an experience and something he was proud of because he got to go and his siblings didn't...plus the food was really good!

In September the holidays were over and it was George's introduction to Junior School. He followed his brother and sisters path to Ravenscroft School. One or two of his classmates also enrolled there but mainly he was to make new friends and set out a new tirade of pranks.

His first teacher was Mr Osmotherly who George believed had to be at least 90 years old. It was a slow first term as he settled in to his new surrounds but the Rudge family was well known there and he was often compared to Louise, Joe, and Rose, all of who had done very well in their classes and George was expected to follow. Sadly, that never happened!

Rose was now in the third form at grammar school and George saw very little of her as she left long before he started his ten minute walk to Ravenscroft. She was a scholar and loved school and would find George an annoyance when she was diligently doing her homework. She was a kind person though and she still kept an eye out for him so he wouldn't get into too much trouble, but she didn't want him to know that.

Rose had passed the 11 plus exam with flying colours and both she and Louise had gone to the same grammar school. Joe chose to go the Technical school at Stratford when he left

Hey Kid

Ravenscroft and really wanted to get an apprenticeship in a trade, any trade. He didn't know what he really wanted just that he didn't want to be a labourer or work in an office.

Things weren't great for hiring young people in those days and Joe never did get that wish but at least the job at Paragon was a start and he knew would move on somewhere when the time was right.

All three of the older Rudge's had been well liked at school by their teachers. Louise and Rose were both exceptional academically and Joe was considered above average in most subjects, especially Woodwork, Metalwork and Physical Education. George had a hard very act to follow.

Christmas was at Tom and Harriet's that year but the air of sadness was still evident when Tommy was mentioned even though they tried to hide it. Tom would still go to the pub with Fred and Nick but the spark of life he had before was barely a glimmer now. Harriet would try to pick up the tempo but, like Tom, she had faded from her old self as well. It had been almost three years now since Tommy died but the sorrow was hanging on like it was yesterday.

They did put on a good show, as much as they could and Fred's seemingly endless supply of Christmas fare continued as food was once again plentiful.

Louise, Joe and Rose all left early to be with friends and George was feeling just a little lonely with little else to do except read, colour in some books and listen to the "old" people.

It wasn't quite like previous Christmases when everyone stayed and George received the attention he thought he deserved. It did change a bit when the men came back from the pub and Fred started with some of his stories. Even Tom had brightened up a bit and chipped in when he further embellished Fred's yarns and told George how, together they captured the Kaiser and 200 German soldiers in WWI!

A quick respite from the stories was held when the King's speech was listened to on the wireless and the usual toast was given. Of course it was really just another excuse to have one more drink!

The Christmas holidays were over and now for George it was just the wait for New Years celebrations and then back to the dreaded abyss of forced learning known as school.

1948

The year started off well with Nick getting a promotion at work and was now a dock foreman. It meant he got an extra £2 a week but more importantly the work would be steadier and he didn't have to work as many weekends.

The other good news was that Doris' brother Harry was on his way home from Australia. He had accepted a position with the British High Commission in Canberra after the war and now his posting time was up. He had been promoted to Lieutenant and in his last letter he told the family that he was staying in the Navy as a career. George had never seen him so he would be a complete stranger when he did arrive.

In June Nick surprised the whole family and he bought a television. It was a 14inch Marconi and the first one on the street. Very few people had televisions then and it made the family feel quite special. There was only one station, the BBC, and it didn't come on until 4 o'clock.
Nick was feeling rather pleased with himself and told everyone he knew that they could come over and watch the Olympic games when they were on. He came to regret that invite when later in the year almost 30 people crowded in the small Nissen hut at one time to watch the Olympics on his TV!

Joe was still not happy at work toiling at boring tasks every day. He was a hard worker and he had a couple of really good friends from school days at Paragon, Billy Baker and Big Bob Bailey. His best mate, Alfie, had got a job with British Railways and moved up to Derby. The "Paragon boys" as they called themselves, were all fed up working there and not seeing a future except for books being bound, packed and shipped out.
One Saturday afternoon they each delivered some startling news to their parents. They weren't going to wait for

conscription so together they decided they were all going to enlist in the Army and make it their career.

Doris, like any worrying mother, did her best to talk Joe out of it but Nick said it may be a good idea and besides Joe would get called up within the next year or so anyway.

It was just three days after Easter when Joe, Billy and Bob took off from work early and went to the recruiting office. They all filled out the forms and enlisted on the spot. Two weeks later they were off to Aldershot for training and the famous Coldstream Guards were three more willing souls stronger.

Times were changing for everyone and good jobs were scarce. Rose was in her last year at school. She decided she wanted to be a nurse like Louise, who was just a year away from becoming fully qualified and still working shifts between her Nursing College attendances.
Between work, study, and Frank Foxton, Louise was rarely seen at home anymore.

The television was a great hit, not just watching the Olympic games but also seeing the news read instead of listening to it and even watching King George VI and Queen Elizabeth celebrate their 25th wedding anniversary.
George's favourite TV show at the beginning was "Muffin the Mule", a marionette mule puppet on a string that was shown as soon as the BBC started broadcasting and was followed by 15 minutes of Harry Corbett with his hand puppet, Sooty.
Another TV station had started called ITV and George abandoned Muffin for "The Flower Pot Men."

Nick had started something with the television and there was always someone visiting when popular shows were on. It would be a few more years before some of the neighbours experienced such a luxury but in time everyone would have

49

a television of their own at home.

In June Harry finally came home. It was almost nine years ago when he left but the family party made up for every Christmas and birthday he had missed.

Fred had performed his usual miracle of producing enough food to feed the country and there was no shortage of beer with a nice tapped barrel brought over from the Trossachs. Even Constable Green, the newest local Bobby, stopped in for a drink and a welcome home toast.
It seemed like the party went on all weekend but no one cared because for the first time since 1939 all of Doris' family were together.

Harry had also brought gifts for all of his nieces and nephews. Unfortunately, he had forgotten that his young nieces were now young ladies and the dolls he brought them were a little "dated" though they still treasured receiving the gift from their long unseen uncle.
Joe received an Aboriginal knife, which was almost a foot long and had to be put away until he came home on leave and George became the owner of a real Aboriginal boomerang with carvings of kangaroo's on it that had actually been used for hunting, or so Harry said!

Harry was based at Chatham Naval Base, which was only a few miles away and he was home staying with Rachelle and Fred most weekends. Like his dad, Harry was also good at telling stories to George about the war in the Pacific and how he made friends with the Aborigines and the walk-about he did with them in the Australian outback. He had certainly learned well from Fred how to tell a story and each one would keep George entertained for hours.

Harry was there for Christmas that year and it seemed like he was Father Christmas himself. He had gifts for everyone and this time the girls received clothes. Not just any clothes, he bought them at Regent Street shops, plus he got some real make-up for them as well. George got a Roy Rogers outfit complete with two six shooters that fired off noisy caps.

He didn't leave Joe out either, buying him two Abercrombie & Fitch dress shirts, and for Fred and Rachelle a weekend at the Thistle hotel in Trafalgar Square. Rachelle and Fred had never stayed in a hotel before so for them it was a really special treat. To top everything off he bought Doris and Nick a new Hotpoint washing machine. No more scrubbing board for them.
He spoiled everyone that year and the favourite uncle was truly number one!

1949

Things had started to look up and there was no shortage of work for Nick, though both Fred and Tom were slowly coming up for retirement and they were both a little concerned that times may be tough for them.

There was a new National Health system the government had put in place with pensions for men over the age of 65 and women over 60. Nick and Doris told their parents not to worry they would do okay. Besides Nick was doing really well at work and was in line for another promotion, this time to a Manager. If that came through they would be buying their own house and Doris could stay home and help look after the parents if need be.

Joe, Private Joseph Rudge as it said on his I.D, had graduated from his first round of training and done rather well. He was home for a few days leave and told everyone he was hoping for a posting overseas so he could travel and see the world. It didn't quite work out that way as a few days later he got his first posting and it wasn't that far away. He was to be stationed at the Tower of London, a mere four miles away! Doris was happy but she was probably the only one.

Things were on track for a great year. Rose was studying hard to follow Louise's footsteps into nursing and would be leaving school in a few weeks, Joe was happy to be in the Army, even if it wasn't the location he wanted yet, and Nick was almost certain of a promotion into management.

Suddenly things changed. Rose was sick, very sick and she was admitted to hospital. There was an epidemic of poliomyelitis and lots of children became very sick from it. She was 16 years old and finishing her exams at grammar school when she became ill. Nick and Doris were with her at

Hey Kid

St. Mary's where Louise worked when the doctors came to them and confirmed that Rose did in fact have polio. Doris was devastated and no amount of consoling her could stop the flow of tears. They stayed overnight at the hospital and left Louise taking care of George until Harriet came and stayed with him.

The next day there was a team sent by the Health authority to the home to do a thorough cleaning and disinfect everything in the Nissen hut as a precaution. Both George and Louise had to go and get checked out at the hospital as well.
In the meantime Rose was treated and put into an iron lung that was supposed to help her breath easier. It was the fourth case in the area in just one week and everyone was on alert, even though they didn't really know what to do apart from consoling each other and cleaning everything in site.

After a few days Rose showed little improvement but she wasn't getting any worse either. Doris had let her work know that she wouldn't be in for a while and they told her that they couldn't guarantee her job. It was a worry but not as big as the worry she had with Rose so she just took the time off and whatever happened they would deal with later. From being on top of the world to the possibility of losing a child in such a short time was a devastating turnaround that no one could have expected.

Rose spent weeks in the hospital and although recovery was slow it was at least recovery. At first she was in bed most of the time but as she got better she could get up and exercise a little. Although she was much better her legs were still weak and she had to wear metal braces to walk and do her exercises regularly.

It took months for things to get back to anything like normal but life was continuing. For George it was the quite period of his life. Not too many jokes and fun stuff went on during those days and Rose was the main focus. The strength of the family rallying around was probably the best medicine that Rose and the rest of them, could have. It was also the quietest school year ever for George. The teachers knew about Rose and luckily for them there was no mood for jokes and pranks present that year.

By the time Christmas came Rose was walking a lot better, though still often short of breath. Celebrations were going to go ahead and a big family get together was good medicine for everyone. Joe managed to get two days leave but was on duty from the 27th and although things had been delayed Nick announced that he would be starting his new position as a Manager in January.

Harry also brought good news as he was being assigned to Admiralty House for a year and if things worked out he would get promoted and become a liaison officer to NATO. Louise had told Rose not to give up on becoming a nurse and she had also been tutoring her so she wasn't too far behind on her schoolwork.

Rose never did become a nurse but Louise's tutoring must have really paid off because a few years later Rose would become a science teacher at a grammar school in Kent.

The whole family were there that Christmas and as rough as the last few months had been there was nothing but smiles from every one of them. It was no surprise Fred came up with enough food to feed England again. It was almost to a point that everyone expected it and no one would ever dream to question Fred as to where it all came from. Everyone had a ration book and though some things were easy to get it seemed that for Fred almost anything was obtainable!

Like every Christmas before the women cooked the dinner and the three wise men went to the pub. Rachelle lit her candles

and the kids were all recipients of presents. That year they were small presents but that was more than many others would receive.
The tradition of Christmas was one of the best times of the year for the family with stories, jokes and smiles in abundance.

No one could have known that Christmas 1949 was to be the last Christmas ever that they would all be together under one roof.

The Junior & Senior School Years

1950

A new decade had arrived and Nick started his new job. Tom retired and his fears of being penniless would become unfounded. He had worked at he Iron Foundry for almost 50 years and on his last day they presented him with a gold pocket watch, a cheque for £50 and two return train tickets to Edinburgh.

Tom had never been to Scotland and if it hadn't of been for WWI when he went to France, he would never have been further than the Isle of Wight! He and Harriet would take a trip to Edinburgh in a few weeks and he would spend at least one day exploring a scotch distillery.

Fred was also on the retirement list at the Glassworks. He was almost old enough but wasn't sure exactly when he would pull that pin, or have it pulled for him.

Like Tom he was in France in WWI and he would say he was a much travelled man, having been to Wales as a in his early years and not to forget the trips to Manchester, one to watch a football match almost 30 years ago and a couple more to visit Rachelle's brother!

Nick was on his way home from work when he bumped into Frank, Louise's boyfriend. They greeted each other and Nick thought nothing of it until Frank shyly asked, "Can I have a word Mr Rudge?"

Nick stopped and deliberately frowned just a little as he looked at Frank deep into his eyes, though he wasn't at all surprised at the way the conversation went.

Frank was more than a little nervous as he stuttered a little at first and, after taking a deep breath said, "I would like your permission to ask Louise to marry me."

Then he stood there looking terrified like a man standing in front of a firing squad waiting for the trigger to be pulled while Nick continued to wear the most solemn of frowns Frank had ever seen. Ten seconds must have seemed like a lifetime when Nick replied, "Good God man I thought you were never going to ask! Of course, Frank, of course you can."

Frank's fear and the butterflies in his stomach made an immediate retreat and a grin appeared that seemed to take up his whole face as he blurted out his thanks.

Louise had met Frank when they were evacuated to Oxfordshire. They were at school together there and Frank was just a few months older than Louise. He came from East Ham barely two miles away and it was there that their flirtatious childhood encounter continued to bloom. They had actually known each other for nine years and they were both going to be 20 this year.

Undoubtedly, Frank would get called up for National Service soon so he thought he had better get on with it and ask Louise to marry him now.

Two days later on Saturday afternoon Louise came home bouncing like she was riding a pogo stick. "Mum, Dad he proposed to me, Frank wants me to marry him." She went on with the whole story and hardly stopped to take a breath. Nick was sitting there with a silly grin on his face. He had waited two days to see his eldest daughter's reaction!

Doris was also in the know of course after Nick had told her about his conversation with Frank but they had both kept very quite. Nick of course couldn't resist a bit of teasing and just sat there and told Louise he would consider it and let her know his thoughts later.

Hey Kid

Later was about 20 seconds, as Louise stood speechless, starring at her father waiting for his reply, which of course was positive.

"So when are we going to make plans for?" Doris asked. "Next Summer? Summer weddings are always nice." "No mum Frank wants to get married this year, September."

It was normal for weddings to be planned over at least a year but Doris and Nick had no intentions of making them wait longer than they wanted to.

Nick was now full of logical questions like where would they live and how much had they saved. The living part was easy. Frank had already gone to the council and managed to secure a one bedroom flat on Barking Road. It likely helped that he had a relative who worked in the housing department at the Council offices but Nick wasn't about to question that.

On Sunday Louis and Frank went to church at St. Luke's. They did go to services occasionally and it's where Louise had her confirmation almost seven years earlier, plus it was the church were her mum and dad and both sets of grandparents were married. Father Bentley was only too happy to oblige and the marriage wheels were set in motion.

Louise and Frank had both been saving and of course had talked about their future together but without Frank actually proposing it was still a dream. Now it was a reality.

Nick and Doris had been thinking of looking for a house to buy but then they thought they had better hold off until after the wedding. One major event a year was enough.

Saturday, September 16th was the chosen date and the plans took off from there. Father Bentley had duly read the Banns and together with Frank's dad Bob they got on with planning the reception. It wouldn't be a huge wedding as Frank only had one set of grandparents still living and was an only child. With aunts, uncles, cousins and friends it came to 72 guests. The local school had a hall that held 100 people, so £50 later that deal was done.

George was almost nine years old and growing quickly but Louise still wanted him as her Page Boy and Rose as her Bridesmaid. She also had two friends from work, Irene and Linda who would be the other two bridesmaids.
George didn't really like the idea of Louise getting married, as he would really miss her spoiling him. Joe had moved out of the house earlier in the year and now Louise was leaving too. The household was starting to shrink.

September 16th soon rolled around and on a sunny, warm, autumn day Louise Rudge became Mrs Louise Foxton.
The party was a great success with the usual would be stars taking over the microphone and singing, if it could be called that, everything from their version of what was at the top of the charts to the compulsory "Knees up Muvver Brown." They made sure everyone got their exercise.
The amount of food and alcohol consumed was of gargantuan proportions, so much so several of the attendees would be sure to have more than their fair share of Asprin and Alka Seltzer the following morning. Others, like Nick experienced a mammoth hangover that lasted two days.

Louise and Frank left in a chauffer driven Austin Princess to their wedding night hideaway and then they would leave on the train for a one-week honeymoon in the seaside resort of Bournemouth.

Much to George's displeasure he was to find out that the reason the usual Rudge family week at the seaside had been cancelled that year because of the cost of the wedding. He started to rethink how much he liked his sister and Frank!

Hey Kid

Louise and Frank had their honeymoon and settled into their new flat and in no time Christmas had rolled around once again.

Christmas Eve was always a favourite of George. Every year they all went to St. Luke's for carolling around the Christmas tree and consumed as much as possible of the rich hot chocolate afterwards. It was going to church without having to put on your Sunday best and that was something that "scruffy" George really appreciated.

Christmas was also somewhat strange for George that year. Rose left after dinner to be with some friends and Joe wasn't there at all. Louise and Frank also came for dinner with but left soon after. Harry was AWOL because of some official Christmas engagement. Fred and Rachelle, as well as Tom and Harriet were there for the day as always and at least all of those present kept the tradition of listening to the Kings Christmas Day message, with the adults of course having their nip for the toast of "God save the King."

As tradition would have it the three wise men again left for the customary Christmas day pint at the Trossachs. They were all so predictable. Fred would have a pint, or two, of Fullers London Pride, Tom would delight in his favourite Bass ale and Nick would have a bitter and mild mix. It would still be a few more years before George became part of that tradition.

1951

George was in his last year of school at Ravenscroft and as the January term started he received his start of term lecture from Doris. This year, she told him, there were to be no more pranks, no playing truant, no fighting, and no being the class clown. Of course George agreed to behave, but then again he agreed last term as well.

The term was only a week old when the first letter arrived informing of George's unacceptable behaviour.

The letter read:

Dear Mr & Mrs Rudge;
As you are aware we have several new students this year who have arrived from different countries, mainly the Caribbean. Unfortunately, George has taken it upon himself to inform two of these boys of some English traditions that have emanated from his own bizarre imagination. He has inappropriately convinced them that they must carry the nicknames of Cocoa and Sambo. He has also convinced them that our school motto, "Semper pro grediens" translates to "The new pupil takes the blame" and also if they drink lots of milk they will become white! In addition he convinced them that a Dungaroo is a real animal and they should be careful going out in the evening in case they get attacked by one of these creatures that lurk in in the dark and eat coloured children.
This behaviour is totally unacceptable and I would appreciate the opportunity to discuss this further with you as soon as possible."

Although Nick saw a funny side to it he had to chastise George and bring him into line. Doris on the other hand was quite perturbed that this had happened so early in the year and

Hey Kid

George would get grounded for a whole week. He was not very impressed with the harsh sentence but this time he had no way out.

A few weeks later Doris had to attend a meeting with the Headmaster as George had now been caught with cigarettes. He wasn't smoking them he was selling them but they didn't realise that. George had been taking the occasional cigarette from the packs at home from Nick, Doris, Fred, and Tom. He took just one at a time and then sold them at school for three pence a stick.

This time it was bad. If he confessed to stealing and selling them he was in big trouble and if he confessed to smoking them he was in the same hot water.

No one was impressed and no matter what he said now he was in deep trouble so he just had to think of something to reduce the punishment as best he could.

His story was actually a good one. He said he had found the cigarettes outside the corner store where an old homeless tramp often sat. He thought the tramp might have lost them so he kept them so he could give them back to him when he saw him next. He told the story so well that he almost believed it himself! There was now just enough doubt in the adults mind and although their belief was a good distance away George's punishment wasn't nearly as severe as it could have been. He was made to stand in front of the whole class and tell his classmates how bad smoking was and then he was made to scrub the boys bathroom, under the supervision of the grumpy caretaker. Finally, he was to stay at school under supervision when the class went on a day trip to Southend-on-Sea and write 200 lines of "I will not misbehave for the rest of the year," and read in total silence.

Two days after the mid-term break another message came

home that someone had put a piece of cardboard in a student's sandwich and George was the prime suspect. He denied any knowledge of that prank and though he wasn't believed totally there was no proof of his guilt this time.
He complained, with some good reasoning. He was the one always getting blamed when anything happened and that wasn't fair. Nick told him it may not be fair but was probably right most of the time!

Luckily the school term would be over soon and he would be going to Senior School in September. His parents could only hope and pray things would get better.

Frank got his call up papers early in February but as he was now married he might get leave not to go for the full two years. He went for an interview and was told if he did six weeks basic training and he joined the Territorial Army, the TA, then he wouldn't have to join up for the regular time. It wasn't that he didn't want to go but he and Louise had started making other plans and Frank had just received an incredible opportunity to go to Africa and be a Manager of a farm there.

Some of Frank's family had gone to Kenya more than 30 years ago and now they were successful farmers. His one uncle, Bob's brother Bert, was now thinking of retiring, or at least slowing down and had contacted Frank about becoming the farm Manager. It was a great opportunity and the money they could make was more than three times what he was earning now.

Kenya was such a long way away and that meant they might not see their families for quite a long time. They discussed the idea with both sets of parents and finally made their decision. It was too good an opportunity to miss. They were going to go.

George was old enough to understand what it all meant and the thought of Louise not being there gave him an ugly unwanted sinking feeling in his stomach and he experienced a new feeling of sadness. He wondered if he would he ever see Louise again. She was almost 11 years older than George and he had always looked up to her and she knew how he felt.

Louise and George had a real brother sister talk and she told George how she would write often and that he could collect the stamps on the envelopes and add to his collection. She also told him he could save up and she would help and in two or three years he could come and visit.
He wasn't happy with her going but he was totally convinced he would be able to save enough to go and visit her.

In typical George fashion he looked at Louise and said "There's a lot of black people in Africa so if you have a baby while you're there, will it be black as well?"

Louise almost fell off her chair laughing and told him no, but if she had a boy she would call him George, just like his uncle. The weeks seemed to fly past and in no time Louise and Frank were ready to leave. The families threw a big going away party for them and in late August, a few days after they said all their goodbyes they left for their adventure to Kenya.

The family was really shrinking now but at least Rose was still there with George and her recovery was going really well. She would still get short of breath occasionally and she would tire easily but her strength was getting better by the day.
She was taking classes at night twice a week as well and if she passed she was going to go to a college in Brentwood. Instead of becoming a nurse she would study to become a teacher instead.

All these events that were happening were fine for everyone else but in George's mind there were too many changes and it was like he was being abandoned. He didn't like that feeling at all.

September was the start of a new school year and a new school. Unlike Louise, Joe and Rose, George did not do very well on the 11 plus exam and he was not going to attend a grammar school. Instead he was condemned to spend the next four years at Ashburton Secondary Modern School.

The school itself was an old dingy building that unfortunately missed most of the bombings in the war and the parts of the building that were hit had been replaced with two barrack style classrooms and an Industrial Arts classroom which housed the wood work and metal work shops.

The main building was still a grim, dour looking structure that was more like a 19th century workhouse than an educational institution with its wire covered windows and gloomy, grubby brickwork.

It was a new challenge for prankster George but he was quite surprised when he got a warning form Grandmother Harriet. "You behave at that school young man." She said sternly to George a couple of days before term started. "No more cover-ups, playing truant or making excuses, you understand!"

She had been more of an ally at Junior School, siding with George most times when he got in some sort of trouble, which was usually once or twice a week.

"But Nan" he would say as he looked up at her with the face of a little angel, "It wasn't me, I didn't always do it. I'm always getting the blame."

Almost all of the time the blame was well deserved, like the time he dipped Jenny Grants blonde hair in the ink well and it resulted in her ruining her white blouse. That time the evidence was stained on his fingers but quick thinking saved him as he "tripped" and started a commotion. As he "fell," he knocked over the ink re-fill jug and quite a few of his classmates suddenly had stains similar to his!

The practical jokes, notes from the school to parents, and the amazingly exaggerated stories that had become a weekly event for George would now, according to his Nan's stern directions, have to stop.

George's partner in crime at Ravenscroft School, Davey Dent, would also join George at Ashburton but someone at the school must have been forewarned as they were in different classes. It wouldn't stop them from their mischievous ways but it would keep them apart enough so disturbances were probably a lot less.

September until the Christmas holidays were unusually quite for George. The school was much bigger than Ravenscroft with four or five times the amount of students and George actually liked his homeroom teacher, Miss Hall. Maybe because he had a schoolboy crush for her and he had not been in a single scrap and had only received two detentions, both for talking, during the whole first term. It was very unusual but it was a relief for Doris and Nick.

Both Christmas and New Years were very quite that year with Nick, Doris and both sets of grandparents making up the adult contingent. The tradition was the same, listening to the Kings Christmas message again, toasting his Royal Highness again, and the same stories of old were told once again. The Fred supplied feast was also the same but this year there were a couple of extra gifts under the tree!

Rose was still home, which George liked but she was much quieter than Louise or Joe. He missed Louise, she was always smiling and fun to be around, plus she spoiled him!

Maybe it was because he was getting older now or maybe

because Louise wasn't there but whatever the reason was, for the first time it wasn't "the best Christmas ever" for George. At least they had a television to watch!

There was news of a different kind over the holidays as well. Joe came home on four days leave on Boxing Day and informed everyone that his battalion were to be posted overseas and they were to leave for Korea on January 3rd.

Doris was far from impressed but nothing could be done or said that would change things. She wondered how long it would be before they saw Joe again and was obviously afraid for his safety. Joe on the other hand seemed to welcome the opportunity and he was ready to go.

With Louise in Africa and Joe in Asia there would be family on three continents and whilst Doris was worrying about them all, George was feeling more than a little jealous and wishing he could travel to some of these far off places for real instead of just in his mind.

1952

The year started off with really good news for the family but devastating news for George. Nick and Doris had managed to buy their own house. They purchased a terrace house not unlike the one they had rented for so long in Wightman Street but this one they would own.

The house was on Russell Road and closer to the docks where Nick was now a Manager. The problem for George was that Ashburton School was on Russell Road and being that close to home would make it harder to play truant and he would have no excuses to be late home as it was two minutes away, if he took his time.

They moved into the new place in March and George had deep feelings of despair knowing that his mum would be able to watch him all the way from home to the school gates.

It had taken George a little while to settle into his new surroundings in the first term but he became accustomed to his situation with his old friends in other classes and having the make new comrades in class 1A.

It didn't take too long for something to happen at the start of the second term when George was given a golden opportunity.

The English literature teacher, Miss Evans, asked the class to tell a story of something funny that happened to them or someone in their family. If only she had known the door she just opened.
Most of the kids told stories about someone ripping their trousers when they bent over or dropping something on their toe. Ronnie Roberts told how everyone laughed when his dad walked into the door and fell on his backside. The only word that came to mind to describe how George felt about the drab,

boring, soporific stories, was "Lame."

When it was his time he reiterated a story that Joe had told him when he and the girls were evacuated.

He told the story of farmer Sam Orwinkle, a pig farmer who told everyone he had a pig that could sing. That brought smiles and giggles in the class, even from the teacher Miss Evans.
As he continued, of course with the normal Rudge embellishment, he came to the part where his granddad was there for the demonstration and after hearing the pig he said, "You call that singing? You must be deaf as a doorknob, that sounded like a wet fart on steroids, and what's more yer pig smells like gypsy's shithouse."

The class was in an uproar with everyone laughing so hard they were almost falling off their seats. Everyone except Miss Evans, that is. She was red in the face and looked like she was ready to give birth to a bag of nails!
As he was quoting someone, George had thought it quite proper to use the full terminology.

"Quite class, quite. George, you get over here. That was totally inappropriate young man. Your parents will hear of this…" and of course they did! For George however, it was success in round one, he had managed to get his teacher quite upset and receive the appropriate recognition he thrived on so much from his classmates.

The expected letter was sent home to George's parents and the expected lecture on growing up and being appropriate followed. Of course it was tongue in cheek for Nick as he found it quite funny but Doris was a little more annoyed about George's pranks and she would take away his television privileges for the next week. For George though it had been well worth it!

Hey Kid

They had only been in the new house a short time when Nick's workmate came by with a delivery.

Horse-trough, Harry Harper, came by with a van and they unloaded six or seven boxes that went straight into the front room to be stacked against the wall. They were marked "Biscuits" on the side but as biscuits don't make a clinking noise when you carry them even George could figure out it was "refreshments."

They received several deliveries like that and even the new furniture was always delivered late at night, just like the coalman delivering his goods. The best delivery was the new television. Nick said it was a trade in and they now owned a new 17-inch K&B with gold knobs on the front. Things were really starting to look up again.

The new place still wasn't that far away from both sets of grandparents and one grandparent or another was often there when George got home, especially if Doris was working. It seemed George couldn't be trusted alone and as Rose was now in Brentwood at the college five days a week someone had to make sure he didn't burn the house down!

It was a cold Wednesday in February when George came home from school to find both Fred and Rachelle in the house and they looked very sombre. He didn't know what was happening and was told to be quite while they listened to the radio. All that was playing was something they called Chamber music and in between the newscaster was talking about the Prime Minister, the King, and messages being sent to Princess Elizabeth who was on a world tour with Prince Phillip.

It was just after four o'clock when Fred turned the wireless off and the television on. BBC still never came on until four in the afternoon, and now George could see what had happened and he realised what they were talking about. The King had died.

There was two minutes silence at school assembly the next day and all they did was talk about the King in every class. A nation was in mourning and the radio, which was being played in almost every class, was like listening to a history lesson between the monotonous music.

It was a very sad time and for two days there were almost no regular shows on the television just newscasts and documentaries. The King's funeral was on Friday, February 15th. The King and his reign plus the new Monarch Queen Elizabeth II had been talked about for almost two weeks at school but on the day of the funeral all the schools closed and lots of the men wore black armbands in respect.

The Rudge house was full on the day of the funeral and everyone in the family watched the event on the television. It was a sad time and George couldn't wait for things to get back to normal.

No sooner was the mourning for the King over then more bad news hit home. Nick and Doris received a letter to tell them that Joe was missing in action.

They all thought that Joe might have been killed or maybe captured by the North Koreans. He had only been there for a little over a month and the news was devastating for everyone. Doris was inconsolable, crying and weeping for days and George took time off from any misbehaviour at all.

For once even the teachers and kids at school were kind and understanding of the situation, which was something new to the now unusually subdued George.

About a week later a sergeant from Joe's Company drove up to the house and told Doris that Joe had been found and although he had been wounded he was doing fine. He was being treated in a Dutch field hospital and he would be sent back to England for rehabilitation. It was like they had won a million pounds and Doris was crying, laughing and jumping around like a frog had got into her knickers. Everyone knew the good news within the hour and there was laughter and smiles from family and friends that could be seen and heard for the length of the street.

Six weeks later Joe was back home on extended rehabilitation leave. He had been shot in the leg and needed a cane to walk but Doris was happy to have him home, especially with the knowledge that he wouldn't be going back to Korea, or so she thought.

George had received two letters recently from Louise and he had steamed off the stamps from the envelopes for his collection like Louise had suggested. He was very proud to get his own letters and it made him feel quite special but also sad that he was so far away from his favourite sibling.

Louise wrote that they were really enjoying Kenya and they had their own maid who lived in a room attached to their house, which was fully furnished and quite big. The heat was taking a bit of getting used to but all things considered they were very happy in their new surrounds.
George missed Louise more than he would ever admit to anyone but he had a plan. He was determined to save up enough money in the next year and then he would go and visit them.

With Joe home, letters from Louise, and Rose at the top of her class in Brentwood College everything was looking up for the family once again.

George was in a great mood and it was time to entertain the class once again. He had managed to catch a rat in a wooden box and now all he had to do was figure out how to get it into the school.

Hey Kid

It wasn't a very big rat but he knew that if things went right it would be a magnificent prank and cause havoc. He put the box at the bottom of his satchel and then picked the threads from the stitching of his bag so he had a "flap" he could pull back. He loosened the end of the box so when he tapped it the box would fall forward enough for the rat to see the light and escape. He was confident that his strategy was faultless and the next morning he just marched off to school in the normal way, except today he had the rat accompanying him.

Everything was going to plan. He hung his satchel on a hook by the door in the classroom and went to assembly with the rest of the class. After assembly they all marched back to the classroom to start their lessons.
As they walked into the classroom they were surprised to be greeted by a policewoman as well as Miss Evans. Instead of picking up their bags as they usually did they were told to go straight to their desk and listen.

A young girl had been molested close to the school and the police lady wanted to know if anyone had seen or heard anything and she also warned the class about talking to strangers.
George knew that was really bad but it was also a huge relief. He assumed she was there because of something he had done!

He thought he had better keep the rat prank for another day as with the police around he would be sure to get caught. Just as that thought came to him there was a horrifying scream. However, it became evident that the rat couldn't wait for George and had chewed its way out of the box and escaped. Everyone started to run around like chickens with their heads cut off and screaming like a load of wailing banshees.

Miss Evans looked like she was scared the most as she climbed onto her desk. The policewoman looked terrified as well and she tried hard to maintain her decorum but she

squealed more than a few muffled yelps as well.
Ironically it was George to the rescue. He picked up a book from his desk and with great aim he threw it and hit the rat first time. It stunned the rodent and the policewoman immediately grabbed the waste paper basket, turned it upside down and covered the rat, trapping it inside.

With all the noise going on two teachers and Mr Jackson, the caretaker had rushed into the room to see what the commotion was all about. Miss Evans quickly cleared the class and let Mr Jackson and her colleagues take care of the invading vermin.

For George it was a miracle! He had gone from the perpetrator prankster to hero all in a few very unforgettable minutes and though he graciously accepted the congratulations that day his heart was beating so rapidly he thought it might just explode.

The only thing he could think was "If only they knew"
For once George was not in trouble and no one would ever find out the truth!

The rat incident calmed George down for quite some time and although still a joker the rest of that school year was considered normal, at least by his standards.

The summer holidays went by very fast with just a couple of day trips to the much visited Southend-on-Sea on the bus and Joe took George around the Tower of London on a couple of different occasions. Joe was greeted there by some of his fellow soldiers and they chatted for a while about Korea and when and if they would be returning there. It was at that time George found out that Joe was going to go back to his unit as soon as he was well enough. Joe swore him to secrecy and George never said a word about it to Doris or Nick.

On one day out George and Joe caught the River Boat all the way to Greenwich from Tower pier. It was a great outing and a good replacement for the trip the family had been planning, which now had to be changed.

They were supposed to have gone to Brighton on the train and stayed a couple of days but hat changed suddenly when Nick's dad, Tom had taken ill so they stayed home.

Nick said it was all the years of working in the Iron Foundry that had made Tom sick and he was very worried about the coughing and shortage of breath Tom was experiencing.

Later in the summer George was to enjoy a fun day trip to Southend-on-Sea. Southend had the longest pier in the world and on the day Fred and Rachelle took George there they rode the mini train to the end of it. George was getting a little older now and his interests were definitely changing though he dare not tell anyone at home that he had a crush on Jeanette Dibble at school!

Fred and Rachelle were having the best of times and George enjoyed being with them even if they did seem to treat him like he was still seven or eight years old at times. Finishing the day with a giant ice cream at Tommasi's ice cream shop was also a huge plus.

Other times over the school holidays George would entertain him self and go out to the local parks with one or two of his school friends. He had known Davey Dent since infant school and they would hang around together and try to stay out of mischief, though that was a very unlikely outcome.

George was still determined that he would save enough money to visit Louise and Frank in Kenya and now he was developing his plan to secure the funds he needed.

First, next year when he was old enough he would get a paper round. That should bring him in about five shillings a week and if he saved most of his weekly two and sixpence pocket money from Nick he could save at least six shillings a week.

Hey Kid

That was good but it wasn't quite enough to meet his time frame. He wanted to go as soon as possible and was known to be a little impatient so there would have to be other ways of making money.

Davey came up with an idea that George thought was brilliant. Scrap metal, especially copper and lead.

People were getting paid quite well for taking scrap into the scrap metal merchant but they were too young and the scrap dealer wouldn't buy from them. Davey's brother Jack however was 18 and for a small cut he would be the seller. Now all they had to do was to plan where to get the scrap metal from.

Tin cans were easy but you needed a large number of them. There were still lots of roped off bombed and derelict houses around. Some of them still had lead flashing from the roof and lead pipes in the outside toilets and there were also the cast iron fireplaces.

Although most of the houses had already been ransacked they thought they would at least be able to get something from a few of the buildings. They had their plan!

They mustn't be seen so they had to be very careful where and when they entered the derelict buildings.

The first house they got into was fairly easy as they climbed over the rubble and then disappeared into the building interior. The fireplace was gone but when they got to where the toilets used to be some of the lead pipe was still there and within easy reach.
They had brought a small hammer and an old pair of pliers that Davey "borrowed" from his dad's toolbox. With the loose rubble not holding the pipe very well it was very easy to procure their first piece of scrap.

Hey Kid

They worked quite hard and within about three hours they had a nice little stash of scrap lead from several houses. They left it well hidden and the next day they brought Jack along to collect and dispose of it.

They never knew what Jack got for it but their share was two and eight pence each. They were happy enough with that and within just over two weeks they had made £4 each. They were in business!

They only had two weeks left before school started which meant they wouldn't have the time to maintain their efforts of scrap retrieval so they decided to get as much as they could as quick as they could. They had become quite expert at it and avoided anyone seeing them so their confidence was high to say the least.

That changed when they dug their way into a house on Ford Street and George found the gas meter still intact. He thought that maybe it would still have some cash still in it but if not there was a nice thick lead pipe going into it as well.

With a couple of swift blows and some vigorous shaking the pipe broke but to George's surprise it was accompanied with the rush of gas leaking out. He knew immediately how dangerous that could be so he shouted to Davey and they both took off like greased lightening.
 They left their stash behind and kept on running, realising their good luck in getting out and not being caught. They decided that maybe they should wait a little while before attempting some more scavenging.

They didn't have to wait too long before making another decision. About half an hour later three fire engines with light and bells blazing were heading towards Ford Street. There had been an explosion and there was a fire in a derelict house. They didn't need to hear anymore about it, they knew the cause. The Police cordoned off the area and evacuated residents from the street behind telling them there was a suspected gas leak or possibly an unexploded bomb discharged.

Later that night it even made the news on television and it was reported that the gas had to be turned off for a three-block radius. The explosion and resulting fire had destroyed any evidence of them being there but had also shattered a lot of windows and damaged a couple of roofs where people where living.

George and Davey swore each other to secrecy and never spoke of it again. By the end of their operation they were both over £9 better off. It was time to shut the business down!

School was now a week away but the focus at home was clearly on Tom. He had been taken to Poplar hospital and Harriet was by his side most of the time. Doris took George with her to visit Tom after work one day. She knew it would be hard on him but she also knew Tom wasn't going to be around much longer and he would like to see his grandchildren while he still could.

George had never had feelings like the ones he had when he saw Tom that day, laying in bed and wires going to a machine made him look like something from a science fiction film.
He had a mask over his mouth and nose and you could hear the heavy wheezing breath like constant high pitched sighs.
Tom put his hand out and held George's arm and as he blinked George could see a smile breaking on his granddads face.
George couldn't stop the tear as rolled down his cheek and Tom shook his head a little and forced out the words "It's okay George", and he smiled at him again.
George hadn't seen Joe come in and as Joe put his hand on his shoulder he shuddered and turned his head to see his brother standing there. Doris told them it was time to leave now as

Hey Kid

Tom needed to rest.

George had never been so quite and never said a word until later when they were all home. He looked at Nick and asked, in a broken sentence fighting back tears, "Dad, Is Granddad going to die Dad?"

Nick was struggling as well and he of course knew what Tom's impending fate was. It was just a matter of how long. He didn't want to give George any false hope so fighting back his own feelings he simply said "Yes George. Yes he is."

George sat frozen, unable to truly comprehend the death of someone so close as he was staring into nowhere. These were new feelings for him and he didn't like them. People died in films and stories and the King had died this year too but this was real. This was his granddad and he wasn't supposed to die.

His face was solemn and drawn with sorrow.

"Can I go see him again tomorrow Dad, please, can I?"
Nick just nodded and told George it was time for bed.

Nick knew that Tom wouldn't see the week out and it was Thursday tomorrow so he had arranged a couple of days compassionate leave from work. The next day in the afternoon they all went to the hospital. Joe, Doris, Nick and George. They were all very silent and sombre on the bus until Joe said, "Do you remember that day when granddad farted really loud when we were with him on the bus and blamed me?"

Nick smiled. He certainly remembered that incident. Joe had been so embarrassed he actually got off at the next stop and started to walk the rest of the way home but Tom, still laughing, got off at the next stop and waited for him and they walked home together.

Everyone chuckled at that memory and they started to talk about some of the fun times they had with granddad Tom. It lifted their spirits for a short time at least and though their loss was imminent their memories were also going to stay with them for many years to come.

The hospital was a cold feeling place but the hospice part was a little brighter and welcoming, if impending death could ever be described as being welcomed. When they entered the hospital room Harriet was sitting there holding Tom's hand. She looked up at Nick and sadly shook her head slightly. The time was soon.
Tom opened his eyes and softly said "You're all here" and after a moment of silence he said, "Where's Rose?"

Nick was about to tell him she was still in Brentwood when he heard, "I'm here granddad, I'm right here." Rose knew she had to be there that day and no studies were going to keep her away from her granddad.

Tom smiled and said, "I love you all, tell Louise I love you all." His chest moved up and down one last time and he turned his head to Harriet and with a final look he smiled. He seemed he was about say something to her but his eyes closed and he was gone.

There was silence, then tears and hugs and Doris put her arms out and ushered everyone out of the room leaving Harriet and Nick to console each other.

For George it was the worse day of his life, not realising everyone else was feeling the same pain. He would have cried more but the lump in his throat was so big that it hurt and the tears started to dry up as the knot in his stomach grew larger. It was the worse feeling he could ever remember having. Everyone except Nick and Harriet, who stayed for a while with Tom, went home.

Hey Kid

It was a very sad time and they spent in silence with their heads lowered. Later hey would talk about the good memories they had of Tom and how things would never be the same without him there but for now it was silence that filled the air.

Fred and Rachelle came by and shared their memories of their old friend as well. George had never realised before that Fred and Tom had known each other since school and even in the adversity of death Fred managed to bring some smiles when he told of Tom's antics in class when they were schoolboys. It seemed like George had inherited his grandfather's penchant for being a prankster.

The funeral was a week later and the church was packed for the service with people from Tom's work and relatives that George had sometimes seen but didn't really know.

Nick had managed to get a message to Louise through one of the shipping companies that had offices in Kenya and he had written as well. Letters would sometimes take two weeks or more but Louise got to know before the funeral. She sent a telegram and Father Bennett read it out at the service. George was feeling quite numb and he never heard most of it but always remembered how it ended.

" ...Be at Peace Granddad. We love you."

Granddad Tom was at peace and Louise's words gave George the feeling of acceptance he needed that day.

Peace was good.

Hey Kid

School was back and George was back, just a little more subdued than past years and maybe, just maybe a little more grown up too.
He was assigned to Miss Hall's class for his homeroom again, the Religion teacher he liked so much. She was young and very pretty and she wore a tight sweater, which highlighted her breast, something George could hardly take his eyes off. He didn't mind being in that class, after all he did still have a crush on her. He still had a crush on Jeanette Dibble as well and he was very happy that she was now in his class.

There were actually a couple of teachers George liked and rarely played pranks in their classes. There was Mr King the Metalwork teacher, although most of the students didn't think of him as a teacher. He was the bloke who taught you how to make things out of metal, like the toolbox George made and would keep for years.
Mr Thomas the Art teacher from Wales and Mr Ray the History teacher from India were pretty good too. On the other side he hated the gym teacher, Mr Birch, with a passion and the Maths teacher Mr Usher was the most disinteresting, drab, sour faced boring person he had ever known.

It was time to get down to business again for George. It was September and nothing would change that. School was here again, like it or not.
For once the opening term was eventless. Maybe because of Tom's passing or Harriet's previous stern warnings but from September until Christmas there was not one detention, punishment, or note sent home.

Christmas that year was the first without Tom but Joe was home and Rose was back from college for almost two weeks. Memories of Tom were a big topic and his picture was out in view for all to see. Like Tommy, Tom was gone but they would never be forgotten and there was a lot more laughter than there was sorrow. All the memories and stories talked about were good, funny, and happy ones.

Harry came home for a few days as well and he announced that he was in line for another promotion and would become a Lieutenant Commander within a year, almost unheard of for a boy from the East end.

George still didn't really know his uncle Harry that well but he was very proud when he saw him in his full naval uniform and he would brag to his friends that Harry was such a hero in the war that he could have defeated the Japanese on his own and one day he was going to be an Admiral.
Of course that was George's imagination as usual but the truth was Harry was a ranking officer and his duties were more about domestic planning and diplomatic events than anything else.
Still, to George a hero was a hero and when that hero happened to be his uncle then he had to be the biggest hero of all!

The one Christmas tradition that did change just a little was this year the Christmas message was from the Queen for the first time. Instead of toasting the King the glasses were raised to her Majesty but the toasts were the same, as were the very generous contents of the glasses.

Joe was very quite about his plans though as he didn't want to hear all the fuss Doris would make if he said anything about being deployed too soon. George hadn't said a word about what Joe had said to him earlier in the year and now Joe's rehabilitation had gone very well and the Army doctors had passed him as A1 fit.
He was ready for active duty again and he had received his orders. In January he would be returning with his Unit to Korea. He would keep that to himself until it was time to leave and the family could enjoy the festive period without further fuss or worry.

1953

It was January, the holiday festivities were over and it was back to the norm. Joe had left for Korea, which Doris wouldn't even talk about and Nick went off to work in the docks as usual. Doris went back to Tate & Lyles every morning and Rose made her return to Brentwood College. It was almost as if the holidays had never happened and they were already a distant memory.

Fred was looking at this being his retirement year and George was saying almost nothing as the dreaded first day of school was coming closer.
George was actually running a bit of a fever the night before school was to re-start and Harriet took him to the doctors instead of school He had just contracted a bug and the doctor gave him some medicine said he should stay home for a few days. First day of school and he missed it, much to his pleasure!

When he did return to school a week later it was just like he had never left. The boredom was dragging him down and the lessons just seemed to last forever. He wondered if prison was like this. He still liked his teacher and he had told himself he would get his courage up and ask Jeanette Dibble to be his girlfriend. It could be an interesting term. Suddenly it was the end of term and he still had not said a word to Jeanette Dibble!

By Easter things had brightened up a little. It was the Queens Coronation this year and everyone was planning something, from a street party to a real shindig at the local pub. All the schools were planning special events as well and decorating classrooms and the main hall was good fun.

What still wasn't fun was the gym class. Birch, the evil gym teacher, and George clashed fiercely and so the contest was about to begin again. George did everything he could to annoy Birch from pouring liquid soap on the gym floor to blocking the toilets with magazine papers. One day George even pulled the fire alarm by tying a long string to the pull station. He cut the string part way through close to the alarm and had the rest of the string behind his back. A slow steady tug set off the alarm and a harder tug followed which broke the string. In the commotion George reeled in the string and got rid of it without anyone seeing.

He was 20 feet away from the alarm pull station when it went off and Birch was only a few feet to his side. No way he could get blamed for that one, so he thought.
After the commotion was over all the children were lined up. Birch immediately picked on George.

"You did that Rudge didn't you" came his angry accusation.
"Me sir? I was here sir, right in front of you sir. It wasn't me sir."
George's smug answer infuriated Birch but he knew George was responsible and he couldn't prove a thing.

George 1, Birch 0

A few weeks later at cricket practice George was facing Brian Horton who was a really good fast bowler. Horton almost bowled George out with the first ball. The second ball was a bit of a bouncer and George ducked to miss it. He could see the grin on Birch's face when that happened. He handled balls three and four quite well but the fifth ball was one George would remember forever.

As the ball came down George leaned just a little with the weight on his back foot and then shifted his weight forward into the oncoming ball. He struck it waist height, through the ball and to the right side. It travelled fast and hard and miraculously hit Birch full on in the stomach. Birch fell to his knees clutching his freshly bruised gut and almost passed out.

Being the sportsman he was, George ran over to see if his beloved gym master was okay. Birch was rolling in agony and George felt like he had just won a gold medal at the Olympics. With the writhing and moaning Birch, surrounded by a group of concerned boys growled out the words, "Class dismissed" and walked, back to the gym bent over like the Hunchback of Notre Dame.

George 2, Birch 0.

George's perfect stroke was the talk of the school and he inhaled every congratulatory comment like breathing in a fresh breeze at the seaside.

He still hated school but the Coronation preparations were fun to be involved in. Lessons went on as normal but everyday something would be said about the Coronation, its history plus the pomp and pageantry involved in it all. For once though it was something that actually interested George!

It was Monday, June 1st when the assembly was held and the headmaster gave a long, drawn out, monotone speech about what the Coronation was about and how lucky Great Britain and the Commonwealth was to have the monarchy. Everyone was incredibly bored to tears by the time he finished.

Classes were very informal that day as the teachers and children finished decorating the school and pictures of the Queen were hung all over the place. Tomorrow, Coronation Day was a holiday so everyone could listen to the proceedings on the radio or watch on television. They would also take part in the street parties that would be going on everywhere.

That Monday was a lesson free day. All of the children were given small flags to take home and wave at their leisure and a feast, if spam sandwiches and vanilla cake and watery strawberry jelly can be called a feast, was laid out in the school. The accompanying milk and weak diluted orange juice was also plentiful but best of all, everyone went home early.

Coronation Day itself was a grand spectacle. Streets were lined with tables full of food, home made cakes and desserts and so much better than the spam sandwiches they suffered the day before. Music was played everywhere and even some uniformed bands marched through the streets.
On Russell Road someone hooked up loudspeakers to their radio and the whole ceremony was blasted out through them. It was "Party Day" everywhere. Even the local bobby had a couple of drinks from Nick's rum stash and old Mr Wright, who Nick said was so old he was at Queen Victoria's coronation 120 years ago, was partying all day.

George thought that Coronation day would be a great time for him to try his luck at getting his first taste of liquor.
He saw his Nans glass of sherry sitting on its own without anyone paying attention to it. He thought it should be easy to purloin. Cleverly he worked his way over to the glass and just about as was to sample his maiden drink Granddad Fred standing behind grabbed his wrist and looked down at George over the rims of his National Health glasses and keeping a straight face said, "George if you drink that it will make you cough, cum, cock yer bum and shit balls of aniseed."

There was George caught red handed and not knowing quite what to say. Then Fred said, "Here you go, one swallow." Fred handed him a small glass of Lambs Navy rum. "Get it down your throat and no more until you're much older."

George knocked back about half an ounce of the rum in one quick go. He pulled a face that was so scrunched up it would make a snapping turtle look attractive. It would be a while before he tried any of the hard stuff again!

The next day George received a letter from Louise, which was always a great thrill and something that brought a smile to his face every time. Each time he received a letter he was even more determined to save enough money to go and visit Kenya.

When they returned to school George finally worked up the courage to ask Jeanette to be his girlfriend. At the first break he saw her walk around the corner and with a deep breath and all his daring in tow he followed her. As he turned the corner with high hopes of a positive outcome he saw Jeanette kissing Terry Dyke from the fourth form. His heart sunk, dreams died, and he experienced his first heartache without even having the chance to say a word to his fantasy crush.

His devastation lasted all of three minutes as Linda Preston walked up to him, held his hand and started talking to him. A brave move by her and George went from heartbroken to having somewhat of a girlfriend in three minutes flat!

He spent quite a bit of time with Linda and he had the experience of his first real kiss that day, something he quite enjoyed to say the least. It was a short lived romance as the school term was ending soon and George never saw Linda until the new term, when she was holding hands with Brian Horton. Romance over!

Summer holidays were on again this year but much to George's dismay they didn't go to the seaside like in years past but instead they went to Kent just a few miles south of the river.

Things were going well for Doris and Nick but what George didn't know was that his parents were saving to buy a car. He didn't even know his dad could drive. Money from the holiday would be saved and they would still get away somewhere.

Hey Kid

What George didn't know was that his next trip would be a Busman's holiday!
The whole family and some friends went including a couple of distant cousins, Billy and Roy and some of Nick's mates from work. George had met them before at different times and he liked them, as they were all jokers and good for a laugh. A couple of them came with their families and everyone crammed into their own small hut, one hut per family.

The accompaniment of would be hop pickers included Horse Trough Harry, Little Alf, Big Alf and Mooney, all of who George had met before at one time or another.

The adults and older kids, including George, would pick hops for about five or six hours a day, then sit around the fire pit eating, drinking and telling stories into the evening.
Doris and some of the other ladies did the cooking and one of the male adults would go off to the Dog & Gun to get a couple of buckets of beer every night while the others were cleaning up.

On the third night Little Alf came back with an empty bucket and a black eye. A couple of local lads had thought it was funny to drink some of the beer and give him a bit of a thrashing, just for fun. Doris wanted to call the police but Nick said they would see to it.

The next day Mooney went off to get the beer and Billy was keeping an eye out further down. Mooney was just to collect the beer like Little Alf had and if Billy saw anyone he would signal the others. They weren't too far behind, just enough to be inconspicuous.

Mooney got the beer and was on his way back again but it wasn't looking like the perpetrators were around this time.
Just when everyone thought it wasn't going to happen again a one off the two younger lads showed their face and started

aggravating Mooney. Billy gave a whistle and the chase was on.

The two youths took off but they ran right into where Nick and Roy where hiding. The first one ran straight into an oncoming fist at the end of Roy's arm. Nick tripped the other one and stood with his foot on his back.

The trapped yob was squealing like a stuck pig and when Nick lifted his foot off he dragged the lad up and had his arm up his back. You could hear the squeals of "Let me go, Let me go" all the way back to the pub.

Roy wanted to give them both a good hiding but they decided that would just cause trouble with the locals. Instead they made them take their shoes off and marched them in stocking feet into the village. They weren't sure what type of reaction they would get, and it could have ended up in a free for all but it didn't.

The lads were yobs and had been terrorising a few locals as well for a while. Everyone laughed at them and the landlord at the Dog & Gun gave Nick and company a free bucket of beer. The two lads were so humiliated and fearful of a real beating that they never got seen again that whole week.

That was the highlight for George, but still worst holiday he ever had. They caught the bus back late on Saturday so it was straight to bed.

On Sunday a grumpy George got up to find out his Nan and Granddad were taking him to Southend-on-Sea for a couple of days. It was only a few miles away and they stayed at Watson's Guest House right on the sea front. At least he would get to go on the pier and to the fun fair, plus he would get some ice cream at Tomassi's Ice Cream Parlour.

Summer was almost over and Joe had returned from Korea. He had only been gone a few months and this time he came back in one piece. He had three weeks leave before going on duty at the Tower of London. Even though he was going to be just a couple of miles away he wouldn't be home overnight again until Christmas, though he would get some day visits in.

Granddad Fred also had some news. He was retiring in a couple of weeks. He had been planning it for quite a while but only he and Rachelle knew the plans, though Doris and Nick were not surprised at all.

Rose had come home for a few days as well as she had finished some exams and taking a break while she waited for the results. Only Louise was missing and George wondered if the whole family would ever be together in one place again. He wanted to go to Kenya more than anything else and still had his goal to save enough money to make it happen. He looked at ways of making more money and finally got himself a part time job with Bob Kneller the milkman.

Every Saturday and Sunday he would get up at 6 a.m. and deliver milk until about 10 o'clock. He got the princely sum of two shillings and sixpence for his efforts but it wasn't a job that would last too long.
 Milkman Bob was a miserable old geezer, always moaning and groaning about something. George was really fed with the grumpiness and after about two months he told Bob to stick the job and find someone else. Bob wasn't very happy but as far as George was concerned he didn't care.

The grouchy sour faced milkman started to yell how useless George was anyway and all George said was "I wonder what your missus would say if she knew you spent over half an hour at Mrs Buckley's house every Saturday morning."

The grin on George's face was about as wide as the Grand Canyon as milkman Bob growled out a marathon of obscenities under his breath and rode off red faced never to be talked to by George again.

The weekdays were long and George was supposed to spend time at his grandparents, though some days Harriet would come over to his house while Doris and Nick were at work. He was too old to be babysat but leaving him alone and trusting him not to get into trouble was an entirely different matter.
George would entertain himself and get up to mischief with Davey Dent and some of the other kids. As long as they stayed out of real trouble everything was okay but they always had to push their luck.

At the bottom of Russell Road was Butchers Road where there was a Catholic church and some shops. There was the barbers shop with old Mr Collins giving short back and sides to the locals and a Second Hand shop which, in reality was a junk shop that sold used everything from used furniture to car batteries.
The other two shops were boarded up and had been since the war. With the shops being so close to home George and his mates had never ventured to get inside, just in case they were seen by one of the neighbours. Until now that is!

With the boarded up stores being on a fairly busy street it wasn't easy to get in from the front but by going down the side of the corner store they could they could get into the back and through a gap where one of the windows used to be without too much difficulty, so they did exactly that.

Davey had some matches and a candle but after the earlier experience with gas leaks they were a little too wary to use that method for lighting, so they would just get in and see what they could. If it they thought it was worth it they would figure something out and come back later.
George and Davey were joined by Ricky and Ronny Rymer the twins from their class and they started their new adventure.

Hey Kid

There were only four or five loose boards over the back window and they quickly pulled them off and got inside. The first room was smelly and damp with just some broken floorboards and piles of rubbish. When they looked in the next room they were amazed to see it was full of furniture and household items. The junk man was using it as storage space.

They laughed a bit then they heard someone open a door. It was the shopkeeper's wife. They backed off and retreated into the first room, ready to make a run for it. It was there they heard her say to someone "So do you like what you see?"

Carefully peeking back in through the crack in the door George got the surprise of his life. She had dropped her dress to the floor and was standing there with nothing but a pair of baggy white knickers on.
They didn't wait to see who she was talking to but when they got out, in about three seconds by Davey's reckoning, all George could say was that she looked like a scarecrow with tits hanging down to her belly and had more wrinkles than the Titanic had passengers. It was a site that could stain a young man's mind for eternity!
They joked about it afterwards but they could never go near the store together without getting into a fit of laughter.

A couple of days later George noticed that the light at been on all the time at Mr Collins barber shop and that was unusual. It was a Wednesday morning when George decided he would go in and see if everything was okay but when he tried the door it was locked. There was an open flap window above the door so he decided to shinny up the entrance take a look inside.

What he saw was old Mr Collins just lying motionless on the floor. He wasn't moving a bit. George knew something was seriously wrong and he had better go and tell someone quickly. As he climbed down he had a very serious thought enter his guilty mind.

Hey Kid

"No way they're going to blame me for that one" he thought and after a few motionless seconds he made his plan.

He walked swiftly up Butchers Road until he came to a telephone kiosk. He dialled 999 and told the operator that someone was hurt really bad in the barbers shop at 132 Butchers Road and that they should send someone quickly. Before the operator could ask any questions he hung up the phone.

She may have thought it a prank call but a few minutes later a police car pulled up outside the shop. George silently watched the action from across the road as two policemen got out got out of the car.

Just like him they tried the door and then one of the officers climbed up just like he had earlier. When he jumped down he shouldered the door a couple of times until it broke open and they both went inside.

It wasn't long before an ambulance turned up but when they wheeled Mr Collins out on the stretcher he was all covered up and George knew for sure that old man
Collins was dead.

There were a few people who had gathered around by then and the police asked if anyone saw anything out of the ordinary going on. George was close enough hear what was being said when the wrinkled scarecrow lady from next door said "Ask that kid over there, he was outside here earlier."

George felt his stomach turn and his eyes widened as he froze to the spot. She was pointing at him.

"Did you see anything boy?" one of the officers asked him. George just shook his head and then said to the police officer in the voice of a very worried sounding tone, "I didn't do it!"

Hey Kid

The policeman looked down at him told him he wasn't
blaming anyone and it looked like a heart attack but he needed
as much information as he could get. Just then the other
officer said something quietly to his colleague.
"Report says it was a kid called it in."

George knew he was now in more trouble than he had ever
known. They hanged murderers and if he got blamed for this
one....

"You called 999 didn't you son."

George was afraid now and really took his time answering.
The blood had drained from his face and he was white as a
ghost. He nodded and said, "But I didn't do anything, honest I
didn't."
The police officer smiled just a little and said, "Yes you did
son, you did the right thing. Thank you."

An extremely surprised George felt a huge wave of relief
encompass his whole body, like he had just been wrapped in a
warm blanket on a cold Winter's day. He stood there in a
stunned silence as the policeman dispersed the gathering and
then asked George where he lived. He pointed to Russell Road
and just said, "Over there, number 8."

The officer walked over with him and Harriet came to the
door. Her first reaction was "George, what on earth have you
done now?"

The officer explained what had happened and told her George
was to be commended but maybe next time he could give his
name to the operator. After taking a few details the officer left
and all George could feel was relief.

Some time later George received a letter from the Police
Commission thanking him and congratulating him on calling

Hey Kid

999 because there was an emergency.

He remembered the incident with the policewoman last term as
well. Good things happened when the police were around,
maybe he should think about becoming a policeman when he
left school!

September was here once again and school was back. Most of
the kids were the same in the class, 3A, and now Mr Heath
was the homeroom teacher. Heath was an okay bloke but for
George school was still the grind of a daily prison sentence.

He seemed to get blamed for almost anything and everything,
though most times till justified and over the last couple of
years he had brought a lot on himself.
He thought what granddad Fred had told him, "George, if
things don't change then they will stay as they are."

There were two new girls in the class, Penny Button and
Jeanette Moore. George was growing up a little and he quite
liked the look of both of them and would have to think of ways
to impress them.

And of course there was the on-going challenge with Birch and
it really was a hatred that was real both ways.
George's first effort of the year to get to Birch was to put a
stink bomb under his chair. The little glass container with its
contents of ammonium sulphide was placed carefully
underneath a wheel of Birch's desk chair and all that was
needed was for the monster gym teacher to sit on it. George
did the dirty deed during a class break when his next class was
gym.

He didn't want to miss the fun. He planned it well as Birch
would always go to his desk at the end of the gym session and
sat down to make his notes. The kids were nowhere close to
the desk so George couldn't be blamed.

Hey Kid

This time however when gym class was done and Birch walked over to his desk he didn't sit down. He first put his hand on the back of the chair and it moved a little. George could see the stink bomb exposed and the trick had failed. It was a huge disappointment for George until Birch took a step forward and trod on the smelly device.
It took only seconds for the smell of rotten eggs to hit Birch's flaring nostrils and his reaction was immediate. He was red faced and furious. He screamed after George and this time he was angrier than anyone had ever seen him.

He pulled George by the ear and immediately accused him of being the perpetrator. Of course George vehemently denied any knowledge of it and there was no way Birch could prove who it was. Regardless it was still George who was reported to the Headmaster and a letter sent home to his parents.

Nick knew his son's mischievous ways and he knew without doubt that George had perpetuated the deed. He lectured him on becoming a young man, telling him it was time to grow up and to stop all this nonsense.

Things seemed to be changing and, as with Birch, George had never seen Nick quite this way before. He really started to have second thoughts about his pranks. Seems like Birch's complaining and hate of George had hit home.

George 2 Birch 1

The rest of that term was one of the most miserable George had experienced. It seemed like Birch was around every corner and George could constantly sense his evil oppositions presence. He would have done anything to get at Birch, and Birch felt exactly the same way about George.

George wisely decided he should probably listen to his dad's advice. He started to grow up a bit that year but the mischievous part of him still lurked inside and for him nothing could beat a good prank. He would just have to choose his battles a little more carefully.

George never had much luck with Jeanette Moore so he dropped the idea of approaching her in any sort of romantic way. Penny Button however was far more receptive and she and George became quite close. She was a lot more sensible than George but she was fun too. A childhood romance was about to blossom.

George and Penny became an item that year and the pranks really died off. They went to the movies together and even went to each other's house with the approval of both sets of parents.

The school term was boring for George though his marks improved somewhat from years past. Miss Hall took over the class for a couple of weeks when Mr Heath was away for some reason and George realised that his crush on his old teacher was still alive and well.

Nick had been working a lot and was now the proud owner of a 1949 Austin A40 Devon for which he paid the princely sum of £120. It was a really proud time for Nick but George wondered if that meant they would ever get holidays again with having the expense of a vehicle to deal with.

Christmas was always a happy time at the Rudge's household and there were cards from Harry, cousins, aunts, uncles, and friends and as usual everyone would of course take time to listen to the Queen's first Christmas Day message.

There were the presents too but Christmas had changed over the years. Rose was only home for a few days as she was going to be spending time at one of her college friends. George had no idea that she had a boyfriend as he thought that her friend Michael was just that, a friend. It seems it was quite a bit more!

Joe was still in the Tower of London barracks but he was due home for leave in the New Year. Louise and Frank wrote religiously and George continued to receive his own letters. Often it would come a day or two before the letter to Doris and Nick but that was because she mailed it earlier knowing it would make George feel special.

Nick's friends didn't come as often to watch the football or cricket on television either but that was because television wasn't as unique as when Nick got the first one several years ago. Now a lot more people had televisions and the government even introduced a tax on them of five shillings a year.

Of course Rachelle and Fred were there in full force. They never seemed to age in George's eyes and Fred's stories and jokes were the best. Fred continued to be the provider of the feast as well and though George would never know where all the food and booze came from he did know that granddad Fred knew everybody in London!

Nanny Harriet was there too, but it was like she was dressed in a cloud of sadness. She smiled and hugged everyone and put on a good show but even George as young as he was could tell she was still hurting from the loss of granddad Tom.

It was a hard Christmas for her being a widow but this year she looked ten years older than before. Nick was really worried about her and he even said that he and Fred would stay home and not go to the pub before dinner this year.
Harriet didn't want that and put on a big smile and told them what nonsense that was. They were both to go. Traditions must be upheld she told them. They were easily convinced. Fred told George that in a couple of more years he would be going to the pub with them, which brought a smile to

everyone. "Well" George said, "The pub would be better than school," which brought a good chuckle.
Harriet braved through the Christmas dinner and George was happy when Penny came by, even though it was for just an hour. That visit of course led to some teasing by Fred and George felt more than a little embarrassed when Rose told him how lucky he was lucky to have a young lady visit him on Christmas day.

Rose was 21 now and by June she would be finished at Brentwood College and looking for work. Nick had always said she was the smartest one in the family and she may even be the first woman Prime Minister, if she wanted the job.

It was Christmas and even though times were changing it was still a good family time.
George would have it last for a month if he could but like all good things it came to an end.

At least school was over a week away before the battle began once again!

George got quite sick between Christmas and New Years and a visit to the doctors determined he had a very sever case of tonsillitis. The doctor would make arrangements for him to have them removed as soon as possible and in the meantime he was fed antibiotics and ice cream. That, he thought, was the most wonderful medicine ever!

1954

George didn't go back to school when the January term started and the doctor had managed to get him into the hospital to have his tonsils out, and in just over a week he was on the operating table getting his tonsils removed at St. Mary's hospital.

It was usual to stay in the hospital for at least a week after any operation so seven days after the operation the recovery time was up and George was duly dispatched home.

The first day back at school he was marched into the Headmasters office. The windows of the Art room facing Russell Road had been broken. Headmaster Brown accused George of being the culprit in the case. No matter how much George protested and denied any involvement it fell on deaf ears. To Brown there was no doubt that George was the malefactor in this instance.

"This time boy, you were seen. Caught red handed and you are going to pay for it. You're first punishment is 12 strokes of the cane, then the police. It's reform school for you my boy."
Brown seemed to delight in sneering down at George and he looked forward to administering the medieval punishment of the cane.
For the first time George was actually feeling frightened at school. They had gone crazy. Who had seen him break the windows? He didn't do it. It was one thing to get caught and punished when you did something but punished for something you didn't do was just unbelievable and George was gobsmacked and had no idea what else to say or do..

Headmaster Brown was wearing the face of a mad man as he started waving the cane around and berating George, who received three or four good swipes of it before he turned and managed to escape by running out the office. All he could hear was "The police will get you boy. You'll pay for this you villainous lout."

No one was home so George went straight to Fred and Rachelle's house. Fred questioned him a lot about the whole incident from the broken windows to the punishment and threats of reform school. He knew his grandson well enough and this time he totally believed George's explanation.

Fred was going to go to the school himself immediately but Rachelle made him wait for Nick. George had three welts on his back where Brown and laced him with the cane and missed the intended target of George's backside. Fred was furious but Rachelle calmed him enough and he knew he must leave it up to Nick.

It was a really long day and every time George heard something he thought the police were there ready to arrest him. At five o'clock Fred and Rachelle walked George home. Doris was there and Nick came in a few minutes later in a rather jovial mood until he saw George and heard the story.

Nick and Doris questioned George almost the same as Fred did earlier. Like Fred they were convinced he was innocent and the claim was unfounded. Nick had a message sent to his boss at the docks to say he had urgent family business to see to and would be late coming into work, if he went in at all.

In the morning Nick waited for school start and assembly to finish. He then he accompanied George to the headmaster's office. Nick's tough stern look that day was something to fear and he was seething that the Headmaster and used such barbaric savagery on his son. He knew however that he must control himself or the consequences would be dire for everyone.

Hey Kid

Brown's secretary announced their arrival and took them into the office. Brown frowned at George and announced to both of them that he had informed his secretary to call the police and that George was to be arrested for vandalism.

Nick started to shake a little and said "My son has welts on his back that you put there. You're a bully and a nothing but snivelling child beating coward and are going to pay for that."

The fear in Brown's eyes even made George think that things may end in a very nasty and painful manner. "First, you barbaric coward, before I teach you a lesson you will never forget I want to know exactly what makes you think my son did something so terrible that you have to beat him like an animal?"

Brown was shaking and afraid but spoke back in a contemptuous sneering tone. "We have a witness who saw him Mr Rudge, a reliable person that witnessed the vandalism your hooligan son carried out." His voice became more angry and condemning but at the same time you could see and hear the fear he had as well.

Nick was calming down as much as he could as he took control of the situation and calmly asked who the witness was. Brown had moved behind his desk and sensing the police were not far away he became very smug in his tone and continued saying it was now a matter for the police and reiterating that they were on their way.

Luckily for Brown it wasn't long at all before the police were there. Nick had an anger and hatred brewing inside and would have beat Brown to a pulp in an instance, but he knew that would have even more serious consequences and that he had to bide his time and control his anger.

The police constable arrived and calmly asked the details of the claim Brown was making. Nick managed to hold his tongue as Brown gladly obliged in a snarky manner that was really starting to get under Nick's skin.

The police officer noticed how Nick was feeling and cleverly placed himself between Nick and Brown, diffusing the situation at least a little.

Brown offered up all the details with the knowledge he was 100% right was relishing in the satisfaction of knowing George would be condemned to expulsion from Ashburton and have criminal charges brought against him.
The police officer asked who the witness was and Brown told him it was one of the teachers, John Birch.

George looked up at his dad with a look of amazement. Nick knew George hated Birch and started to get a very uneasy feeling about all of this.

"Well" said the police officer "Better get him in here."

Brown had the secretary go and inform Birch that he was needed and in the meantime the police officer started to question George.

All George could tell him was that he didn't do it and he didn't know anything about it. He really didn't know anything about the broken windows so that was all he could say.

Birch entered the office with a grin like the cat that swallowed the canary. He was immediately asked about the whole situation and how sure was he that George was the person he saw at the window breaking incident.

Birch, with a self satisfied smirk on his face, told the police officer how he stayed at the gym a little later that day and at about 4.45 he saw George throwing rocks at the windows and causing considerable damage. He ran out of the office but by the time he got there all he could see was George running away and a whole row of windows smashed.

"And the date sir?" the officer asked.

Birch told him it was Tuesday January 7th.
Nick's eyes widened with surprise and immediately he looked directly at Birch and he asked him, "Are you sure?"

Birch's snide, condescending reply was "Of course I am, I know what I saw and I know he's going to get punished for it. He'll get what he deserves this time."

The officer then looked at George and asked what he had to say for himself but before he could answer Nick said "Nothing. He has nothing to say but I do."

It was Nick's turn to gloat as he starred straight into Birch's eyes and said, "On Tuesday January 7th my son had his tonsils out at St. Mary's hospital at 2 o'clock in the afternoon. So can you tell me how he made a two miles trip here in less than three hours from the start of his surgery and threw rocks at windows while he was under a surgeons knife?"

Nick stared Birch straight in the eyes and glared at him with a look that could have killed instantly and in the angriest of voices said, "Well man, can you?"

Nick was ready to pulverise Birch but managed to keep control of his temper very well.

There was a silent pause then the officer calmly asked Nick if he was certain of that date. He could also see Nick was getting gritting his teeth and becoming really angry as he thought that his son had received a beating and was accused of something he could not possibly have done.

Hey Kid

Nick assured him and told him he could check with the hospital if he cared to. The police officer looked Birch and sternly said, "Looks like you have made a mistake sir."

Birch flew of the handle and started screaming, ranting and raving and shaking with anger. He went into a rave and screamed like a whirling Dervishes. He was frothing at the mouth as he angrily reiterated, "It was him, I saw him. It was him I'm telling you."

Birch was about to burst a blood vessel and was completely out of control.

George was also shaking now and stood close to his dad as the police officer, along with Brown tried to calm Birch down but he was like a mad man possessed with a demon.

Birch suddenly lunged at George with his hands out ready to grab him around the throat and strangle him but as he did Nick hit him hard with a solid right hook. He went reeling backwards and was out cold.

Brown then started to raise his voice in panic and yelled at the police officer,

"He hit him. You saw him, arrest that man."

The officer had no intention of arresting Nick.

"Self defence and reasonable force" the constable said and told Brown he would be making a report to his superiors at the station and that it would be forwarded to the school district. Brown and Birch's conduct was out of line and he told them they both may face charges for their collusion in trying to entrap an innocent child and for violence against a minor.

Birch came around and slowly got to his feet and as he looked across the room and saw George standing there he started to rant again, but this time as he came forward the police officer put his arm into a half Nelson and told him he was under arrest.

In the meantime Brown's secretary had heard all the commotion and called the police station telling them she thought an officer was in trouble.

Two more police officers arrived a few minutes later and assisted the constable but not in the way either Brown or his secretary expected.

Brown was also taken to the police station to be cautioned along with Birch. The officer spoke to George in a very calming way and told him that he was sorry George had to go through all of this and that everything would get sorted and not to worry.

Later that week they heard that Birch had a breakdown of gargantuan proportions and was institutionalised. He never returned to teaching.
Brown was immediately suspended as well and a new head teacher was appointed for the rest of that term.

George was shaken up by the incident in a way he had never experienced before but he could feel nothing but relief, even though he had experienced a true weakening of the knees for the first time in his life.

He wouldn't return to school for another few days and when he did he was nervous that the other teachers would hate him and make life uncomfortable for him. Much to his surprise they were all very good to him and the new temporary Head teacher was one to keep everyone in place. No more pranks that term for George and the rest of the year was extraordinarily quite.

Hey Kid

Thankfully, in George's mind, school eventually broke up for Summer holidays in July but the whole time from the Birch incident until then it was like a huge dark cloud had descended over every class and every pupil. Even the teachers who were usually fun to be around were far more subdued and professional in the way they acted their classrooms than ever before.

The one exception was Miss Hall. George continued to have a crush on her but unfortunately, only took her class for Religious Instruction classes three times a week.

He had done very well in his History and Geography classes. He wanted to learn first about Kenya then the whole of Africa so he had actually paid attention for a change. He had been saving his stamps since Louise left and had expanded his assortment to include a few more countries and was soon accumulating a very nice collection.

It was a strange consequence but the stamps were one thing that actually kept George busy and out of mischief, plus he would read a lot about the different countries and he became very adapt in history and geography. The end of term report George got that year was the best one he had ever received.

It was July and that meant holidays. This year they would go to a Holiday camp in Norfolk called Golden Sands. The only problem was George was the only child going. Harriet was asked to go but she said she just wanted to stay home, as did Fred and Rachelle. So it was just Nick, Doris, and George. They would drive there in Nick's nice Austin which was a real treat, at least until they found out that George was prone to car sickness!

What George didn't know at first was that Penny Button and her parents would be there at the same time and it turned out to be a great holiday week.

Hey Kid

George and Penny spent most of their free time together and George didn't even mind when Nick would tease him about his "girl friend." Both sets of parents thought it was cute. They must have forgotten what it was like to hit puberty and have your hormones run wild, to say nothing of wandering hands!

When they returned from the holiday George was still determined to save enough money to visit Louise and Frank and he continued his savings goal running errands for some of the neighbours.

One day he went to Jackson's the greengrocers for old Mrs Roberts who lived at number 16. She gave him her list and a £1 note. The grocer, Mr Jackson, filled the order and gave George change for a 10/- note. George argued with him that he had given him a £1 note but the miserable old man Jackson wouldn't give in.

George thought Mrs Roberts would accuse him of stealing the money but when he explained she told him not to worry. He had pulled that trick before and she would deal with it. George felt both glad and sad. She gave him a shilling but the thought someone would cheat an old lady made him very angry. George may have had a mischievous streak but no one, he thought, should steal from an old lady. It just wasn't right. He would have to plot revenge!

For a young man George was actually very patient. He bided his time well but when the opportunity arose he took it. George had devised a plan. He would make a hook from some scrap metal, tie it to a rope then ride his bike past the greengrocers. He would then throw the hook to catch the leg of the stall outside the store keep riding, which would result in the fruit and veg making a new home on the pavement and infuriate Mr Jackson.

He did a couple of dry runs to practice though he would have to hone his throwing skills if the plan was to work.

Hey Kid

Luck, or karma, was on his side and an even better opportunity arose that would help him execute his plan.

The Post Office van pulled up to deliver a parcel to the shop next door to Mr Jackson's store. George put his bike against the wall and quietly walked up to the side of the stall and dropped the hook and a quick manoeuvre with his foot meant it was in position. He made a hoop in the other end of the thin rope and walked swiftly past the van and hooked the rope over the bumper. With that done he was on his bike and down the road far enough not to be seen but a vantage point close enough to witness his justice.

It worked like a dream. The Postman walked out of the shop and got into the van. He felt nothing as he drove off leaving the potatoes, carrots and cauliflower to make their road dance debut.

With the assistance of a lorry driving by the moving vegetables were quickly transformed into artwork on the tarmac. Justice was further served as old man Jackson came running out of the store, more like a semi fast hobble, and fell straight on his arse. Victory was accomplished and justice was done.

George had also managed to get a part time job with Davey Dent. Davey's uncle had a market stall in Rathbone Street market and the boys could earn a little bit extra giving him a hand. It was only a Friday and Saturday job for about four hours a day but it was more income that would make his Kenya trip a reality.

He would still earn a few shillings doing weekday errands as well and he would always have a huge inside smile every time he had to get something from Mr Jacksons' shop, where he always made sure he had the right change.

In July a letter from Louise and Frank arrived. Wonderful news, Louise was almost two months pregnant.

George of course received his own letter from Louise with the same news except she added "I hope you remember that I said I would name the first child after you. Well it's going to be George or Georgina, UNCLE George."

That made George feel proud and special and it also made him want to get to even more.

What she told Nick and Doris but not George was that the political unrest was increasing and there had been some bad things going on. It wasn't affecting them yet but a renegade group called the Mau-Mau were causing a lot of problems. It had been on the news but it didn't seem like it was a big problem and the government would sort it out very soon.

Having Louise so far away was hard on Doris and she would get teary eyed whenever there was a letter or news from overseas. It was probably hard on Nick also but he never let it show, at least not in front of George. Now the worry of something going wrong so far away was an additional concern.

By the time school was back in September George had saved the amazing sum of £37. He knew that passage was £42 so he would soon have enough. All he had to do was figure out the time he could go.

At last it was George's final year at school and decisions were being made on what career path he would take. George decided that he was going to either join the Navy or the Coldstream Guards like Joe. Unfortunately he would have to wait almost three years before he could do either of those things.

Jobs were hard to come by for Secondary Modern school children and most of those graduating at just 15 years old would only find jobs as labourers or, if they were lucky, apprentices. The job situation was starting to improve across the country a little and construction work would be increasing over the next few years. George would have to give some real thought as to what he wanted to do at the end of term.

Hey Kid

The students found that there were several new teachers when they returned. Miss Hall had left, much to George's disappointment, to get married. Birch was gone of course and Brown didn't return either. The new head was a woman, Miss Warner who looked like she could go a few rounds with a heavy weight boxer, as long as they were no taller than five feet four inches like her!

Miss McMahon was the new English teacher and she was quickly nicknamed Miss Holland because she had no noticeable boobs, she was flat, just like Holland!

There was also a new gym teacher, Mr Peterson and he was more like a drill sergeant when it came to the activities he planned but he was fair and approachable unlike his predecessor.
The last new teacher was Mr Grant and he was as black as the Ace of Spades but spoke with a very posh accent. He was also George's homeroom teacher.
George would mimic his posh accent until one day Mr Grant mimicked Georges Cockney accent. Everyone laughed so hard but he was the best teacher they had in years. At last, thought George, a teacher with at least some sense of humour.

Nothing was out of the ordinary in the first term. George was even doing better in gym class and the new Drill Sergeant actually turned our to be a pretty decent fellow. George was also smart enough not to try anything either. One gym teacher notch was enough for a lifetime.

Christmas was at Fred and Rachelle's for a change and it was also the Christmas that Rose announced that she and Michael were going to get married.

They had both secured jobs in Kent at different schools and wanted to get married before the beginning of term next September. It came as no surprise to anyone and over the next two weeks everyone would meet Michael's family. They were quite well off and his father owned a building company that was doing very well.

The wedding date was set for July, once again quicker than most weddings, and of course it was to be at St. Luke's, the same church Louise was married in. Once again wedding plans were on the way and, once again George's holiday would fall by the wayside.

Christmas was very quite from past years. Harriet put on a good face but again, she wasn't the same as before and it seemed like she was fading away by the month. Joe came home for Christmas Day and Boxing Day and he had now been promoted to Lance Corporal. He had to go back early on the 28th and left before George was awake but he did leave him an envelope full of stamps that he had managed to collect for him.

Joe had told Nick that he had heard rumours that the battalion were going to be shipping out soon but he had no idea where or when. They both thought it best to say nothing and not start Doris worrying anytime soon.

The one tradition that changed this year was that Joe accompanied Nick and Fred to the Trossachs for his inaugural Christmas pint with the men of the family. George wondered what that was like and started to look forward to the time he would experience the traditional walk to the pub.

What George did experience was spending the next day with Penny Button and they were now seeing quite a lot of each other. George didn't say much about it as he didn't like the teasing and smart remarks but he was very much liking his time with her and experiencing his first "falling in love" feelings.

1955

In January George returned to Ashburton School for his final
year and he couldn't wait for the unjust prison sentence he had
served to be over.
The family heard from Louise again but this time it was with
both good and not so news. The good news was Louise had
given birth to a 7lb 4oz baby girl, Georgina.

George had his own letter as usual and he was really proud
now to be an uncle and wanted to visit Kenya even more.
The bad news was that a couple of their farm hands had joined
a renegade group called the Mau-Mau and part of the operation
had been burned to the ground. Louise didn't go into great
detail and made it sound more like an inconvenience more than
anything else but to Doris it was a dangerous catastrophe and
she was worried for their safety over there.

Louise told them that the troops had made some arrests but
things were still a little uneasy. They had police staying near
the property and they were all hoping the renegades would be
stopped very soon. The authorities had arrested their leader,
Jomo Kenyatta, but the farm operation was being affected and
they were making back up plans.

Everyone back in London was following events very closely
though Doris was a nervous wreck and praying for Louise and
Frank's safety.
They were really worrying times for the family and were made
even worse by not being able to do anything.

In February things continued to slide downhill when Harriet
was taken ill and had to be hospitalised. Doris and Nick would
go to the hospital every evening and Rose would go at
weekends whenever she could. George would visit after
school sometimes with Doris or Rachelle and Fred and he

would tell Harriet everything that was happening at school with the usual amazing Rudge embellishment of course. Sometimes she would hold George's hand, look lovingly at him smile but she was getting too weak to say very much and when she did speak it was so quite and George would just smile and nod at her without really knowing what she had said.

A few days later Doris and Nick took George with them to visit Harriet and they took a huge cake that Rachelle had baked. It would have been Harriet and Tom's 45th wedding anniversary, though it was unlikely Harriet would have been aware what day it was. At least some of the patients and nurses could share the cake and the staff had been really good and Harriet was being well cared for by them so Doris and Nick used the opportunity to show they appreciated their efforts.

Doris was quite serious when she was talking but Nick would try and joke a little and try to make people smile a little during the visits. They were nervous jokes that helped to cover up his feelings and fears. Nick knew his mum was dying and it hurt but Tom had always told him that laughter was the best medicine ever.
There was no laughter, just agreeable smiles but some humour seemed to make the situation just a little more bearable.
George asked Doris why they called the ward a Palliative Care Ward and Nick intervened and told him that Nanny Harriet wasn't coming home and the ward was a special place where she could live comfortably and quietly until her time came.

George choked up and said little except "Then she'll be with granddad again, right?"

Nick's eyes filled with tears and with the lump in his throat it was too hard to speak so he just looked at George and nodded.

Harriet knew what was happening when she held her hands to

Hey Kid

George's face and whispered to him what a bright future he had in front of him and how she and granddad Tom had always felt so blessed to have him as a grandson.

Her words were quite and muffled and George still struggled to hear her but he knew what she was saying. She kissed George on the forehead, told him she loved him, and told him he would be a huge success. She laid back and fell asleep and Doris took George downstairs while Nick sat with his mum just a while longer.

Harriet fell into a coma later that night and never regained consciousness and two weeks later she was laid to rest with Tom and Tommy.

The times weren't good at the start of the year but there was a wedding to arrange and George had to be thinking about work and what he wanted to do for a living.
Things had to carry on, plus George had to finish school.
Just a few weeks to Easter and then the final run in until July when George would be freed from his "sentence."

He decided that he would have to leave one last mark, take one final memory away from that dungeon of education that was called a school. He would bide his time for a while and devise his academic Swan Song to be one that was remembered by everyone.

He was reasonably quite in class, though still had a witty wisecrack to make when the time was right and he was still the class joker. Everything was seemingly normal up until a few days before the Easter break. George had devised a plan. It would involve the toilets and this would be his best and last hoorah.

The toilets were located in an outside building at one end of the school playground, with the Boys one side and the Girls the other. The entrances were at opposite ends and there was a storage room in the middle separating the two parts of the building on the inside.

George discovered long ago that the storage room door was a little warped and that he could slide a thin piece of metal between the door and frame and put enough pressure on it to move the lock and open the door.

He was to use the fireworks that he had saved from Guy Fawkes Day. He had about twenty "Bangers" that he could use. He tied them together with an elastic band put them in a plastic bag and joined the blue paper fuses together so they would become as one.

The plan was to get into the ceiling above the toilets and wait for one of the girls to come and sit down. There was just enough room to see through and be able to reach in and dispatch his delivery. He would light the fuses and drop the fireworks into the tank at the top. They would explode and scare the person using the loo. With a bit of luck they would get soaked as well and scream with fear.

George did a couple of dry runs and the whole plan worked to perfection. This prank was to be the "crème de la crème of all pranks, one that he would be able to brag about forever. He chose the girls toilets because they always had to sit, so he was assured that as soon as one unsuspecting young lady came in he would have his victim. The girl's toilets were closest to the part of the storage room where the door was as well so his escape route would be quick and he would be able to enjoy the fruits of his devious plan from the outside.

March 1955

It was early March and it was time to put his plan into action. He had taken notice that at every break the toilets were well used so it should be no problem carrying out his deed and obtaining the expected results.

He was one of the first out at recess and he got into the storage room without anyone seeing him. As in his dry runs he was above the first toilet quickly, laying in wait for his prey.
He only had to wait a very short time before Ruby Collier from his class came in and sat on the throne. George flicked the lighter, lit the fuses and dropped them in the water tank.
Ruby could hear the fuse but before she realised what was happening there was the loud bang and that's when it all went wrong.
George had not given a thought to the fact that the toilet cistern was made from cast iron and the attached water pipes were lead. The cast iron tank immediately cracked then broke pulling the lead pipe with it.
Ruby was not only getting soaked she was also hit with a piece of flying cast iron and the water was gushing everywhere.

George almost died on the spot. His long awaited and well-planned and perfectly executed Swan Song had backfired. He had really screwed up this time.

Ruby was running out of the toilet with her navy blue knickers hooked over one foot and was screaming like a wild banshee. George retreated at lightening speed and ran out of the toilets, almost needing to use one himself as the fear of what was going to happen almost made him crap in his own trousers!

He was amazed and devastated to see there were already lots of people around and teachers bustling into the playground.

Hey Kid

He was ready to surrender, wave the white flag and concede defeat. There was no way he could beat this one but he then surprisingly noticed that everyone was heading away from the toilets towards the gates.

George couldn't believe his luck. A gang fight had started with about 40 kids from Faraday school coming to Ashburton to fight.
Inter school fights were common and the timing of this one was amazing luck for George. As fast as he could George immediately melted quickly into the crowd and was now just another student caught up in the mob. The police were there in no time and everyone who wasn't rounded up by them or the teachers was ushered back into the school.

The playground was getting flooded, running with water that was spewing from the toilets like the Trevi Fountain had moved there.

The commotion with the fight settled somewhat as the police and staff managed to separate the warring factions. Most of the pupils, including George, had been ushered back inside and so far no one seemed to do anything about the free flowing water that had now started to form puddles the size of small ponds over the old tarmac that was the schoolyard.

George had no idea if anyone had seen him exiting the toilets or if Ruby Collier had seen him at the scene. He continued to live in a state of fear for what seemed like an eternity but he wasn't caught -yet.

All the students were gathered into the assembly room and a head count was taken. The police had detained several kids from both Ashburton and Faraday and the fight was over.

George's heart was pounding like it would leap at of his chest any moment as the Headmistress stood at the podium on the stage with a police officer next to her and gave the sternest of lectures to the students.

"The police will be pressing charges and making more arrests from this unbelievable act of unwarranted and needless show of violence. If you were involved you had better come forward now, or you will face even more sever consequences."

All George could do was wait it out. He wasn't involved in the fight but if he was seen by anyone coming from the toilets he was a dead man.

The next day at morning assembly the lecture continued but luckily for George the caretaker, Mr Jackson, swore he saw one of the Faraday boys running from the toilets. Ruby Collier received cuts to the back of her head and legs from the pieces of broken cast iron but said that she had seen no one. Thanks to Ruby being too afraid to look up and Jackson's poor eyesight George had got away with his final prank.

The Easter break couldn't come fast enough for George and he was now laying so low he felt he could have crawled under a snake's belly. He wasn't used to being quite and paying attention but his experience and natural survival instincts had kicked in and he took notice of them.

At home things were still moving forward as the wedding was planned and much was said about how Rose would be a beautiful bride but the worry of what was happening in Kenya was a dark cloud of worry for Nick and Doris. George hadn't understood much about it but it was now being talked about on the news quite a bit and even he was starting to wonder if Louise was safe.

At school George had been nothing short of perfect for weeks and was still not about to rattle any cages. He was glad that he was leaving Ashburton soon and he would never have to see the inside of that depressing institution again so he decided just to bide his time.

The whole time from Easter until July George continued to be inconspicuous and although being far from the ideal student he was certainly more sublime than ever before.

Like his classmates George had been applying for jobs and was to have a couple of interviews before the end of school. One was at Pratt's Electrical store where they were looking to train television repairmen and the other was at Paragon where Joe had worked. He really didn't want to work there after hearing Joe's stories.

In reality George wasn't really interested in either one but he decided he would take the one at Pratt's first if he was offered it.

Towards the end of the term George was summoned to the Headmistresses office. For once he was at a loss and had no idea what he had done or what was about to happen.

Miss Warner may have looked like a professional boxer but she knew people, especially young people and she knew Ashburton School wasn't the right place for George. To George's surprise he was one of several pupils called into the office for what turned out to be a friendly lecture on his future.

He was very surprised when Miss Warner told him she had been paying attention to his behaviour and had watched his abilities the whole year, and that she recognised that he had a lot of potential. No one had ever said that to him before. She told him he was one of the most capable students she had ever taught and if he learned to channel his abilities correctly instead of wasting them, he could go far in life.

"George" she said in a very serious voice accompanied with a stern but not accusing look, "You have a sharp mind and excellent life skills. Use them well and channel your imagination into your real life. If you have a chance to make something of yourself, and I believe you will, you must make sure you take it."

George didn't know what to say. Only Miss Hall had ever really said anything positive to him in all his school years. He was actually stuck for words until he managed to mumble out "Thank you, Miss."
After he talk he got up and was leaving when she said, without looking up from her desk, "George, use your brain for something constructive and no more bathroom transgressions in the real world...and close the door after you."

George was absolutely gob smacked. Did she know he was responsible for the toilets being damaged so badly? How could she? Why didn't she say anything?

George never would figure it out but she must have seen something in him that few others, if any, ever did.

Thursday July 14th 1955 was a day that would live on in George's mind forever. The day his sentence was over and he was released from school!

It was also the day that Penny Button told him that her parents were emigrating to New Zealand. George was both surprised and heart broken. She would be leaving for the other side of the world in just a few weeks and he would never see her again.

The lump in his throat was like he had swallowed an oversized grapefruit and he found it hard to fight back the tears he felt welling up.

Penny put her arms around him and they just hugged for a while saying nothing. She told him how sorry she was and how she only found out the night before herself. She said they

could write and maybe one day he could emigrate as well. George wasn't convinced that would ever happen and all he could say was "But Penny, you can't go. I love you."
The tears slowly rolled down her face as she told George she loved him as well.

"We will see each other again George, I know we will, I promise."
He knew she meant after she had left but at least they did see each other several times over the next month but then she was gone. They wrote for months to each other but gradually the letters would stop and the first love of his life would eventually fade into no more than a distant memory.

Two days after school broke up on Saturday the 16th of July, Rose and Michael were married. George was dressed up in his best suit that Denny Mincer had made for him and he, along with everyone else, was ready for the celebration.

The sun was blazing down that day and, Rose was fidgeting like she had ants in her pants, was giggling like a schoolgirl and could hardly stay still.

It truly was a great day for Rose and Michael and they looked like the perfect couple. For Doris there was still the cloud hanging over her as she thought of Louise and what was happening in Kenya. She tried not to let it show but the tears were too hard to fight back at the reception when the Best Man read out the well wishes.
When he said there was a telegram from Kenya, Doris welled up again as he read the message:

> "We miss you Rose. Wish we were there.
> Congratulations to the best sister in the world and
> Frank, the luckiest man ever.
> Love always
> Sis, Frank & Georgina."

Hey Kid

The tears again rolled down Doris' cheeks and though she smiled through them on the inside she was really missing Louise and the granddaughter she had never met more than ever.

There were a few more toasts to the couple and the party was on. It was different from Louise's wedding, with the absence of Louise, Joe and of course Tom & Harriet but there was enough drinking that several toasts were made to all of them! Joe was home for the wedding but he was soon to be on his way to unknown parts. He said hid unit was leaving in a couple of days but he didn't know exactly when and he would let them know them when he could.

The newlyweds left about nine o'clock but the party went on until the early hours of the morning, until the second keg of beer ran out!
Rose and Michael were off the next day on their honeymoon in the highlands of Scotland for the next two weeks.

On the Sunday the family got together as a cleaning crew and made the party hall look decent once again. It wasn't to be the easiest of jobs for some, such a Nick who would have rather stayed sleeping off the previous nights experience but everyone pulled together and it didn't take too long before the hall was respectable again.

It was after the clean up that Fred took George to one side and told him that he was to come over in the morning and they were going to meet someone about a job. Fred said he had some contacts and it may be a really good opportunity for George.
George wanted to ask questions but Fred just told him to wait and see and he would explain more later.

George had no idea what it was all about but as it was his granddad and because Fred he knew everyone in London, or so it seemed, he would comply with the command.

George dressed in the same clothes he had worn for his other interviews and looked quite respectable when he reported as instructed at 8.30 in the morning.

Fred and George walked up to Barking road and boarded a westbound bus into downtown London. Fred didn't say much except they were to meet the son of a dear old friend who, if impressed enough, just may offer George a position but as what he didn't say.

About 20 minutes later they got off the bus and walked about two minutes to a café. It was a small place nestled in an old Georgian building and not very appealing to George's eyes. There were four booths and about eight small round tables, all with red and white chequered table clothes on them. Fred ordered two cups of tea from the good looking busty lady with a European accent behind the counter and they sat down at the farthest table and waited for his mysterious friend to make his appearance.

A few minutes later a very well dressed stout gentleman walked in and walked hastily came up to Fred, holding his hand out ready to greet Fred with a vigorous handshake and a huge smile.

"Fred, it's so good to see you. It's been too long."

"Indeed it has Bernhard, indeed it has. How is the family?"

Bernhard, as George now knew the man's name, and Fred engaged in small talk including uninteresting questions of each other's life situation for what seemed an eternity but eventually they settled and Fred completed the introductions.

"George, this is the son of a very old friend of mine so please shake the hand of Mr Bernhard Finkelstein, QC."

"Pleased to meet you sir" said George, still wondering what was going on.

Bernhard asked George a few questions about what he liked to do, his hobbies, and his plans for the future and then the conversation turned to Fred and questions were asked and answered about family and friends again.
It soon became obvious that Fred had been a good friend with Bernhard's father during WWI and that they remained friends after, though George had never heard anything about the things they spoke of.

With all the small talk over the conversation became a little more serious and Bernhard, or Mr Finkelstein as George would call him, had been talking to Fred about hiring a new clerk in his firm and George was now being interviewed for the position.

Of course George had never even thought about an office job of any sort but now he would listen and maybe fit the bill.

After a 20 minutes question period, which George considered more of a "grilling" Finkelstein, explained a bit more about who he was and what he did. He was a senior Barrister who was a Queens Counsellor with the Law Firm of Snodgrass Snead Finkelstein and Gold. The position he was considering George for was vacant due to the previous employee continually not meeting expectations and when Fred had found out he was looking for a replacement he suggested George as a candidate.

Finkelstein became quite serious when he reiterated the position and explained it in more detail.

"George, this is am important position that requires quick

thinking, organisational skills, determination, honesty, punctuality, and flexibility. Do you posses those skills?"

George attempted to answer, "Yes…" but Finkelstein continued by saying "Of course you do, your grandfather has already assured me of that.

"The position includes many facets from running errands, completing research both in the office and at the library in the Courts of Justice, to delivering and retrieving important legal documents." He then light-heartedly said "And sometimes even bringing me my tea. The position can be one of extreme interest and could lead to you becoming a legal assistant, or better if you have the Mettle for it."

"So, what do you say, are you interested?
George looked up at his granddad and the eternal silence of three or four seconds seemed like an hour had gone by.

George hesitated momentarily and the thought that went through his mind was something that Fred had said to him a long time ago and it seemed appropriate right now.

"George, if you are ever offered the trip of a lifetime
don't ask questions about where it's going and when,
just jump on board and experience the journey."

"Yes sir, yes I am very interested."

"Good" came Finkelstein's immediate reply.
"On Monday, September 19th you will appear at my office at 9 a.m. sharp. At that time you will report to Miss Allard who shall show you your station and instruct you in your immediate duties. I will address you when it is convenient."

"The remuneration is Two pounds Five shillings a week and you will receive two shillings a week to assist with your transportation costs. You will wear black shoes, grey flannel trousers, a white shirt, black jacket and a black tie, tied in a full Windsor knot. Cufflinks must only be gold or silver in colour but plain with very little or no design on them."

"You will be on probation for three months during which time you may be dismissed without notice or any reason being given. After that period, if it is agreeable to both of us you will be offered a more permanent position with incremental increases in salary annually. The term will expire when you are conscripted for your National Service or should you not be conscripted for any reason your position and terms of employment shall be reviewed and discussed at that time.

Between now and your employment, I require to read and familiarise yourself with the contents of these two books."

With that Finkelstein reached into his briefcase and handed George a copy of "The Annual Practice of British Law" and a copy of the Rules and Regulations of the Libraries of Her Majesty's Royal Courts of Justice.

George's head was spinning and he wasn't sure what he had let himself in for and he had certainly never read books like the ones he was given.

Everything rushed through George's head like a tornado had been let loose in his brain and his thoughts were blowing around haphazardly in an endless storm.

George thought "This bloke is a Jekyll and Hyde who swallowed a dictionary, laughing like a schoolboy with Fred then as serious as a judge handing down a death sentence two minutes later."

George had always trusted his granddad and was certain if Fred had anything to do with it then it was a good thing, so he stayed quite and just nodded his head in agreement with the instructions he was given, even if inside his head he struggled to know what was really happening.

Fred and Bernhard finished their personal conversation and exchange of memories of years gone by and George duly thanked his new future employer, shook his hand and held his breath a little as he tried to calm the butterflies in his stomach at the same time trying to clear the tornado in his head, or at least slow it down a bit.

On the ride home Fred explained a little more to George about his relationship with the Finkelstein family and how Bernhard's father was actually Fred and Tom's commanding officer in WWI. For once he didn't go into any major detail or embellishment of the story in his way but instead was a little more serious and just said that things happened in war time and in the trenches in France that changed men's lives and friendships were born that lasted a lifetime.

He also explained to George that Mr Finkelstein was a well-known Queens Counsellor, which meant he was a very high up in his profession and was a Barrister who had very well connected clients. He was considered an extraordinary legal authority in the City.

There were other Barristers and Solicitors that worked at the firm under Mr Finkelstein and in time George would get to know them on one level or another but for now he had a job, books to read and a future to consider. It had been a morning of tense experience for George as he realised the days of pranks were over and now he was to get ready for the real world.

This kind of job was something that he had never even given any thought to but it wouldn't take long for it to become quite interesting and eventually, life changing.

Hey Kid

No more pranks, no more goofing off, and no more childhood. That was all behind him now, George Nicholas Rudge, the scruffy kid from the slums of the East End didn't realise how his life would change and how big this opportunity really was.

George arrived back home and excitedly explained news of the job offer to Nick and Doris. They were all as surprised as George, Fred hadn't said a thing about it to any of them. Everyone was happy for him as jobs weren't that easy to find and this sounded like a great opportunity.
Nick said he would gladly pay for some new clothes and of course teach George, who had only worn a tie about six times in his life, how to tie a proper full Windsor knot.
Doris was the doting mother who told George how proud she was and happy for him and she mentioned that he really was as smart or smarter than his brother and sisters. George thought that was just wishful thinking!

The congratulations and celebration suddenly came to an early conclusion when there was a knock at the door that was answered by Doris. There was a postman standing there with a telegram in his hand.
It brought memories of the telegrams and visits that were so well known and unwanted during the war and the blood drained from Doris' face as she looked at the unwanted man in front of her and turned a ghostly white.

"Telegram for Mr and Mrs Rudge," said the postman and Doris, suddenly feeling faint and shaking nervously, took it from him. She knew it must be something bad about Joe and she didn't have the nerve to open it.

She walked in to the living room where George and Nick were still talking and smiling and silently held out the delivery for Nick to take. The smiling stopped and the serious feeling of fear replaced was now present in both of them as they stood in silence starring at each other in trepidation.

Nick opened the telegram and read it out:

> *"Leaving Mombasa July 21 stop*
> *Frank injured but ok stop*
> *Arrive Southampton Aug 3 stop*
> *Letter coming stop*
> *Love L, F & G*

Something was wrong but they had no idea what. Nick said all they could do was wait for the letter and he would also go and see Frank's dad and see if he knew anymore about what was happening. He didn't have to wait too long as there was a knock on the door barely 30 minutes later. It was Bob Foxton with more news.

Frank had managed to get a phone call to his dad and explain the situation in Kenya.
The first thing Bob said was not to worry about them, as Frank, Louise and Georgina were safe. They had booked passage on the Windsor Castle and they were coming home.

Unfortunately, Bob's brother Bert had been killed by the Mau-Mau and some of their farm had been destroyed. Frank had fallen in the escape and injured his arm and broken some ribs but he had been patched up and he was doing fine.

They were at a safe hotel in Mombasa, along with Bert's widow Ann, that was being guarded by British troops and policemen and there were with a few other people who had suffered from the renegade Mau-Mau as well.

It sounded like things were under control but it didn't stop either of the families worrying about what catastrophe may happen next.

Plans had to be made for their homecoming and Bob would be contacting the Foreign Office in the morning to get more information if he could.
It didn't take long to get organised and it was decided that both Nick and Bob would drive their cars to Southampton to be there when they all arrived

Bob had room at his house for his sister-in-law Ann and thought he would be able to arrange a small flat for Louise and Frank for a month or two at least. It all seemed to be working out and now all they could do was bide their time and wait for the Windsor Castle to arrive.

It was of course a sleepless restless night for them all and everyone was feeling down. In the morning they would spread the news to Fred and Rachelle and get word to Rose and Michael and Joe as well.

George's new job news seemed to him to be put way on the back burner and was of little consequence for the time being. Much to George's relief that wasn't the case. As hard as it was for Doris to concentrate she would help George with his studying and research as much as she could and she would say, "It's all going to work out. Everything will be fine soon." The fact that she said it about fifty times a day made it obvious how worried she really was.

A week had gone by and no letter had yet arrived but they did have news of the Windsor Castle that everything was on schedule so that was a relief.
The next day Joe was home on three days leave and he had more news. His unit was being posted overseas and they would be leaving in a few days. Doris cried and almost fainted when he told her where the posting was.
Kenya! They were going to reinforce the troops there and help

quash the uprising. That was the plan at least.

Doris went up to her room and sobbed. She fell on her knees
and prayed for the safety of her children like she had never
prayed before. She wondered why were they being singled out
for such punishment and she was at the lowest ebb she had
ever experienced. Life to her was all about her family and the
feeling that she could lose any one of them was almost too
much to bear. But she was resilient and dug deep to find the
courage to handle whatever was thrown at them. They were a
family, her family, and they would pull through it all.

It was that same determination that spread through the whole
family and the one thing they knew how to do best was to
succeed. Nick had told George when he was younger that as
long as the family were pulling together they would overcome
anything.

On July 28th Joe left for Kenya on a troopship and ironically, it
was more than likely he would pass Louise somewhere on the
high seas. He and his unit would sail out of Portsmouth just a
few miles away from the port at
Southampton.
On that same day the letter from Louise arrived with the
Saturday post delivery.

This time there was no special letter for George, just a short,
hurriedly written account of what was happening at the farm
and what plans they had made. She explained that a renegade
group had attacked the farm and with the help of some of their
loyal employees they had managed to escape. On the way off
their land a smaller group attacked them killing uncle Bert and
badly injuring Mfundo, the farm's lead hand and Bert's long
time friend who was helping them.

Before that Frank had been hit from behind and fallen, injuring
his arm and breaking some ribs but Mfundo managed to beat

off the attackers that time.

When they got closer to Nairobi they were met by some British police and taken to the hospital. The police recovered Bert's body the next day and a funeral was arranged to take place just a couple of days later at St Michael's Anglican church.

There would be three funerals that day as the attacks had become worse and many of the white farmers in that area were fleeing their homes.

From Nairobi they arranged passage on the Castle Line and after Frank was treated and let go they went to the bank to retrieve some documents that Bert had always said to take with them if they ever had to leave the country in a hurry.
The next day they left on the train for Mombasa. There were soldiers riding on the train for the whole journey and the Pavilion hotel they would be staying at was well protected, plus there had not been any incidents in Mombasa involving the Mau-Mau, at least not yet.

Aunt Ann was distraught but with the help of some sleeping pills and Louise close by she was handling things as well as could be expected.
Mfundo was left behind and also being treated in the hospital. They were told he would be well looked after until he was well enough to go. The other workers who fled with them all disbursed, not wanting to be captured by the Mau-Mau and they may never return for fear of persecution or even death.

With that Louise had told them all she could in a nutshell and signed off just saying "We arrive Southampton on the Windsor Castle August 3rd. Love you all."

It was a relief to know they had survived and the extra information made Doris feel just a little less tense but the worry wouldn't go away until she could see them all for themselves. August 3rd couldn't come fast enough.

August 1955

It was a sunny morning on August 1st and everyone was eager for tomorrow to arrive. George had been diligently preparing for his new job, even catching the bus to see how long it would take. Doris had been just as diligent in helping him as well but today was different. Today though she felt her heart beating harder and would even allow herself the odd little schoolgirl giggle when she thought of Louise. In 24 hours she would be seeing Louise and Frank and meeting her granddaughter for the very first time. Today was a good day and tomorrow would be better.

The Port of Southampton was about 120 miles away and the Windsor castle was due to dock before noon. They knew it would take up to a couple of hours to disembark but the two vehicles left at 7 a.m. and were parked waiting for the ships arrival by 11 a.m.

With binoculars the ship could be seen clearly about two or three miles away and shortly after noon she steamed into the harbour and docked.

There were almost 100 people waiting to greet the passengers but the security guards kept good control and everything was very orderly until the passengers started to disembark. People would jump and scream and wave their hats in the air as they saw their passenger coming towards them. Doris was no different and she was fidgeting like a teenage girl waiting for her first date to arrive.

Hey Kid

It seemed like an eternity but at about 1.15 Nick caught site of
Louise pushing a black pram and at the same time Bob saw
Frank and shouted with happiness and relief "There's my boy,
there's my boy!" and he broke through the crowd to get to
him.
Nick and Doris quickly followed and huddled around Louise,
almost squeezing her last breath out of her. They all had tears
rolling down their faces accompanied with smiles so big they
would make the Cheshire cat jealous.

Doris held her granddaughter for the first time and the tears
started all over again, this time with Nick telling her that if she
kept crying like that they could float all the way home!

Bob's face grimaced and tears filled his eyes as he hugged
Ann and shared her grief in knowing his brother hadn't made
the journey. It was a bittersweet moment but Ann was strong
and was quick to say that Bert loved Kenya and now he is at
peace there.
The commiserations were accompanied by the joy of a
reunited family and in the following days there would be many
stories shared and more smiles than tears.

The luggage consisted only of four suitcases and Georgina's
pram. They had left the farm with almost nothing but one of
the maids, Beauty, had managed to get some clothes and
personal items to them before they left for Mombasa.

Nick strapped the pram to the roof rack on his Austin and got
two suitcases in the boot and Bob loaded everything else in his
car. Louise and Georgina travelled back with her mum and dad
with Frank and Ann taking passage with Bob.

They had made the decision earlier to drive back to Bob's
place in East Ham as he had arranged a flat for Frank and
Louise close to their home and Ann would be staying with him
and his wife Jane.

Hey Kid

Both families were waiting at the Foxton residence in eager anticipation of the African arrivals and Rose was so excited she was fidgeting about and couldn't sit still for more than a few seconds at a time.

It was a little more than three hours later when they stepped out of the cars and the front door of Bob's house was flung open with families appearing like clowns popping out of a Jack in the box.

Rose and Michael were first in line on the Rudge side and waiting impatiently. She was holding a welcoming bouquet of flowers for her big sister but she dropped them as Louise came close and Rose cried like a babbling baby as she held on tightly to her sibling.

Jane bolted like an Olympic sprinter to put her arms around Frank and George was left behind, surprisingly quite, standing back and nervously shaking. He was wondering if Louise would remember what he looked like!

As George was standing there watching the proceedings he saw that Fred and Rachelle had arrived and suddenly Rose stopped jumping up and down and held her hand to her mouth and said "Oh God, I think I just peed myself."

There were howls of laughter as the embarrassed Rose, was helped into the house by Michael and then Louise turned to see George. There was a silence accompanied with a huge smile as Louise looked towards her little brother, held out her arms and grabbed him.
"Look at you" she said. "You're taller than me and so handsome too." George hugged her and tried to fight back his tears but as one unstoppable renegade drop rolled down his face Louise pulled out her handkerchief and wiped it away saying, "Oh George, looks like you have something in your eye."

Hey Kid

All George could do was smile. Louise really was his favourite and even though he may not get to go to Kenya now at least his big sister was back.

After a couple of more hours things were settled and the welcome travellers were allowed to unpack and relax as arrangements were made for the following day and the visitors all bade farewell, for now.

Over the next couple of weeks normality would take over and the visits would not be so emotionally charged. George had his studying to do but still had lots of time to listen to the stories about Kenya and he felt an enormous amount of pride when he was referred to as "Uncle George."

Frank had brought documents back with him that were to do with a listed company and foreign investments and he had to have some serious meetings with the bank and solicitors.

It would turn out in the months to come that Frank had been made a full partner in the business with his uncle Bert and they had been wise enough to diversify quite a significant amount. Ann was obviously Bert's heir but as they had no children of their own Frank was named in both their wills as the sole inheritor when they died but he was now the major shareholder in the business.

What to do with a company based in Kenya was now the dilemma and meetings with the solicitors felt like they would be a major headache to Frank, but one he would have to endure over the next few months.

Joe was now the one writing letters back home and like Nick's letters from WWII they were very heavily censored. Unlike Nick's letters though they did come quite frequently and the good news was that he was safe.

George recognised that so many things were changing around him and he was no longer the schoolboy that could just play pranks and have fun. Now he would have to grow up and act like an adult. Something he wasn't sure he really wanted!

Hey Kid

However, he was determined to make something of his job opportunity and though he still didn't fully understand what the job really was and what it entailed he was ready and willing to give it his best shot.

After all Granddad Fred had said this would be an opportunity of a lifetime and has he had never lied to his grandson, so it was time to trust and go forward.

The Work Years

September 18th 1955

Fred and Rachelle came by on Sunday afternoon to see George on the day before he was to start work and wish him luck. He was more than a little nervous but looking forward to the challenge before him. A short while later Louise came by with Georgina as well and she presented him with a Schaffer fountain pen and told him to use it well and that it would bring him good luck.

George had taken the number 15 bus several times and had his route planned to perfection. The bus took 40 minutes and stopped at the top of Shoe Lane where the offices were located just 50 yards away on the corner of Shoe Lane and Plum Tree Court. He would catch the bus at 8.05 and be at the office before 9.00 a.m.

He would get to know that route very well over the next few years. Tomorrow though was a little different, it was to be his first ride as an official employee.

On the Monday morning, September 18th George caught the number 15 bus as he had in his trial runs and just on the planned time he disembarked at the bottom of Shoe Lane and took the short walk to the office.

He had been up to the front of the office on his trial runs but he had yet to go inside. Entering the building he could see the Victorian style lifts that would take him to the third floor where the offices are located.

With a deep breath and some trepidation he entered the lift, pressed the button to the third floor and he was on his way. The offices were nothing at all like he had expected. The front door was a huge solid wooden portal with ornate brass handles and a lock that must have had a key six inches long to open it.

Hey Kid

George entered the office, first noticing their high ceilings and Victorian décor. A very attractive young woman was sitting at the huge oak reception desk and sorting through some documents.

"Good morning" she said, "May I help you?"

"I'm to report to a Miss Allard" was Georges' somewhat nervous reply.

"Ah, you must be Mr Rudge. Just take a seat and I will inform Miss Allard that you are here. She shouldn't take too long."

George appreciated the fact that a very attractive young woman had greeted him and he watched with impish glee as her appealing sensual steps followed the corridor to one of the offices, returning swiftly and telling him to wait and he would be seen presently.

He sat on the comfortable red leather armchair and waited for Miss Allard to appear. It seemed like an hour had passed and the occasional glance and a smile from the young lady at the desk was all that was happening, though she was easy enough on the eyes to enjoy the passing time.
In reality only a few minutes had passed when a middle aged lady dressed in a black pencil skirt, white blouse and short black jacket entered the waiting area. She was stern looking but not unattractive and probably just a year or two younger than his mother. She walked confidently up to George, held out her hand as he stood up and said, "You must be young Mr Rudge" in a rather posh and very confident business like voice and before he could answer she followed with "Mmm, a lot younger looking than I expected. Come this way and I shall go over all of your details."

George followed her half a step behind down the long hallway that was decorated with paintings and framed documents adorning the walls, to an office that was home to a desk similar to the one in the reception. It was decorated with a set of inkwells towards the front, a writing tablet and a blotting pad and it was perfection with not one thing out of place.

There were two smaller red leather chairs in the room and a lamp with a rather gaudy, tasselled shade standing in the corner and two large scenic paintings gracing the walls. Before she moved to her chair behind the desk she held out her hand once again to George, smiled just a little this time as she shook his hand for the second time and said, "Welcome to Snodgrass, Snead, Finkelstein and Gold. Now let's get down to business."

George, shaking her hand a second time, somewhat nervously and just said "thank you." It appeared the first handshake was the professional greeting and the second more of a welcome. He took a seat as directed and waited as Miss Allard opened a folder with his name on it and started to write.
"I see we have here a copy of your birth certificate, and your NHS number. We also have a letter of reference from a Miss Warner. That's all in order. Good. Furthermore I have here some documents for you to read and sign. The first is an agreement that you will be employed by the corporation and that you agree to all the terms and condition hereto."

George took the document from Miss Allard and was about to sign it when she abruptly stopped him.

"Stop." Her command came like an order from a sergeant major addressing a wrong doing subordinate. George looked up wondering what he had done wrong and he started to feel quite intimidated.

"This is a firm of Law, George. All legalities will be adhered to, which includes employees and clients reading any and all documents and legal material presented to them and you will only sign such documents when you have read and fully understand their contents. Is that clear?"

George was quite taken aback. His first effort at anything had obviously missed the target.

"Yes ma'am." He replied.

"It's Miss Allard, not ma'am and you will learn around here that people are addressed by their title and name, excepting Messrs Finkelstein, Gold, Snodgrass and Snead who you may refer to as Sir. Are we clear on that?"
George had butterflies in his stomach hat were starting to flutter like a murder of crows and was thinking he may just get fired the first day of work!

"Yes Miss Allard, I understand and it won't happen again."

George read through the papers presented to him, or at least appeared to, and signed them. He had no idea where they had got a copy of his birth certificate but he assumed Fred had provided that along with his NHS number.
He really wasn't feeling like he had made a good first impression and was wishing Miss Allard would at least crack a bit of a smile like the nicer, pretty young lady at the reception did.

He nervously handed the forms back and Miss Allard examined them quickly and placed them back in a folder with his name on and placed them on her desk.

Quiet quickly she seemed to mellow a little and told George he would like the firm and in a much friendlier tone told him she was glad to see a fresh face there and she was looking forward to working with him.
She informed George that Mr Finkelstein would be addressing him in due course sometime later in the morning. She then

told him that, later she would go over some of his duties with him and introduce him to some of the other members of staff that he may be interacting with and, finally she will show him where he would be stationed.

"You're much younger than we usually experience here George, and I must say I'm a little surprised that Mr Finkelstein would consider taking on someone of your youth. He must have seen something extraordinary in you. I hope your time here will be rewarding and beneficial to both you and the firm. Now come, I shall show you around."

The offices were much larger than George had imagined from the outside. They occupied the whole of the third floor and the décor made him think of grand places like Windsor Castle and Buckingham Palace that he had once seen pictures of, or even he Houses of Parliament that they visited on a school trip a couple of years ago.

The rooms had high ceilings with ornate gold coloured chandeliers adorning them and the two large doors to each office, one of which was embossed with the name of the occupant on a large ornate brass plaque. About half way along the hallway Miss Allard showed George into what had to be the smallest room in the building. This was to be his station.

The room next to his was the tearoom, a room to which he would become very accustomed to in the next few weeks and would be the only place he would see some of the other people who worked there.

Miss Allard informed him that almost everyone was busy at present and that he would get to know them all in good time, however the only people to give him any instruction would be her and Mr Finkelstein. Her previous more friendly tone had now changed again and was somewhat more stern and monotone. George was getting a sinking feeling, like a huge hole was about to open up and he would be the one falling into it.

As he looked around the room he saw that there was a desk

that was somewhat smaller than the others he had seen, two chairs in front of the desk, neither of which looked anything as comfortable as the last two he had sat in, an old black leather chair behind the desk and a whole library of books that completely filled one wall. On the other wall were shelves that housed numbered boxes, each labelled with a name, date, letter and numerical code.

George was really starting to wonder what granddad Fred had got him into and he wasn't sure he would even see the day out in this crusty old atmosphere and a roller coaster changeling, which Miss Allard seemed to be. Just as those thought were running through his mind the young lady from the front desk walked in and handed Miss Allard a piece of paper. As soon as she read it she started to walk out of the room, then turned to George and said "I am very busy, George. Dorothy will take over from here and she will instruct you on what is expected from you until Mr Finkelstein directs otherwise."

With that she turned and walked out of the room and George prayed that Dorothy wasn't cut from the same cloth as Miss Allard and would at least be able to produce something of a smile.
His prayers were immediately answered as she said "Hello George I'm Dorothy Hawkins. Don't let Miss Allard worry you, her bark is far worse than her bite. Actually she's not bad at all she just likes to run a really tight ship and she does a good job doing just that."
"I must say you're a little younger than I thought you would be. How old are you?"

George was now thinking that maybe his youth was going to be a problem. No one had mentioned it before but now two people in a short time had brought it up and it was something he hadn't been prepared for. However he did like the look of Dorothy. She was very pretty with long black hair and piercing, deep blue eyes. He had heard everything she had said but was fantasising just enough to stumble over his answer. He wanted to say, and almost did blurt out, 36 B, which is what he guessed her bra size to be! " Fifteen Miss Hawkins, I'm 15."

 "That is young, and it's Dorothy between us, and Miss Hawkins only when a client is present. I think you are the youngest person to ever start here. Before you I was the youngest starter here and I was 17 when I was hired on here almost five years ago."

"Now don't worry about this dreary little dungeon, you won't be spending too much time in it after a while. Come on let me show you around the place. But, first just a word of caution. If the door is closed on an office, do not enter. You can phone from the inter office line if it is important but never just knock and enter unless you are expected."

He told her that Miss Allard had taken him around but as they had time she insisted that she would show him again and explain a few things as they walked around. The truth was she really wanted to get away from her desk for a few minutes and this was a good opportunity.

The Arabian tent of an office they were in was truly massive and it seemed to go forever. As they walked down the corridors Dorothy explained who occupied each of the offices they passed but there was no way George could remember all those names, at least for now.

There were so many paintings hanging on the wall the George couldn't help but think they had taken a wrong turn and walked into the National Gallery.

George came to like Dorothy during their office tour and as well as being pretty she was also quite jovial and very sociable. He was actually a little disappointed when she told him that she was in engaged to one of the young solicitors in the office, Sebastian Brown, so his new little crush was shot down and went up in flames as quick as an old wooden chair

Hey Kid

on Guy Fawkes Night.

Back in the room that Dorothy had called the dungeon they chatted for about an hour. She gave George a lesson on the history of the company and what it was like to work there saying how she had enjoyed all the time she spent there. She told him again that Miss Allard was a seemingly tough old bird but actually she was quite soft on the inside and was the best ally to have in the company. She also explained that George would sometimes feel like he was not much more than a courier and he would be running from one building to another and could be carrying enough envelopes and folders to make him feel like he had joined the Post Office.

It was almost 11 o'clock when Miss Allard came back to the dungeon and she thanked Dorothy for taking care of George and told her that she may return to her position. Dorothy smiled at George, said she would see him around and left him in Miss Allard's company.

Miss Allard asked George how he enjoyed his tour of the office and if he was comfortable but before he could answer in full she told him it was time to meet Mr Finkelstein and off they marched to his office.
She knocked and entered immediately on the closed door so it became obvious to George that the rules Dorothy had explained to him did not apply to Miss Allard. Sitting at his huge ornate oak desk in an equally large luxurious leather chair he said, "Thank you, Sophie" at which time she gave slight nod of the head, turned and left the room.

"Welcome George, to what I hope will be a very successful and rewarding experience for us all. Take a seat."
George had felt nervous when he first met Miss Allard and then became a lot more relaxed when he was in Dorothy's company and now, sitting in a chair that had experienced a 1000 bums before his, the nervousness was returning.

Hey Kid

For the next hour he would listen to Mr Finkelstein's instructions and expectations. Like Dorothy, Finkelstein talked about the history of what he referred to as "The Firm" and the excellent reputation it held in the city.
He asked George if he had read the books that he'd given him at the first meeting and he also asked some questions from the books, almost as if it was a quiz which, luckily George passed with flying colours.

Finkelstein told George that later Dorothy would be taking him to the Royal Courts of Justice library where he would be registered and be given a library card. He was told that this wasn't just any Library card as only selected guests were allowed in the hallowed library in that building.

The nervousness was starting to fade again and George experienced a personal rarity by listening a lot more than he spoke. After the meeting George was a lot clearer on what he's duties were to be. They included, among other things being a courier as Dorothy had told him, a researcher and an assistant. He was to find out that "assistant" really meant occasional shopper, tea provider and errand boy and also accompanying his boss when Mr Finkelstein would appear in court for a case.

Three thirty came and George was told by the "Governess/boss lady" Miss Allard that he could go home and she would see him in the morning when he would actually start work. He thought for a moment that there was the hint of a smile from her, but then again he may just have imagined that.
George was of course grilled by all of his family members on how he did, did he like it, had he made some friends, was there anyone else his age there? The questions seemed endless but by the end of the week it was old news and thankfully for George everything was almost normal again.

The weeks before Christmas went past quickly and a lot of

the family focus had been on Louise and Frank as they were trying to settle back in England. Most of their marriage had been spent in Kenya and getting back to the work and ways of London although not difficult was taking a little time.

Frank's aunt Ann was settling in and very well and had adapted quickly to being a widow although Frank and Louise knew things were very different for her from the farm in Kenya where she had spent over 30 years. Most of the time she had a stiff upper lip that was so common amongst the Victorian English and she always appeared content, though she spent quite a bit of time on her own in the flat.

Frank and Louise didn't realise when they left Kenya that uncle Bert had been making arrangements for several years in case events would lead to them vacating the country in a hurry. His plans in business were made to make life a lot easier for Louise and Frank and he also wanted to insure that Ann would live well with the rest of her life.

Bert had listed a holding company in many years ago and although Frank knew he was full partner in the farm, he didn't really know the full extent of what he was a full partner of with Bert's dealings in England. Ann was providing a little information but the business side of things had always been Bert's job and she wasn't able to be a big help, though she was a great support.

Frank's earlier meetings with the bankers at Barclays and the solicitors, Morley & Co who Bert had retained in England years ago, had given him a lot of information to digest and now he was getting ready to handle things.

The company was trading in goods from several countries in East Africa such as, Nigeria, Uganda and Tanganyika. Although things were not looking good in Kenya at the moment and there was some unrest to be concerned about in most of Africa, Bert had realised that the export business would still thrive and, given time, grow. They also discovered the account at Barclays had far more funds in it than Ann, Frank, and Louise could ever have realised.

There was still a lot for Frank and Louise to come to terms with but the decision was soon made that Frank's dad, Bob would join them in the company in a part time position in a few months after he could make some arrangements with his own business and he could bring his expertise to the table. With Bob's experience, Frank's eagerness to succeed and Bert's plan for the future things looked pretty positive and if it all went as planned they may just make a success of things.

Christmas was coming very fast and, like the last couple of years it was changing quite rapidly. Joe was still away in Kenya and he wouldn't be home for quite some time. Rose and Michael were enjoying their teaching jobs in Kent and would be spending Christmas Day with Michael's family. Louise and Frank would come to Christmas breakfast and then go back to East Ham to spend the rest of the day with Frank's family and George would be home with his parents and grandparents. It didn't look like it would be the best of Christmases.

On Christmas morning things went as arranged. Louise, Frank and Georgina were there by nine o'clock quickly followed by Fred and Rachelle. Presents were opened and stories shared and right at 11 o'clock Fred announced it was time to go to the pub for the annual Christmas day pint. Fred, Nick and for the first time, Frank walked off to the Trossachs to fulfil the Christmas day tradition and leave the rest of the family to fulfil their traditional duties.

George was a little miffed and knew he wasn't old enough to join them but sitting around with the women wasn't something he cherished either. He was missing Penny as well who was probably on a hot beach somewhere in Australia and he was feeling quite left out for once. This growing up business wasn't at all what he had expected!

Louise could see how George was feelings and was quick to come up with her own little idea. "Come on George, let's take your niece for a stroll before we leave."

Before George could say yes or no Louise was putting Georgina in the pram with a thick woollen blanket over her and she was ready to go. George grimaced a smile, put on his jacket and off they went.

They walked for a while and ended up outside the Trossachs. Louise told George to stay with Georgina because she just wanted to have a word with "those three very inconsiderate men on the inside."

If that was supposed to make George smile it didn't work but about four minutes later Louise came out holding a gin and tonic in one hand and a pint of Fullers bitter in the other. "Here you go George, first Christmas pint with your big sister."

George was gobsmacked but he suddenly had a smile on his face that worked its way up from his mouth to his eyebrows as he took the pint glass from Louise. He didn't say anything at first, he couldn't with the lump in his throat but he was just like someone who had won the Irish sweepstakes, and the lump was soon washed down his throat by the accompanying beer.

It was cold outside but with Georgina wrapped up well, Louise and George didn't care. Louise was giggling and laughing as she watched her not so little brother down his first pint of beer in public and Christmas Day changed immediately for both of them.

It wasn't too long before the three wise men exited the pub and they were all smiles as well. Fred looked at George, who was expecting a sarcastic wise crack from his granddad, and said with a big grin on his face "Good lad, but next year you will be on the inside and buying the first round." He knew he was a long way off legal drinking age but it wasn't unusual for that law to be broken in the east end. He started to feel more grown up and just answered his granddad with a cheeky grin. With smiles all round they made their way back home, and said their goodbyes to Louise, Frank, and Georgina then, as in every year past, they listened to the Queens Christmas message and got stuck in to Christmas dinner.

Boxing day was quitter than usual and George took off to meet up with his old mate Davey Dent. They didn't do much except hang around and share stories of how their new jobs were going. Davey wasn't having such a good time at his job and was considering looking into migrating to Australia on the £10 emigration programme.
Dave was a few months older than George and was already 16 years old. That was old enough, if he had parental permission, to go Australia. George just looked at him and he said, "Bloody Nora, Dave, is everyone moving out?"

The thoughts came into George's mind, first Penny Button, now Davey, who was only referred to as Dave now he was a part of the adult workforce. Who the Hell's going to be left around here?

George was starting to feel that the world as he knew it was starting to crumble around him and it was a feeling he didn't like at all.
Dave followed through with his application and less than two months later he was on a ship sailing for Australia. Not knowing if he would ever see, or even hear from his mate again George's only thought was that he would now be missing one more friend.

1956

The start of the year was welcomed in with cold, wet and rainy weather accompanied by endless dark clouds drifting across the sky like smoke belching from hundred's of factory chimney's.

Friendless George, as he was thinking of himself now Dave was gone to Australia, was spending much of his time in the library at the Royal Courts, often copying papers that he did not understand. Dorothy was there some of the time to help and that at least made the day the little brighter. She may have been engaged but she was still available to the eyes and imagination! She reassured George that in time he would understand a lot more, especially once he was able to see some of the cases that were being tried in court.

That experience wasn't to take too long as he was sat near Mr Finkelstein in a case where the firm where defending their client in a lawsuit.

The client, Sir Geoffrey Montague-Smyth owned a yacht moored on the River Thames near Chelsea. A couple, Mr & Mrs Anderson were walking past the yacht when a window on the boat seemingly exploded and injured both of them. The woman had panicked and fell, hitting her head and receiving a concussion. The gentleman received cuts to his arm and face. They were suing Montague-Smyth for negligence and trying to claim £5,000 in compensation.

As soon as Finkelstein started to speak George realised what the research and photocopies really meant. The prosecuting attorney had put their case forward to the magistrate and it seemed like they would be awarded damages with no questions asked. That however, wasn't going to happen.

Finkelstein quickly got to the point stating it could not be proven why the window exploded but the insurance adjusters had deemed the most likely cause was from a foreign object striking it. It could have been a passing boat throwing up an unknown article or a bird dropping a pebble from a great height, there was no way of knowing so the law of negligence, according to Finkelstein, did not apply.

The Andersons solicitor retaliated, saying that excuse was nothing but nonsense and the window should have been protected.
George was starting to get really bored but was suddenly impressed when and how his boss spoke,

Without looking any further at his notes Finkelstein calmly replied, "I refer to Fardon v Harcourt-Rivington, January 1932 tried in this very court."
"The House of Lords determined that a person or persons shall not be liable if they failed to guard against "fantastic possibilities.""

With that closing argument the Magistrate recessed for 15 minutes, obviously to check the case mentioned. As they were waiting George realised that the case mentioned was one he had researched with Dorothy and Finkelstein had memorised the significant parts. It was a small and rather insignificant case for the firm but as George would come to realise it was the clientele that could be significant and not the case itself. Upon the Magistrates return he addressed the court and immediately found for the defence.   Case dismissed.

That was George's inauguration to Mr Finkelstein's prowess in the courtroom. It turned out not to be as boring as he expected but it wasn't very exciting either, though listening to Finkelstein was an experience. There would be many more interesting times to come, but at least he saw the results of his own work.

Back at the offices Finkelstein thanked George for his part in the case and ability to follow instruction. George took that as quite the compliment as he had heard Finkelstein wasn't known to say too much about his junior's efforts and his expectations were very high of everyone around him.

He also explained to George that although the case was trivial he enjoyed an afternoon of simplicity in the court, plus it always helped to have friends in high places.
George also realised that what was said in the office, told to clients, and mentioned in court may have been the same story but certainly told in very different ways.

After seeing Finkelstein in action several times he realised that some of the qualities of being a top Queen's Counsellor included being able to bluff like a good poker player and having the ability to be somewhat devious, in addition to being a good storyteller. Maybe, thought George, his boss took lessons from Granddad Fred!

Dave sent a letter back to George, who had been spending a lot of time in the library as well appearing in the court with Finkelstein several times, telling him about the trip and how nice Australia was and also suggesting George consider going there. As with Penny the letters would become few and far in between over time, and losing friends was a fact that George soon realised was part of life.

So far Finkelstein had won every case and his comprehension of the English language truly amazed George. Even some of the other legal types in the court could be seen looking at a dictionary to find the definition of one or more of the words Finkelstein used.

It was indeed a real experience to listen to a person who had obviously memorised the Oxford English dictionary and had the ability make some of his "learned friends" feel very inadequate!

Hey Kid

George felt very lucky, as Dorothy would often be available to help him with the research and they had become close friends as well as work colleagues. One afternoon at the office she asked him if he had plans over the Easter weekend and if he would like to join her, Sebastian, who he now also knew quiet well, and some friends on Saturday for a party in the park.

George didn't have anything special planned, especially with the family focus being on the Frank, Louise and the time they were spending with legalities of their own type, plus he would be pretty much alone after dinner anyway. He hesitated for a second but before he could answer that he would be happy to join them she said, "I'd like you to meet my younger sister, Penny. She's a little shy and, well she, um, well you'll see. It will be a good time."

That was an up and down moment for George as he thought if she was anything like the gorgeous Dorothy he would love to meet her but the memories of his first love, Penny Button, streamed into his thoughts like a cascading river.

Dorothy didn't wait for any answer and she just said "Good, Then we shall see you at three o'clock Saturday afternoon at Temple Gardens by the Embankment."

Just a little lost for words and searching for an answer George just nodded and spit out an "Okay," and then he started to wonder what "you'll see" meant. Was she the ugly sister, or maybe she had a wooden leg or something equally as bad?

Saturday afternoon arrived and being true to his word George dressed in his smart casuals and walked to his usual workday bus stop. He boarded the number 15 bus as he had done so many times since starting work with Mr Finkelstein and company and he immediately noticed the difference in the Saturday passengers from his normal workday travel companions. There was not one of the regulars to be seen but instead a different group of people consisting of what looks like mums and dads taking the children on a Saturday outing or maybe off the shops.

Over the last few weeks he had "named" all his regular fellow passengers and guessed at what they did for a living, from Ahab the Billingsgate fishmonger to Titsalina Bumsquash, the fat lady who took up two seats. She thought she must have been a mud wrestler or a female bouncer! At least his imagination helped him pass the time on the bus!

It was a little different for George as he passed his normal stop and disembarked from the bus, a couple of stops further than usual on Fleet Street and he took the short five minutes walk to Temple Gardens and he arrived there a few minutes before three.

He didn't have to wait long before Dorothy, Sebastian and Penny showed up. Dorothy almost looked like her usual self, only she was wearing a rather flowery dress that showed more cleavage than he had seen before, which was very enjoyable, though he had to be careful not to stare!
Sebastian also looked totally different and George had never seen him without wearing a suit and tie. Today he was wearing jeans and a sweater and carrying a knapsack. He looked very different than when he was in his office attire and George actually liked him better this way.

Dorothy greeted George in a happy and somewhat playful tone, a hug and a totally unexpected kiss on the cheek. "Hi George, so glad you could make it. "This is my sister Penelope, Penny to family and friends."

George couldn't believe his eyes. She was absolutely stunning, about the same height as Dorothy and wearing a navy blue skirt and a white cardigan covering her cream

159

coloured blouse.

She looked a lot like Dorothy with the same dark hair, piercing blue eyes and flawless skin only she was younger and even prettier. George reached out his hand like a gentleman and said "Pleased to meet you Penny, Dorothy has told me about you." That was an exaggeration to say the least because Dorothy had said very little about her sister, ever.

Penny smiled and shyly held head down just a little as she looked to George and said "Nnice to mmeet you Ggeorge."

There was a deafening silence for a second or two as Dorothy held her breath and waited to see what George's reaction would be when he heard Penny stutter. She was now thinking that she should have told him but then he may not have come. She stood there, silently hopping, with baited breath. Whatever thought went through George's mind when he heard Penny no one would ever know as he simply smiled and said, "You look very nice Penny, I've been looking forward to meeting you."

Had George turned and looked at Dorothy he would have seen her biting her bottom lip and then silently sigh with great relief and had he looked even closer he would've probably seen, and heard her heart beating loudly through her expanding and then deflating breasts. He would've also noticed Sebastian look at Dorothy and give her a nod and a smile. But he saw none of that. He was far more fixated on the gorgeous young lady standing in front of him.

Of course he had noticed the stutter but for some reason it was totally irrelevant to him. First impressions count and his first impression was that Penny was someone he would like to get to know a lot better.

Sebastian broke the silence and announced that he had a bottle of wine and some sandwiches in his knapsack and also a set of bocce balls. He suggested that they have some fun and play a game of bocce on the Green.

There wasn't actually much room in Temple Gardens as it was more of a place people walked through to enjoy the flowers and the shrubbery, or maybe sit and read, but there was a good green patch and you don't need much room to play bocce.

The teams were a foregone conclusion with Sebastian and Dorothy teaming up to challenge Penny and George. Sebastian was the only one you had any idea how to score and it was an hour of good fun as each side declared they were the winner. After the game Sebastian pulled out a blanket from his knapsack and laid it on the grass.

As they sat eating sandwiches and drinking wine out of thin paper cups they chatted about work and other things but Penny didn't say very much. Dorothy had tried to bring her into the conversation but it was easy to tell she was feeling a little embarrassed and not really sure of herself.

George had noticed that as well and he started talking about Frank, Louise and his niece, Georgina and how they had to leave Kenya in such awful circumstances. He told them about his brother Joe and that now he was over in Kenya and was part of the policing action. He didn't want to get too serious but it seemed that Penny quite interested.

Looking at George and quite serious she said "Your pparents mmust have been vvery scared for them." George told her they were but they were very proud of them as well.

Dorothy was looking on and was feeling quite emotional. It

was obvious that this meeting had been set up to introduce
Penny to George and she certainly didn't know what the
outcome would be, although it looked like things were
going a lot better than she could have expected. Sebastian
told her later that even a blind man could have easily seen
George was attracted to Penny the moment he saw her!

George hadn't given it a thought that no one else had
shown up until Sebastian said they were meeting their
friends at the Blackfriars pub and he invited George and
Penny to come with them.
Dorothy's eyes suddenly widened a little as she realised
she had not thought about their age.

She looked at Sebastian and said, "They aren't old enough
Seb, we better go and tell the gang we have a change in
plans."

Before Sebastian could answer George piped up
And said, "No, you go it's fine. Penny and I can maybe take a
walk along the Embankment and stop at the Wimpey Bar
or somewhere for coffee or tea and a snack, if that's okay
with you Penny" as he turned and asked her.
She smiled, nodded and said "I wwould really like tthat." So
the deal was done.
Dorothy didn't know whether to jump in the air and
congratulate herself on her matchmaking prowess or give
George a big hug and a kiss. Luckily she did neither but she
did say they would have to meet up and go home together.

"How about we meet outside Blackfriars tube station at 9.30?"
she suggested. It was all agreed.
Dorothy and Sebastian walked towards Blackfriars and George
and Penny walked the other way towards the Embankment and
headed for the Wimpey Bar.
It was a short walk, only about ten or twelve minutes to the

Hey Kid

Wimpey Bar, famous for its tasteless bland coffee and small, somewhat overcooked hamburger with chips but at least it was very convenient and comfortable. They sat at the window table where they could watch the many boats go by on the busy river Thames.

It was just after 5 p.m. so George and Penny had four hours to get to know each other and he really liked the idea of getting to know her. She did look like Dorothy but her eyes were even bluer and her skin was flawless. She didn't have Dorothy's look of confidence and she wasn't as outgoing either but she did have a smile that was warm, inviting and an uncomplicated natural beauty.

They chatted about all kinds of things like their families, Kenya, and the places they wanted to travel to but it was George who did most of the talking, which was very unusual for him when he met someone new. He didn't mention the last Penny he knew but she did pop into his thoughts a bit as he was talking to this Penny. He was wondering if this newfound friend would also be taking a one-way trip to a far off land in the near future.

He knew Dorothy had nobbled him just a little but it didn't bother him, he actually thought it quite funny and even more, appreciated it. The more he looked at Penny and the more he talked, the more gorgeous he thought she was.
They could see the sun starting to go down over the power station on the south side of the river as they sat silently for a few minutes soaking up the moment.

Penny was struggling a little to say too much and was feeling embarrassed at the fact she stuttered. She would look at George and try to say something and then she would lower her head and the words wouldn't come out. Then she would pick up and chat for a while but then suddenly stop. George wanted her to feel more relaxed and feel comfortable so he also sat in silence for a while and smiled at her until he found the courage to say what was on his mind. He was far from a romantic but this time he chose his words well, though they could have been straight from a romance novel!

"Penny, I know that we have only just met but, well…I don't want to be too forward, but you really do have the most incredible eyes."

Penny blushed then grinned just a little as she embarrassingly shrugged her shoulders. "Thank you," she replied slowly, without stuttering. Still feeling a little embarrassed but also curious she had to say what was on her mind as well. She was looking quite nervous as she said, "But G G George you don't ss seem to mmind my ss stutter. Why?"

George looked at her with a surprised look on his face and he wasn't really expecting her to be quite so candid with him.

 "I don't know. It's you I suppose. It's part of you. I just think you're very nice and …"

She reached across the table and cupped his hands in hers looking at George and said "I think yy you are the nnnicesest pp person I have ever mmet," and started to talk more easily.

George could only smile back and the accompanying silence said everything. The time ticked away faster than he wanted it to. The had sat in the Wimpey Bar and shared four cups of coffee, which neither of them really liked and they sadly consumed two of the overcooked hamburgers. It was time to start strolling back. Penny didn't want her big sister coming to look for them.
Their conversation had covered all kinds of topics, from history to careers. Far more than either one of them would have expected but none of which they ever remembered as their real thoughts were elsewhere.

Hey Kid

Penny was a little more than a year older than George and she was attending a college in Hackney. She was learning secretarial work but she really wanted to be a teacher. The college had a speech class she attended three times a week and they had told her to forget about a job as a teacher as she would never be able to communicate probably with children. George thought that was both sad and really harsh. He told her that his sister Rose was a teacher in a grammar school in Kent. He could have a talk with her and see what her thoughts were. That suggestion made Penny smile and feel good, as it also meant that she was going to see George again, and that was something she wanted.

As they started to walk back along the Embankment George closed the small gap between them and reached down to hold Penny's hand. Even after all the talking and smiles that had happened in the last two or three hours he wasn't too sure of himself and hoped she wouldn't pull her hand away.

She didn't, she took his hand and squeezed it a little and at that moment they were both wearing their hearts on their sleeve. They didn't too say much on the walk back as they were both digesting everything that had happened in the last few hours. What was going through George's mind was "I hope this Penny stays."

As they approached Blackfriars station they saw Dorothy and Sebastian waiting for them. They were like two deer's that were caught in the headlights of an oncoming vehicle and they froze momentarily still holding hands and neither of them wanted to let go.
Dorothy was looking very happy and maybe even a little tipsy, which George found humorous because at work everyone was so prim and proper but he had never seen Dorothy in a social setting. "So, did you two have a good time?" she asked.
She got a nod from Penny and a "Uh Uh" from George as they finally stopped holding hands.

Hey Kid

Dorothy looked at both of them and wasn't quite sure what to say but she had a good feeling about the two of them hitting it off. Then she asked, "Are you catching the train or the bus George?"

He told her the train was easiest from here and he would go through to Plaistow and catch a bus from there. Dorothy and Penny would go to Mile End so they would be on the same train for a while and Sebastian would catch the bus across Blackfriars bridge to Southwark were he stayed.

Dorothy said her goodbyes to Sebastian while George and Penny walked into the station. They didn't have to say anything but neither of them wanted to stand around while Dorothy and Sebastian sucked face either!

The three of them got on the tube train and said very little, though big sister Dorothy did keep digging. They had seven stations to go and George had 11.

Just before they got to Stepney Green station George looked at Penny and said to her "If you're not busy Wednesday night maybe we could meet again. As long as you're not busy that is."

Dorothy wanted to jump in and say that Penny wasn't busy but the matchmaker's work was done and now

George and Penny could work the rest out for themselves.

"Yes Ge George I'd llike that" and so the relationship began.

As the doors opened at Mile End station and they were about to disembark Penny turned to George and kissed him. "See you WWednesday" she said and it was hard to tell who had the biggest smile, Penny or George, ...or maybe Dorothy!

On Easter Sunday Rose and Michael were back home for an Easter dinner visit. It was a very small event in comparison to the family dinners of just a few years ago when there were so many people some of the kids ate from a plate on a tray while sitting on the couch.

George wasn't particularly concerned about Penny's stutter but the fact she had been told she could never become a teacher because of it really bothered him. He thought he would ask Rose for her opinion, and that's just what he got!
After dinner George spoke to Rose and told her he had met somebody and that he had a question for her. Nick had always said that Rose was the smartest one in the family and he was right. As she was the teacher and so smart George knew she would be the best person to talk to about Penny.

Rose and George weren't as close as he was with Louise but he did believe his dad when he said that Rose was most certainly the smartest one in the family. Plus she was his sister and he knew he could trust her.
To say Rose had an opinion on the matter of telling someone what they couldn't do was the greatest of understatements.

"What! Somebody wants to stop somebody else becoming something they want to be because of a perceived physical impairment? Those kind of things really make me really angry."

The subject had obviously hit a sore spot with Rose as George, after seeing her face turn red with a look of fury, was now waiting for the flames from her mouth to engulf him as if he were standing in front of a pissed off momma dragon.

"Do you know how many famous people have stuttered?"
It was obviously a rhetorical question because before George could even hazard a guess she carried on.

" I can tell you, George. You can start with King George, Lewis Carroll, Winston Churchill, Isaac Newton, and my Headmistress, Mrs Turner."

Hey Kid

It seemed like George may have opened Pandora's box and Rose certainly had some strong opinions to voice on the matter.

She took a couple of seconds and a deep breath then calmed down a little. They spoke about it at some length, with Rose of course doing most of the talking. George not only received an education on the subject, he really appreciated Rose right then and what she had to say.
Rose also told him they could talk about it any time and if he wanted her to meet his friend she was more than happy to do so.

George didn't feel he could take it any further right then so he thanked his smart sister and told her they would talk some more at a later time, after he met with Penny again.
They re-joined family and got on with the Easter visit, only now George had something more to think about.

Tuesday morning George went to work like any other day and after sitting at his desk for about 15 minutes Dorothy entered the room all in smiles.

"So George," she said, sounding somewhat like one of the Barristers in court, "What did you do to my little sister on Saturday to make her act like she had just won an Olympic medal?"

Dorothy was smiling and obviously happy that George and Penny had got on but George was more than a little embarrassed as Dorothy was questioning like a police interrogation, and he certainly didn't want any teasing at he office.
He just looked at her, shrugged his shoulders, smiled and didn't say anything.

Dorothy just smiled and said, "Well as you are picking her up

tomorrow I thought you had better have this," and she handed him a piece of paper with the address written on it and told him that 7 o'clock would be just fine.
She smiled at George again and left to get on with her work, leaving him to his job and his thoughts of Penny.

George didn't bother going home from the office on Wednesday afternoon, as he never got home until 6.30 Anyway so he stayed at the office until about 6:15 and then made his way down to the tube and took the train to Mile End. Penny and Dorothy lived with their mother, Lil on Rhonda Grove just about three minutes walk from the station so George was a little early.
Their house was bigger than the house he lived in and he walked nervously up the four stairs onto the stoop and knocked on the door. Penny must have been laying in wait because the door opened almost immediately and she was there ready to go. As she greeted George a larger mysterious figure loomed behind her.

It was George's first big fear, her mother, who softly said "Nice to meet you George. Don't get into any trouble and don't get back too late. Okay?"

Penny's mum was a little on the large side and was wearing a black dress and a coloured apron, just like his own mum wore. She was holding a rolled up newspaper in her hand and George's first thought was that she would whack him with it! Luckily that wasn't to be. She gave Penny a kiss on the forehead, told them to have a good time and disappeared into the house.

George had no idea where they were going, he hadn't given it any thought and for a while they just chatted and held hands as they walked towards the park. Penny had the advantage over him, as George didn't know the area that well so he just followed her lead. They walked for a few minutes more and then sat on a bench outside The Morgan Arms. George tried to make some small talk but Penny had a serious look on her face.

"This wwas my ddad's ffavourite pub."

"Was?" replied George.
She closed her eyes and nodded slowly. George knew immediately by her solemn look that her dad must be dead.

"He he wwas killed …in Germany."
It wasn't something that George was really ready for and all he could think to say was how sorry he was.

Penny looked at George, still holding his hand and rested her head on his shoulder. "My ddad would hhave liked you." She said, and with a lovingly but almost sad smile she kissed George on the cheek and said they should walk some more.

They walked, talked and stopped at a little teahouse cafe called "Nan's" where they spent the next hour and a half talking and sharing a pot of tea that neither of them touched.

George had butterflies in his stomach again as he tried to make conversation. He really liked Penny and was hoping she would feel the same way about him but she was so beautiful and she was older than him he had his doubts. He thought that his age might put her off of taking him serious. Time would prove that he couldn't have been more wrong.

Penny had a night classes every Wednesday and Thursday but this was Easter break so no classes this week. Friday night was family dinner, something that was a long-standing tradition in the Hawkins family, so they arranged to meet Saturday.

George suggested he pick her up in the afternoon and maybe they could go to the movies later in the evening. She quickly agreed and a short time later George was walking her back home. It was almost 9.30 and even though Penny had turned 17 years old her mum had given her a curfew and they both thought it best not to break it on the first night!

George left Penny at the door to her house and they kissed goodnight. This time though it was a longer, lingering kiss which made George's heart swell and pound, to say nothing of other unseen body parts.

This, George thought, was the best encounter with a girl he had ever experienced and he walked off to the Tube station on a cloud, smiling all the way and feeling like Jack the lad.

Tuesday nights and weekends would become a regular occurrence for George and Penny in the future, which of course brought some of the expected teasing from Nick and Fred, but he really didn't mind. After all it was he who had a girlfriend.

The Incredible Case of Sir Basil Perry

Early on Tuesday morning Sir Basil Perry was in the office with Mr Finkelstein.

Sir Basil had come to the office in a real panic. He was a tall, gaunt man who looked like a smile hadn't graced his face in a long time. He was serious and surly looking with a downturned mouth and huge sagging bags under his eyes. He looked like a long Shar-Pei on two legs.

His story was that a couple of days before, he was pulling off his driveway and glancing down at some notes on a pad, which was on the passenger seat. That lack of concentration led to him to not notice the bus in his path and he drove straight into it.

No one was hurt except for a couple of small bruises experienced by the passengers as the bus driver hit the brakes hard but Sir Basil was charged with "Driving with undue care and attention."

Normally that would just be another accident and Sir Basil would get a fine along with his insurance company picking up the cost of all the repairs but this wasn't the norm.

Sir Basil was due to be announced as the next British Ambassador to Holland but even the slightest blemish on his character before the announcement was made would lead to him not getting the job.

Finkelstein was a very well known QC and taken on a cacophony of "people in high places" cases in his career but never one as odd or as minor as a motor vehicle accident that was so obvious who was at fault.

However, because it was Sir Basil and because the consequences were so serious he felt obliged to help a man he had known for more than 30 years.

Hey Kid

His first strategy was to be one of stonewalling and delay as once Sir Basil was in the position of Ambassador it was unlikely that he would be removed for a motoring infraction.

His second thought was to get the case moved from a Magistrates court to a Crown court where the case would be heard by a judge and jury and therefore, take a little longer to get to court. A change of plea to "Guilty" on the day of the trial would annoy the prosecutor who would see it as a waste of time but it would offer the delay that was needed.

The plan worked and the case was to be heard in Crown court but unfortunately there had been some case changes and this case was brought forward and would be tried very close to the time Sir Basil's announcement was to be made.

A request was made to the insurance company for all their documentation and also to the police for copies of their reports and the statements made at the time of the accident.

George was about to witness what would become one of the most simple but bizarre cases ever to come to court. Finkelstein's best chance was to get this to a 50/50, no fault accident with blame equally shared, but that may not help Sir Basil.
George had the task of putting the statements into chronological order by the minute from when the bus left the last stop until the collision occurred. Finkelstein was clutching at straws hoping to find something he could use, or abuse.

The morning of the accident there were three London Transport employees on the bus. They were the driver, Mr Davis, the conductor Mr Roberts and, a Bus Inspector Mr Baines.

Sir Basil stated that he drove off his driveway at exactly 7.00 a.m. a time he confirmed as the bells from the church across the road were chiming the hour. As he drove off he hit the bus in the area of the front wheel, causing the bus to make an emergency stop. A London Transport safety officer was called to the scene, as were the local police. Sir Basil was charged and the bus was towed away shortly after.

Finkelstein had very little to work with and was sure Sir Basil's cause would be completely lost unless he could find a way delay the case even more.

George went through the notes and spotted something that may just have been of interest. The bus inspector said in his statement that the accident happened at 7.05 a.m. but Sir Basil had said it happened at 7.00 a.m.
He wasn't sure if it was significant but he brought it to Mr Finkelstein's attention anyway.

All too soon the court day was to arrive. The judge instructed the jury that this case may seem minor to some people but the law in England allowed a person to be tried by their peers if so desired and the person charged in this case had executed that right. From the tone of the judge's monotone voice he sounded very impartial but Finkelstein knew him and was aware that the right honourable judge was just a little frustrated at the farce of challenging such an obvious case.

Finkelstein looked over at the young solicitor the Crown had sent and received a condescending look in return.
The inexperienced young counsellor knew this was a cut and dry case and would be over in minutes and he couldn't help but wear a cocky smile.

The charges were read and Sir Basil was asked to enter his plea, which was "Not guilty."

The prosecution called the first witness, Mr Davis the bus driver. He asked his account of the incident, which was the same as his statement to the police. Very quickly the prosecutor announced he had no more questions and Mr Finkelstein had his turn to question the driver.

"What time did this accident occur?" he asked

"7 a.m. sir" came the reply and when questioned if he was sure of the time he replied he was because he could hear the church bells ringing seven."

He thanked the driver and said he had no more questions of him.
The prosecutor said he had no more witnesses as the case was so obvious and he wondered why the courts time was being wasted.

The Judge then asked if there were any witnesses for the defence and Finkelstein called the bus conductor as a hostile witness.

Finkelstein asked him the same question about the time and he also confirmed it was at 7.00 a.m. He then asked the conductor how the driver knows when to leave a stop to which he replied, "I ring the bell and then he knows he can go."

The prosecution had no questions and with that Mr Roberts was dismissed from the witness stand.

Mr Finkelstein then called the Bus Inspector, Mr Baines, supposedly a second hostile witness.

Like the others he was asked what time the accident was and like the others he replied that it was at 7.00 a.m.

He was then asked how the driver knows when to leave a stop and he gave the same answer as the conductor.

Finkelstein then asked who rang the bell the day of the accident. Baines hesitated for a second and said "I did, I always ring the bell when I'm on the bus as the inspector."

The door was then opened and Finkelstein made a meal of things, producing the statement made by Baines that said the accident happened at 7.05 and not 7.00 as everyone else had said. He then produced the bus schedule that had stops by time.

The bus was indeed due to arrive at the stop at 7.05 and the bust stop before was a holding stop. A stop where if a bus is running a few minutes early it waits there until it is back on schedule.

Finkelstein turned to the court, looked at the jury and then turned back to Baines and said:
"I suggest, Mr Baines, that you rang the bell in error because your watch was running a little fast. You sir risked the lives of every passenger aboard by ordering the driver to leave before it was time and as a consequence of that unforgivable error an accident did indeed occur."

Baines was tongue-tied and the prosecutor objected to the line of questioning. The judge overruled the objection and with no more questions Baines left the courtroom.

It was time for the closing arguments and the prosecutor addressed the jury saying Finkelstein's tactics where no more than theatrics and they should dismiss such nonsense and let common sense rule. He was so angry he was shaking and finished with the words "I am confident you are all smart enough not to fall for the nonsense the defence has fed you with."

Finkelstein was far more charming, first apologising to the jury for the prosecutor's unprofessional behaviour in suggesting that their intelligence may be questionable and then thanking them for their understanding of the evidence.

He then continued, "Ladies and gentlemen of the jury, it would be unforgivable for a person to be punished for the negligence of another. Had the inspector acted in a proper manner in carrying out his duties and held the bus at the stop for just two minutes longer so it would arrive on time then this incident would never have happened. By failing to act adequately as a trained employee in an important and responsible position, the inspector endangered lives of people he did not even know. By his action and he traumatised people, including the bus driver, the conductor, the passengers and my client, who has suffered distress because of this incident.

"Yes, there was an accident but it was avoidable and I implore you all to see justice done and that a victims of this incident not be punished because of the negligence of the real perpetrator, bus Inspector Baines." He then thanked the jury for their diligence and understanding before returning to his seat.

The judge, certainly not believing what he had just heard stayed impartial and simply directed the jury on their responsibilities and the bailiff escorted them to jury room to make their decision.

George accompanied Finkelstein to into the hall where they stood by one of the many life size statues of famous people that adorned the hallways of the court and they were soon to be joined by very nervous Sir Basil who was looking very concerned at what the outcome may be.

Finkelstein had done all he could and George was thinking that, although this was a serious case for Sir Basil, a comedy could have been written about such a far-fetched excuse for an accident happening. George thought back to his mischievous school days and even he had never come up with such a preposterous excuse!

The jury were out for less than 20 minutes when they returned to the court. Sir Basil felt the ambassadorship he so desired just sinking into an abyss like a coffin being lowered slowly into a grave.

The judge asked the jury foreman if they had reached a verdict to which the answer was "Yes." He then asked them what the verdict was and his face, which had been totally emotionless throughout the proceedings, was suddenly somewhat betrayed, as his eyes grew wider when he heard "Not Guilty."

He took a deep breath, thanked the jury and without further ado he said, "Case dismissed."

The young prosecutor was fuming and stormed past Finkelstein on his way. Had the look of fire in his eyes been real flames Finkelstein would have been reduced to a pile of smouldering cinders. Instead he was able to give the semblance of a somewhat condescending smile and a slight nod to his young adversary, which totally disguised the inner belly laugh he was experiencing.

Sir Basil shook Finkelstein's hand vigorously, and he was the Shar Pei who had just been given the biggest biscuit he ever had. He beamed a smile and thanked Finkelstein as if he had been given the gift of eternal life. Just like George, Sir Basil couldn't believe his luck either.
Finkelstein smiled but unlike Sir Basil he was very calm and matter of fact. He had done his job and if he was very pleased with himself he didn't show it.

"A pleasure" he said calmly and looked at Sir Basil and George, and said, "But don't thank me Basil, it was this young man he saved your skin. You may want to remember him, he's going places."

George was well taken aback. A compliment like that from someone who was only one step lower than God in the legal community was amazing. Sir Basil then thanked George with the same vigour, still sporting a silly schoolboy grin.

"I'm sure we shall meet again young man." And with that he almost danced down the hallowed halls of justice and disappeared to share his celebrations with whomever he could.

George had been in court with Finkelstein a few times but this one really took the cake. Finkelstein had somehow pulled the wool over 12 so called intelligent peoples eyes. It was incredible as far as George was concerned, even unbelievable. The jurors were actually convinced that a man who was 100% guilty was innocent because a bus was on the road at the wrong time. He couldn't discuss it with anyone, amazed as he was but it was something he would remember and chuckle about many times in the future.

Less than two weeks later it was announced that Sir Basil Perry was appointed as Her Majesty's Ambassador to Holland.

July 1956

It was George's birthday this month and he would be 16 years old, a year and a bit younger than Penny. At the office only Finkelstein, Dorothy and Miss Allard knew how old George actually was. Everyone else there assumed he was about 17 or 18 years old and luckily birthdays went unnoticed at the firm.

There was always something of a fuss made in the Rudge household when it was somebody's birthday. It usually consisted of a Fred produced cake, family, friends and the men going to the pub regardless of whose birthday it was!

This year though George didn't really want to have a birthday party. He was starting to think he was just a little too old to partake in such childish events plus he was told to bring Penny and he was more than a little afraid of being embarrassed. None the less he duly complied and a birthday gathering was arranged.

Things had been going very well between George and Penny and today would be a really big step for him, as she would meet his whole family at one time and in one place for the very first time.
He knew they would like her but he was still nervous about the comments and wisecracks he may have to endure, to say nothing of the possible embarrassment. He prayed Doris wouldn't get any baby pictures out and that Fred wouldn't come up with too many exaggerated stories.

Of course he was also hoping Penny would like them as well. Penny caught the train from Mile End to Plaistow station at 12 o'clock and George was waiting for her as they had arranged. It gave them at least a little bit of time together and Penny was also quite nervous at the prospect of meeting the whole family as well.

Hey Kid

When they arrived Fred and Rachelle were already there as were Louise, Frank and Georgina. George introduced Penny to everyone and thankfully there were no smart arse remarks made, though that didn't stop his expectations of someone embarrassing them soon.

Louise and Frank weren't able to stay too long. Things had been going very well with the business but they had more reams of paperwork to get through and other legal documents that had to be seen to in the next few days so they would spend a couple of hours and then take the leave.

They wouldn't leave before Louise had talked to Penny and got to know her just a little and later pulled George to one side and said to him "George, she's beautiful and really nice. I'm proud of you bringing her here, you must be a nervous but don't worry the silly comments won't happen today. They will wait until they know her a bit better then embarrass both of you!" She had a big smile when she said that but luckily that was the only teasing he received that day.

Of course he was still very nervous, especially of what Fred may come out with. He loved his granddad but knew Fred had a rather dark sense of humour as well.

Louise had to leave early but she told George that when all their work was done he must bring Penny over for a visit with just them one evening very soon.

A few minutes before Louise left, Rose and Michael showed up. They came in their new car and were quite eager to show it off. They had purchased in grey coloured 1952 Ford Prefect for £50 and were really happy to show everyone that they were moving up in the world.

George went through the introductions one more time, so now Penny had met everybody, except Joe of course and of the

Hey Kid

chatter continued.

Rose had been very keen to meet Penny and talk to her about Teacher training after her recent conversation with George.

When Doris said she needed to go to the store for some more milk Rose took the opportunity to say that she would go and maybe Penny would like to go along with her for a walk. The store was only a couple of streets away but it took about 45 minutes for the two of them to return.
George wasn't to know what transpired in their conversation for a while but both of them seemed pleased with themselves so he assumed it was something good.

It wasn't much like a birthday party but more like family get-together, until the birthday gifts made their way to the table. It became painfully obvious that George had been in need of some new clothes.

He unwrapped the first parcel, which was from Louise and Frank and revealed a new white long sleeved shirt and a smaller parcel that said on it "Happy Birthday uncle George." His first ever gift from his niece was three pairs of socks.

Rose handed him a card and inside there were two theatre tickets for "My Fair Lady" at the Drury Lane Theatre for next Saturday. George had never been to the theatre in the West End and the only plays he had ever seen before were pantomimes around Christmas time. Before he could say too much Rose laughingly said, " I have just checked with Penny and she is free next Saturday."

They all laughed but George felt his face getting a little red as well. Fred and Rachelle gave him his first new shaving kit, a Gillette razor complete with brush and soap. He didn't shave every day and he had been using one of Nick's razors up until then.

182

Hey Kid

Doris produced a card from Kenya. Joe had sent it weeks ago to make sure it got there on time and it contained a postal order for 10 shillings along with a birthday greeting and some stamps from Kenya and Uganda. George still had all of his stamps but hadn't paid much attention to them for some time, though he was still quite proud of his collection.

Penny reached into her handbag, pulled out a small parcel and handed it to George. He opened the package to find a new blue tie and tie pin. He was starting to wonder about this "clothes and dress better conspiracy!"

Finally, Nick handed George a small envelope with two ten shilling notes and a £1 note and said "If you're taking your young lady to the theatre you had better take her for dinner too."
It really did seem like a birthday conspiracy but obviously George didn't know that everyone else knew Rose was getting the tickets and they must have wanted to make sure he was dressed properly as well!

It had been a great afternoon and, thanks to Nick scoffing three huge pieces of cake, the remains were hardly enough to feed a few hungry sparrows. Everyone had a good visit and about 5 o'clock Fred said they had to go home, but he was actually making a stop to conclude one of his little deals at the pub.

George said he would take Penny home at about 6 o'clock so they could catch the train and spend some time alone but Rose stepped in and said she and Michael could drive them to Mile End and drop them off. That turned out to be a great idea. George sat in the front of the car and Rose chatted to Penny about teaching. Rose was full of ideas and knew the system really well. She even invited Penny to come and visit King Edward grammar school where she was teaching and told her she could arrange a meeting with her headmistress, Mrs Turner who she described as an absolute inspiration.

Hey Kid

Penny was excited to say the least and the conversation continued as if Penny and Rose had known each other for years. Even after the car had stopped and they all got out to say their goodbyes they continued talking for a few more minutes.

Eventually it was goodbye and Rose gave George a kiss on the cheek, something he couldn't remember her ever doing before, and said "Happy Birthday brother" and whispered to him, "She's a keeper!"

On Friday it was to be George's turn to face the jury as Penny had invited him to meet her family at their weekly gathering. George, like Penny a few days earlier, was a little nervous. She had told him that there was always a large number in attendance and this week it was at their house on Rhonda Grove. Now he knew how Penny felt coming to his place for his birthday.

Friday came all too quick and at 6 o'clock George knocked on the door and was welcomed by a smiling Penny. He was introduced to everyone but the only names remembered where the two grandmothers, granny Hawkins and Nanny Nelson.

Dorothy and Sebastian were both there and when they were somewhat alone Sebastian told George not to worry about the gatherings as he had a list of excuses he could give him to not attend regularly in the future.
Sebastian smiled and George wasn't if the offer was serious or not but as it turned out even Penny had her own excuses and was determined not to condemn George to the sentence of the weekly tribal event.

George followed Sebastian's lead and left when he did, with a smile and a quick kiss from Penny. He had a feeling of relief that his introduction to the Hawkins family has gone okay but he was glad it was over.

Hey Kid

George picked Penny up early on Saturday afternoon and they took the bus to the Strand where they walked around for a while before stopping in at Rules, one of London's oldest restaurants. It was very fancy by their standards but after spending over £2 on a very small meal they at least found out how richer people lived!

My Fair Lady was a play to remember and Penny had never enjoyed herself so much. After the show she told George she was going to call Rose on Monday and she wanted to meet her again and find out if teaching really was a possibility for her. George was delighted at the prospect but at the same time hoped it didn't mean Penny moving away to college like Rose and Louise had a few years ago.

After the call Penny and Rose didn't waste any time and arrangements were made to meet at King Edward School the following week. Penny was to bring all of her school results, her final marks and the confirmation of her GCE's she had completed, and she was to come prepared to spend the day.

It would take a little over an hour to Welling station on the train and Rose would be there to meet her and take her to the school. Everything went to plan and by 10.30 that morning Penny had received a tour of the school and was ready to meet Mrs Turner, the headmistress.

The school was magnificent and the people she met there were very friendly. The thing that really concerned her was that some of the students she saw looked as old as her.

Mrs Turner was an older lady, a little wrinkled in the face but extremely graceful, very well spoken and she was dressed impeccably. She asked the secretary to bring in tea for three and invited Penny and Rose to take a seat sit on the very comfortable looking old cloth covered chairs.
"Well Penny, it is a pleasure to meet you and Rose tells me

you have aspirations to join us in the teaching profession."

Penny was very nervous and as comfortable as Rose and Mrs Turner had made her feel her heart was still pumping like she had just run a marathon.
"Yyes I very mmuch would." She managed to nervously say.

Mrs Turner ignored the stuttering and went on to talk about commitment, dedication, and listening to the calling we all have inside.   She looked through Penny's qualifications without saying very much or giving any facial clues as to what she was thinking.

"Very good" she said as she looked towards Penny. "The thing is Penny, do you have the drive and passion to make happen those things that will shape your future and the future of those entrusted to you?"

Penny was about to answer when Mrs Turner continued talking without waiting for a reply. She told Penny what a success Rose was and how she had started very young as well, and that now it was time for the next generation to make its mark.
"It is time for change," she said. "Your generation must take up the challenge and mould the students of today into the leaders of tomorrow. I was born when Queen Victoria was still on the throne and I have witnessed many changes in education and there are many more to come. But it will soon be time for old fuddy duddy's like me to move on. So, Penny do you think you posses the intestinal fortitude to help initiate positive change in young people by ensuring they are properly educated?"

She felt like it was an interrogation but somehow wasn't intimidated. Mrs Turner's voice was quite calm and even with the intensity of what she said Penny felt strangely comfortable. She hesitated for a second and then said in a very confident voice, "I do Mrs Turner, yes, I do."

She didn't notice herself but the fact Penny didn't stutter struck Rose immediately.

Mrs Turner smiled and surprised both Rose and Penny when she said "Parlez-vous francais, Penny?"
Although she wondered why Mrs. Turner addressed her in French she actually did know a little so she answered "Je fais madame mais pas très bien. " *(I do ma'am, but not very well.)*

Mrs Turner smiled and said, "My dear, you remind me of myself of almost 50 years ago. I also stutter and I still persevere to overcome it. Today maybe I can pass my experience on to you.
First, learn a language other than English. You obviously have some French so study it more. The new words and their pronunciation help you as you have to use the part of the brain that helps you concentrate. Then you must also read as much as you can and embrace every word, speaking out loud, slowly and with passion.

Also, do not use contractions. People may feel like you are a snob when you say "I do not want to" instead of I don't want to" but you will get used to sounding out each word and finally my dear, do it at your own speed. Like me, you may never lose your stutter but you will control it. I do."

Rose was actually surprised at the straightforwardness of Mrs Turner's talk to Penny and how relaxing but still inspiring she was, talking almost like an old friend and advisor but with such passion. The meeting was a great success.

Mrs Turner was on the Board of Governors at Brentwood College where she had first met Rose, and was willing to help Penny get a place when the next term started in September if it was at all possible.

Hey Kid

There were some hurdles to cross but luckily Penny would have a lot of support from family, or families, and from Mrs Turner, who also said that if Penny became an accomplished enough student, she may consider her for a student placement at King Edward when the time came.

Penny couldn't wait to tell everyone, especially George who would have mixed feelings but she knew he would also be very supportive, especially after she would tell him that the day she met him was the best day of her life.

It had been almost a month since Penny visited King Edward School and submitted all the documents for the application to Brentwood College but she hadn't heard a word. She had spoken to Rose who told her to be patient but she wasn't feeling anything except anxiety.

When she thought about it she had only known George for three months but it seemed like he had always been there with her and she hoped that he was feeling the same.

July rolled into August and school had broken up for the summer holidays but there was still no word from the college. To make things worse Penny was due to go to Brighton with her mum to spend a couple of weeks with aunt Agatha, her mum's sister. They had gone every year since the end of the war and it had become their annual family holiday, only Dorothy hadn't attended for the last two years. Penny really didn't want to go until she heard if she had been accepted or not.

Mrs Hawkins reluctantly agreed to let Penny stay home and as Dorothy would still be there everything would be fine so on Saturday August 4th Mrs Hawkins caught the train to Brighton from Victoria station alone.

The following Wednesday George would stop off at Rhonda

Grove to visit Penny and as he approached the house he saw her sitting on the top step holding her head in her hands and he knew the news wasn't good. He walked slowly up the stairs when suddenly Penny jumped up and said "I've been accepted George, I'm going to Brentwood."

She flung herself at George and wrapped her arms around him and held him tight to her body. He could feel the palpitations thundering through her breast with excitement and he started to laugh, in part helping to disguise the thundering feeling he was getting as well.

"Never a doubt" he said, still holding onto her.
Now she had to make arrangements. The letter had said that she was not able to stay in residence as Rose did because everything was already booked. That meant travelling every day. It it was only a 45 minute journey from Mile End but Rose had told her how beneficial the study groups in the evening were and now she may miss out on those. Right at this time though it was a minor detail and Penny was busy in her mind planning the next three years of post secondary school.

George stayed until about 8.30, after the news had been shared with Dorothy and Sebastian who had come home an hour or so before and were holding their own little celebration alone in the front room. They told Penny and George that they are the first to know that they had decided on a wedding day and it was to be next Easter.

She also told them that she and Sebastian wouldn't be home Friday or Saturday as they were going away for a couple of days together, a celebration of sorts, but Penny wasn't to mention a word to their mum. Then she said, "You two will be okay alone here together won't you?"

She smiled, kissed Penny on the forehead and left.

Hey Kid

Penny looked at George and said, You cccan stay? I don't
want to bbe here alone." Of course he said "yes" immediately.
George knew it would be easy to get that past his parents but
he would make a plan.

He didn't really want to lie to Nick and Doris sot he just told
them that Dorothy and Sebastian had a lot going on and asked
him to stay over if he could. To his surprise they didn't
question him at all about it and Doris even said she would
make sure he had enough clean clothes for the weekend.
It suddenly dawned on him that he hadn't told them Mrs
Hawkins was in Brighton so maybe that's probably why no
embarrassing questions were forthcoming.

They sat cuddling on the couch for a while Friday night,
watched TV and talked about things neither of them would
ever remember.
At about 10 o'clock Penny told George she was tired and
would take him up to show him where he was sleeping. He
had been hoping it was going to be in her bed but she took him
into Dorothy's room and told him Dorothy had said it was
okay for him to sleep in there.

After some more hugging and holding each other Penny left
the room and George, as much as he didn't want to be, was a
gentleman and just climbed sadly into bed.

The lights were all out and it was very quite in the house when
just a few minutes later Penny came quietly back into the room
and dressed in the flimsiest of nightgowns she slid into bed
with George. She put her arms around him and laid her head
on his chest and almost in a whisper said, "I love you."

George had memories of Penny Button just last year and
remembered what had happened to her after she said those
infamous words but this felt different, more real and the
feelings he was now experiencing were something very new to

him, and it just all felt so right. He held on to her and kissed her as he said, "I love you too Penny Hawkins, more than anything I love you."
They made love for the first time and stayed in bed until almost 10 o'clock the next morning.

They were both walking around very pleased with themselves, like they were on a cloud and both inwardly congratulating themselves on their adult experience.

Penny, most certainly being the more sensible of the two, became very serious and told George that before anything else happened he would have to go to the Chemist by the station and buy "some of those things." George looked a little embarrassed but also immediately agreed and went shopping, alone, a short time after.

It was Sunday afternoon when Dorothy returned and the first thing she asked was if they had a good weekend to which Penny said, not wanting to give anything away, "Yes, it was good thanks. How about you." Dorothy smiled and said just one word. "Good."

With the smile on her face there were no real surprises and she was probably thinking it was very good, for all of them. George made his way home for Sunday dinner and was accompanied by his dirty laundry, which he duly passed on to his mother.

Louise and Frank were there for dinner and talking about the long drawn out meetings with the solicitors that were becoming a real bore. They were fine financially but getting one thing and another approved and not even meeting anyone from the contacted company that was dealing with the imports and exports was becoming very difficult for Frank to hold his patience. His solicitor had told him that a meeting was soon to be arranged with Bradley, Chase & Wills the shipping agents but it still may take another few months to get fully sorted so they just had to bide their time.

It was frustrating for them but Bob Foxton was now also helping a lot and in the not too distant future things would be very different for them and they would be busier than they ever could have imagined. For now though they had to be content with the slow progress that was on going.

Louise looked at George and when no one was around she said, "What have you been up to, George, you've got a look about you like you've inherited a fortune."
"Me? Nothing really, just work stuff and Penny going to Brentwood, thanks to Rose. Nothing much else."

Louise just smiled and George wondered how the Hell she knew anything at all.
"Mmm, nothing is it. Okay. Guess you must have been in the sun a lot, being so red that is."
They just looked at each other with smiles that told their own story and Louise winked at him and said, "C'mon little big brother, let's help mum clean up."

Later George went to bed not thinking about work the next day but with other thoughts swimming in his head as he visualised and relived his weekend experience a hundred times over. Eventually fell asleep with a huge grin accompanying his dreams.

August was very slow at work for George and many of the senior staff had taken holidays, leaving some of the juniors to complete the smaller tasks that had been left to them.
Mr Finkelstein had obviously not gone far because he would drop into the office twice a week, though he said very little and after checking the mail and any messages he would usually gone in an hour or so.

Hey Kid

Mr Reynolds was the only senior in the office full time for most of August and he never said more than "Good Morning" or "Goodbye" to anyone except Miss Allard.

For Penny however, August was busy. She met with Rose several times and borrowed some books from her and purchased others. Rose would also coach her and give her a few tips about some of the instructors and what they were like to study under.

It was a really exciting time for Penny and although George wanted her to succeed in every way he was also a little apprehensive that he would not be seeing as much of her, which would turn out to be true.

Throughout September to December things were seemingly normal. George was getting on well at work and had been given a pay raise of 5% and was really getting an education in research and in how to read people, thanks to Finkelstein who took pride in explaining his adversaries mannerisms and expressions.
He also accompanied some of the other barristers on occasion and was becoming very familiar with the ancient legal system.

Dorothy and Sebastian had been busy and had sent out or delivered invitations for their upcoming Easter wedding and Penny was getting stuck in with her classes at college.

At home Nick was now in charge of over 100 men in the docks and work was picking up at a fast pace. Joe had written in October and said he was going to be home in January, which Doris was over the moon about and her brother Harry had announced he was going to be visiting for Christmas and would be accompanied by his bride to be, Margaret. He had let Fred and Rachelle know months before but tasked them to say nothing until he came home.

Hey Kid

Rachelle and Fred were still always there when needed and neither ever seemed to be in anything but a good mood. The big family news of the year came from Rose and Michael. They announced they were expecting their first child and were planning to buy a brand new house. From the pictures it was luxurious with three large bedrooms and a garage, plus it was completely detached.

For Louise and Frank business was still going well and the solicitors had told them they were now only weeks away from finalising all the complicated UK company papers and then they would be working full time and not tied up in a bureaucratic, hodgepodge jumble of indecipherable government paperwork.

Christmas celebrations that year were some of the best ever. George took Penny to St Luke for the Christmas Eve festivities and she stayed over, unfortunately for George in the spare bedroom, and experienced Christmas day with what Louise referred to as the "Crazy Gang." George didn't join the elders at the pub that year as was mentioned last Christmas but instead he and Penny went for their own walk. They did however, raise a glass of sherry for the obligatory toast to Her Majesty after the Queen's speech.
Fred provided much of the feast once again but this year Harry provided more champagne than anyone of them had ever seen as he introduced Margaret to the family who was an immediate hit with everyone. They hadn't decided on a wedding date yet but Harry told them that it wouldn't be too long before they made it legal.

George reciprocated Penny's Christmas Day visit on Boxing Day and was introduced to about 20 of Penny's rather loud relatives, most of whom he met for the first time, including her uncle Ed who was quite outgoing to say the least. They got on very well and Ed reminded George very much of his granddad Fred, always a funny comment and he seemed to know

Hey Kid

everyone!

Christmas 1956 was a time when it seemed like everyone was happy and things were going well. It was almost like they had hit the jackpot and life was as good as it could get. That Christmas, George was a very happy young man.

1957

By the second week in January Doris was getting more than a little bit antsy waiting to hear from Joe. She had been hoping that he would have been home by then but instead of Joe walking through the door a letter arrived that said plans had changed and they were being posted elsewhere with immediate effect.

Doris was heartbroken. She sat down on the sofa and sobbed for a while, waiting for Nick to come home.

She told Nick the news when he came home and he things only got worse when he told her he was the bearer of even more lousy news. The workers at the docks had voted to strike and it looks like his job could be at risk, at least for the next few weeks and things may get tough financially. He was management now but he still had a lot of long time friends who worked in the docks and he was very hesitant about crossing the picket lines if it came to that.

About an hour later at 6.30 things got even worse when Bob Foxton drove up with Louise. Michael had phoned Louise to say that he and Rose had been in a car accident.

She said they were both doing okay and were in the hospital being examined. The doctors were keeping very close tabs on Rose because of the baby. They didn't have many details but it appeared Rose was dropping Frank of as she did twice every week when an out of control vehicle sideswiped them. Apparently the driver had a heart attack and he was dead at the scene. They were taken by ambulance to Gravesham hospital in Gravesend and Michael was going to call as soon as he had any more news.

Nick didn't wait for any more information he just grabbed Doris by the arm and headed for his car. It took about 40 minutes to get there, though it seemed more like two hours in their anxious, fretful state.

As they ran into the Emergency area they saw Michael sitting there with his father. His arm was in a sling and his swollen face was sporting blue-black bruises. He looked afraid, like the fear of God had possessed him and that worried Nick beyond words.
He could say very little and was fraught with worry about Rose and the baby. Michael's dad was able to bring Doris and Nick up to date.

Rose hadn't suffered any broken bones but she had been trapped in the car until the Fire Brigade managed to cut her out. She had several lacerations but none of them too serious. The only thing the doctors had told them after she was admitted is that her injuries were not life threatening but there was some internal bleeding that they had to control.
After about an hour of worrying, pacing, and telling each other that she would be okay a doctor came out to talk to Michael.

Her condition was serious in as much they had to wait and see as far as the baby was concerned. The family was allowed to see her, but Michael was told to make any visit brief.
Rose was sitting up and starring into space as they entered the room. Her face was bruised and she had a tube in her arm and another larger one that disappeared under the blanket and was taped to her abdomen.   Considering her experience and the pain she was in she was in better spirits than they had expected, forcing something of a smile that became wet as her tears slowly cascaded her face. Doris was trying to put on a brave face but Nick knew she was a wreck and after a brief visit they left Michael holding their daughters hand and telling her everything would be fine. They waited for any more news in near silence the waiting room and just hoped and prayed for the best.

Meanwhile George had returned home and was feeling quite

chipper as he had been re-reading a note, more like a letter rom Penny, but he walked in he saw Louise siting there and by the look on her face he knew immediately knew something was wrong.

"What is it Lou, what's happened?" he said. He thought something bad had happened to Joe. His heart started pounding and his legs weakened as a thousand terrible thoughts seemed to rush through his mind at once.

Louise told him about the accident. His stomach felt like it turned inside out and his knees felt like they were being held up with jelly. He started to blabber out some questions, "Is she, is…"

"She's okay George, it's going to be fine." Louise was calm and composed on the outside but her stomach was also in free fall as well.

She knew what his reaction would be like and that he would tend to panic and think the worse. He may be getting close to six feet tall and he was getting used to being treated more like a man than a boy but Louise knew her big little brother better than most. He was a young man but he was also still an impressionable 16 year old who he had an imagination that would make him jump to all kinds of conclusions.

Louise and George sat there for an eternity waiting for Nick and Doris to return. George, in frustration and anger said that they should have a phone at home. Very few people did but this was one time it would have been welcomed.

It was almost midnight when the front door opened and Doris was the first to walk in the room. Here eyes were red raw and her face gaunt and white. She wasn't crying anymore, there couldn't have been many tears left in her but she continued sobbing as she tried to spit out he news. She started to talk in broken sentences but Nick stepped in and took over. His voice was monotone and sad as he forced the words past the lump in his throat. George had never heard him like that before but Louise had years ago when she was a child and his best friend had died.

"They're okay and Michael is at his parents place tonight. They're keeping Rose in for a bit but she's going to be okay as well." There should have been smiles and relief at that time but the invisible black cloud of impending disaster that engulfed the room told Louise there was more to come.

Fighting back the emotional pain and tears as much as he could, Nick continued, "She's lost the baby.
The silence was cold and everyone seemed unable to move, as if time was standing still deep in a dark, soulless, abyss. The seemingly eternity of a deathly silence was broken by George who said something so far beyond what anyone would have thought.

"But she's alive dad, my sister is alive and she's going to be okay because she's strong and she has us, Michael and us."
"Right dad?" he said, speaking through his own tears as he looked up to Nick.

Nick had forgotten the time when he told George that a family like theirs never had to fear anything because together they could overcome anything. It was years ago when he was a child but George didn't only remember it he used it at the perfect time and the tears of sorrow became the fuel of strength as they would all pull together and make sure Rose got whatever she needed to get past this painful day.

In the morning George walked to the telephone booth on Barking Road and called Miss Allard. He explained what had happened and she told him to take what time he and the family needed. She normally carried a voice that was almost emotionless, like a toned down Sergeant Major but this time George could hear they empathy in her voice and he was learning that people are not always what they appear to be. Nick went to work briefly rather than phone and then he stopped at Fred and Rachelle's to let them know what was happening.

They drove the short distance to East Ham, picked Louise up and all four of them headed to the hospital.

Michael was already there with Rose when they arrived and although there was sadness and grief the strength of being together, and grieving together made things a little easier to bare. George held up a bunch of flowers that they bought just outside the hospital.

"Don't let anyone see them Rose," he whispered.
"I pinched them off some old lady who was sleeping at the other end of the ward."

There was a laugh from everyone, and a loving clip on the ear from Doris but that jovial gesture was more than welcome as it made the sorrow just a little easier to deal with right then.

It was easy to see the emotional pain but Rose was stronger than people realised and she would get back on her feet very quickly.

She told George he must tell Penny, as they were supposed to meet tomorrow and go over some of her course work.

Nick drove back through Brentwood on the way home and dropped George off. He would come home on the train later and get a chance to see Penny.

George waited for her near the college entrance passing the time with his thoughts on what the future was going to bring for them. More fantasies than thoughts and they were constantly interrupted by the thoughts of Rose, lying injured in a hospital bed.

Hey Kid

Eventually Penny came through the college doors and when she saw George she beamed a huge smile and came running towards him. She dropped her bag to the floor and put her arms around him and just hugged him. The smiles didn't last long as George told her what at happened.

Penny had become very close to Rose in recent weeks. She was much more than a mentor, she had become a really good friend and Penny was just beside herself as George told her the whole story.
They walked to the station and George went back to Mile End with Penny on the train. By the time they got there they had talked enough to solve every problem in the world but the sad feeling of Rose being in the hospital and losing the baby overshadowed everything.

She told George she wouldn't be able to study that evening. She couldn't concentrate knowing Rose was in the hospital so they went to Nan's Tea Shop for an hour or so and just talked some more. The mood was somber for a while but George's new found knack for changing the moment came to the rescue again as he used the sugar on the table to spell, upside down, "I love u," which brought a smile and a reciprocal "I love you."
It had been a long day, one that no one would forget anytime soon.

A couple of days later Rose was allowed to leave the hospital and go home. She left with Michael and his parents and told everyone not to worry because she would bounce back and would call Louise often so she could keep everyone informed. It seemed like an eternity but the pain stopped soon enough although the emotions never left.

Fred and Rachelle had their own news to share as well. It wasn't exactly bad news and it seemed like something was happening to everyone so now it was their turn.

Hey Kid

They had received notification from the Council that they were to be relocated, just as Doris and Nick had been several years ago, only this time they wouldn't be housed in a Nissen hut but rather a new flat.

Many of the streets around them had been demolished and new homes built but their street had been saved from the wrecking ball. They had lived in the same rented house for more than 40 years but as it was a three bedroomed house the Council wanted it for a family and they were to be housed in a one bedroomed flat. It wasn't what they wanted but they had been expecting it and were prepared for the move.

None of that seemed to matter a couple of days ago when they heard the news about Rose, but of course it didn't change anything and in just a few weeks they would be on the 6th floor of a new block of flats just half a mile away on Barking Road.

The news did get better later that year as Rose recovered and got back to work and Penny did extremely well at the college. The strike earlier in the year didn't materialise as predicted but the possibility was still looming. Joe had been writing quite regularly and his unit was not posted as they had been told and he was still in Kenya, though it didn't look like he would be coming home anytime soon.

Things had been going well for Louise and Frank as far as running the business was concerned and they had learned a lot from Bob. With the help from his dad, Frank had started to get a good understanding of most things and was feeling confident that he had a grasp of things and that everything would be running smoothly very soon.

That was until the solicitor told him there was still some important business that needed his attention in Kenya.

EASTER 1957
The return to Kenya

Easter was quieter than most years with Fred and Rachelle moving into their new flat, Joe still away and Penny studying every spare moment she had. Things had been relatively normal at work for George and he was hoping for something more interesting to come up very soon.

Maybe it was because things had changed or maybe it was because George was growing up but Easter was just a few days off work and things were soon back to normal.

Frank's solicitor had told him earlier there were some issues with farmers who were re-organising in Kenya and making long-term deals with the government. They were keeping a close eye on events there but Frank was feeling he had enough to do where he was.

They had left the Foxton farm thinking the Mau-Mau would have destroyed everything and was given up as a loss but they were wrong and now, almost a year and a half later, there were be some different opportunities to investigate.

The solicitors strongly advised Frank to go back to Nairobi and meet with the white farmers group and see what opportunities he could take advantage of.

He was very hesitant about returning to Kenya and he wouldn't take Louise and Georgina for sure, plus it was 18 day on the ship so he could be gone a long time, which was something he wasn't prepared to do.

The solicitors did eventually convince him to go but not by ship. BOAC had flights to Nairobi four times a week. They flew to Rome, then Cairo, Khartoum, and on to Nairobi but because of the conflict in the Suez they would go from Rome to Malta then Khartoum-Nairobi. With stopovers in both Rome and Malta it would take three days.

Frank left in May and when he eventually landed in Nairobi where Ronald Kamou from the solicitor's Kenyan office was there to meet him and check him into the Stanley Hotel in the business district. The next morning it was down to work.

Ronald had copies of all the legal documents pertaining to the farm and from two more bank accounts held in Nairobi that Frank had no knowledge of.

Before the meeting that had been arranged Ronald gave Frank an in depth explanation of the current situation. The major items were the land transfer programme and a syndicate of farmers who had some spectacular long term plans. It was a lot to go over in a short period of time but the solicitors had really done their homework so life would be a little easier for Frank.

At about 10 o'clock that morning the syndicate members started to arrive and 30 minutes later 12 of them, some like Frank with their legal counsel, were sat around the huge mahogany table. Frank recognised several of them and was very happy to see Mark Houghton there who was someone he knew and was a good friend of Bert's.
For several hours they discussed what the future was going to be for foreign landowners, with some of the naysayers painting a picture of gloom and doom whilst others, like Mark, were saying it was time to seize the opportunity and grow with the changing times.

After some haggling and what some referred to as just nonsense talk Mark Houghton stood up and said,
"Coffee beans, maize, sugar cane, and cooperation that's where our future is."

Another farmer brought up the Land Transfer programme and

said that everyone could lose all they had and they need to stand their ground.

For Frank it was a headache and matters he couldn't wrap his thoughts around. It was the same after lunch and at about 6 o'clock it was decided to quit for the day and they would meet again tomorrow.

Frank felt like Santa Claus on Boxing Day, relieved it was over! "Thank God" was the only thought in his head, and then he realised they were meeting again tomorrow.

Mark Houghton came over and invited Frank for drinks and a bite to eat at the hotel lounge, an offer that was quickly accepted.

Mark explained in much easier terms exactly what was going on in Kenya and told Frank that the most likely outcome was the country would get independence. India, Pakistan and Ceylon had already become independent and Ghana had also negotiated with Britain and was to become independent next year.

Mark's prediction was that in the next 10 years most of the African countries would be on their own so the choice was to drop everything and run or to make lasting agreements that would benefit both sides.

He also explained to Frank about the land transfer programme where the white farmers would have to relinquish huge amounts of their land to local farmers and receive very little compensation in return.

However, there was a good side to it. If some of the farmers started the process before it became law they would have a head start, gain trust, and ensure the land would go to people they picked and not to government appointed people who may be corrupt and would be harder to deal with.

Hey Kid

Frank was thankful for at least some insight but it had been a long day and the bed in the room was calling his name. A hot bath and a long sleep was all he wanted.

Too early in the morning the phone rang by Frank's bedside. It was Ronald and time to go for breakfast and then round two of the Kenyan white farmers African boxing championship, or so it seemed.
Frank was wondering if he had made a huge mistake going to Kenya. They had been doing fine back home and the prospects were looking good. Maybe he should have left it at that.

It was easy to see that there were many different opinions and some of the syndicate members wanted to hold on to their land and fight to the bitter end but common sense prevailed with most of them. Things were changing and unless they changed they would become non-existent in a few short years.
The land programme was high on the agenda and the meeting started to become a blur to Frank, who had no idea about some of the things they were discussing.

When they broke for the day Mark took Frank to one side again and told him that he could see how frustrated he was getting but tomorrow the old guys would really get down to brass tact's so Frank must be prepared.

They ordered a couple of refreshing pink gins and sat in the old red leather armchairs by the window and at least had a good view of the gardens, which in itself was both welcome and relaxing.

Mark started the conversation and got right to the point.
"Look Frank, here's the real situation and how it has to play out. The old chaps think they are still fighting in the Boer war or something but most of the syndicate knows what's coming. You own an Import Export company and some land here. We

all have land but we will not be able to keep it all to ourselves much longer the way things are developing. We, the white farmers, have to make other plans and that is where you come in."

"We need to come to terms with the local government first then the big boys. We will lose a lot of the farms to the blacks, no doubt about it, but they still need to sell their crops.
Now, because of the laws, the time, foreign residency, and a myriad of bureaucratic bullshit, we can't just up and create or own companies abroad. Besides anything else there are too many hands in this pot and agreements could take longer than the second coming."

"You have what everyone here needs and its something that can make you a rich man, if you're fair. Tomorrow the talks will change and some interesting offers are going to be on the table. Now, your uncle Bert helped me out a lot in the early days and to be honest if it wasn't for him I wouldn't have made it. So, it's payback time."

"They are going to make you an offer to take the contracts to get all the crops, mainly coffee beans and sugar cane, over to the UK. We can cut out brokers and some other hangers on here and you can handle the European trade.
With good long-term contracts in place it will also be easier to deal with the land transfer programme because there will be less work and guaranteed income for the new black farmer.
What they are going to want, and need is warehouse space and their own overseas office in England. I believe the offer will be a fair one and is to include an annual contract fee at a fixed price plus a bonus of 1.5% of the syndicates joint annual profit."

Frank was sitting with his mouth open and listening intently, saying nothing.

Mark continued his thoughts, "You need to be ready. Talk to

your boy Raymond, he probably has a good idea what's coming anyway, and make a counter offer. I believe the contractual agreements will be very fair but you still have land here that the syndicate could use in their portfolio so you could counter with your land thrown in and ask for 2 ½ %. They will counter and settle for 2%."

"This can work if you want it too Frank. What do you think?"

Frank's firs reaction was, "I think I need another drink!"
A few moments of thought and Frank told Mark he had to wrap his thoughts around so much information but if all what was said was true then he would be very interested.

Day three started off and Frank was waiting for the arguments to start again but they didn't come. Everyone was much more amiable and it was to be a day for business.

As Mark predicted an offer was to be made. Kendall, the one who had done a lot of the talking over the last couple of days, asked for silence and said they would turn the floor over to their legal counsel to summarise things and propose a plan.

There was silence as Cornelius Hyde, the distinguished Barrister, took the floor and gave his speech, which echoed tones of Mark's talk the previous evening.
He then looked directly at Frank and said, "Mr Foxton, it has come to my attention that you may be pivotal to some of the proposed plans that everyone here has been discussing. After much consideration and lengthy discussion we shall propose an offer to you that should be considered one that will create a mutual benefit to all present."
With that he went on to propose almost exactly what Mark had said the night before.

Frank had been wondering if this was all a good thing or was it some type of set up that he couldn't figure out.

Hey Kid

Hyde finished his talk and the room was silent as they waited for Frank's reply. Frank said nothing for a few seconds that seemed like hours to some of those present, and then he said, "Thank you Mr Hyde. May I suggest, we take a short break so that I can discuss this matter with my representative here, Mr Kamou. Shall we say one hour?"

Mark Houghton was smiling on the inside as he saw Frank had paid attention to their earlier conversation and he was feeling that everything would work out.

Frank and Raymond Kamou sat in the drawing room off the lobby. It didn't take more that a few minutes for Raymond to say what a good deal it was and that he hoped he could continue as Frank's representative in Kenya. With Frank in England he could be the number one legal representative in Kenya with a job for life.

"This is an amazing chance, sir," he said whilst hosting a grin like he had won a jackpot. Then Raymond explained how things would work and he was on the same track as Mark. Frank's only thought there was what if Mark and Raymond were collaborating, but his gut was telling him this was genuine, and if not what did he have to lose? The farm was already considered gone as far as he was concerned and he and Louise could survive on the business back home anyway. It wasn't a big risk.

Frank had developed trust in Mark and although blunt and boisterous, he seemed very genuine, and he was a good friend when Bert was alive. He decided he would take a chance and make a counter offer as Mark suggested.

Raymond was a little nervous that the deal might fall through if the counter was seen as too much but he reluctantly agreed and they made their way back to the meeting room.

Hey Kid

Raymond stood first, shaking a little but holding himself upright and confident, as he looked straight at Cornelius Hyde. Raymond was the only black person in the room and he had experienced dealings earlier in his career with the formidable Mr Hyde. He announced that they would like to make a counter offer and quickly outlined the detail of 2 ½ %.

There was silence and Frank was expecting reasons being given why they would not accept the counter. Nothing was being said but Hyde was looking around at everyone there. Finally Frank saw Kendall give the shortest of nods and Hyde said, "Two percent and it's a deal."

It seemed like it was a play that had been rehearsed and when Frank agreed there were smiles and handshakes with all the farmers congratulating each other on finally agreeing to terms. Hyde announced "Congratulations gentleman, the documents will be with my learned colleagues by 9 a.m. tomorrow and we shall meet again here in three days."
There was now some time to spare so Mark offered to take Frank out to the old farm so he could see for things himself. Frank had expected it to see overgrown wasteland and rotting crops but he was to be surprised.
As they drove up they could see the maize was high and way to the south end the wheat fields were full.

"After the big riots those of us who came back started to make things work again. Bert's share, your share, of all this is being taken care of by Kamou's firm."

Frank looked amazed. He had no idea and if the solicitors in London had told him he hadn't understood.

They drove through the gates up to the house, which had been damaged in places. Some of the windows were boarded up with corrugated metal sheets. The stoop was still in one piece though some of the railings were missing and the front door was open behind a mosquito netting. The front room was being used as an office and was furnished with a desk, two chairs, and a filing cabinet but most of the other furniture was gone.

There was a noise coming from the workshop, someone was using an electric drill. They walked over and to Frank's amazement there was a man working on some farm equipment. It was Mfundo.

Mfundo looked up to see Frank standing there and his eyes widened to the size of frying pan lids accompanied with a mouth that opened so wide it could have been mistaken for Blackwall Tunnel.

"Mr Frank, Mr Frank you back," screamed the familiar and friendly face as he dropped the drill and ran in his hobbled fashion to greet his old boss.

Mfundo started to talk as fast as bullets leaving a Gatling gun. "How's mama Ann and miss Louise and Baby G. Are they here?"

Frank's answers weren't what Mfundo had hoped for but he was pleased beyond belief to see his old boss and tears of happiness rolled down his face as he laughed and cried at the same time.

Holding on to Mfundo's shoulder Frank turned to Mark and said in a broken voice "This man saved our lives, Mark. He's a hero."

Mark knew the story and told Frank that's why they had made sure Mfundo had somewhere to go after he healed from the injury he received that night. He also told Mark that it was people like Mfundo that they wanted to be involved with the Land Transfer. No corruption, no government buddy schemes, just people you could trust.

It all started to fall into place that week for Frank and now he understood more and he knew for sure that Mark was on the level.

Mark explained that when Kenya gets its independence and the transfer of lands goes as planned then they will be creating a new class of Kenyan, the small farm owner. Larger than the yeoman farmers in the outlying areas who supply the locals, the small farm owner would be a supplier to the syndicate Mark was talking about and a new middle class would be created.

Frank was all for it and although he would never see Mfundo after he left the farm that day he would maintain contact with him through the business for many years to come.

Back at the hotel Frank booked a phone call back to England and the next morning he explained everything to Louise and Bob and told them he expected to be on a plane back within a week.

Before attending the next planned meeting he visited Bert's grave at St. Michaels and was greeted by Father Duncan, or Father D as they called him, who he remembered well. During their conversation Father D mentioned something that came as a surprise to Frank. Aunt Ann had made arrangements a long time ago with the church to be buried with Bert when the time came and Frank had no idea of that wish.

Father D told him it had all been arranged way before Bert's death and Ann had been very generous to the church over the years. Now when it was time all Frank had to do was to get her there!

After everything they had done for him and Louise he would be sure to follow through on that wish.

The three days were up and the final meeting began. Raymond had explained everything to Frank and an expensive hour-long phone call to the solicitors in London had Frank feeling very pleased with everything.

The contracts were exchanged and a celebration lunch had been arranged. Every farmer there was relieved and happy as a new chapter had begun for all of them.

The next day Mark drove Frank to Eastleigh airfield to catch his flight back to London. He was glad to be going back home but he knew the work had only just started.

Armed with a few small gifts and carrying a bank draft for the sale of the land for £20,000 and a promissory note in the sum of £10,000 for establishing a new warehouse and office Frank was on his way home and with more money than he had ever seen.

It wasn't that long until the summer holidays when Frank arrived home but instead of time off he and Louise would be warehouse shopping. Frank wanted his dad to become a full time partner now but it meant Bob giving up his own small, but successful business. He had already taken a lot less of a role since he started helping Frank earlier and he decided it was time to take a leap of faith and join Frank in his new venture.

Back at the Rudge household Joe had written and he already knew that once again he wouldn't be home for Christmas. The good news was Rose's recovery. She was doing really well and the depressing times where she thought of nothing but losing the baby were becoming far less. She was still off work but the decision had been made that she would be off the rest of the year and return to King Edward's at the start of January term.

Rachelle and Fred were starting to feel a little more at home in their new flat, but it would never be the same as the old place.

Hey Kid

Fred said it was a house not a home but they were still together and they would be happy there anyway.

George visited them and said it was set up just like the old place, only a different view. You could see the Docks, the Glassworks, and the corner of the Iron works where Tom had worked. Rachelle's candelabra, was at the centre piece on the mantle, the old Railway clock was hanging on the wall, and their wedding photo was on the other wall above the table. Just like old times.

Penny had been doing really well at the Teachers college and she had taken Mrs Turner's advice and was learning French as well. George's visits with Penny were now down to mainly weekends with the occasional weekday evening thrown in for luck but their romance was still on a high at least.

There hadn't been many interesting cases as of late for George and he was getting a little bored with the research but there were a few fun times as well.

He got to meet Mrs Bracegirdle who came into the office every December 1st or thereabouts, to confess to the murder of her husband in 1935.

He had choked to death when he ate some of her Figgy pudding just before Christmas. She was certain it was her fault so she turned herself into the police. The Coroner's report of "Accidental Death" was not acceptable to her and she told them she had to be charged.

Finkelstein was called and even he couldn't convince her it was an accident so they held a "trial" at the office with Mr Gold as the judge, Mr Snodgrass as the prosecutor and Mr Finkelstein as the defence. She was found guilty under extenuating circumstances of delivering too much of a consumable product and given a sentence of probation. Every year since then she has turned up at the office to report to her designated probation officer, Bernhard Finkelstein!

College closed for the holidays, though Penny would spend a

lot of time studying and the office closed on December 23rd, not to re-open until January 2nd   Miss Allard would still go in almost everyday to sort the post but everyone else was given an extra break. George thought it was due to the lack of work but he would find out in a few weeks it was just the calm before the storm.

Christmas 1957

Christmas was at Doris and Nick's that year but only Fred, Rachelle, Penny and George were there for dinner.

George had stayed over Christmas Eve and had breakfast at Penny's then they caught the bus back to Russell Road on Christmas Day.
There was also a change in tradition as Penny was asked to join them at the pub for a lunchtime Christmas day pint. It didn't matter that she and George were still both underage as it was very unlikely anyone would have said a word to Nick or Fred. That just left Doris and Rachelle to do all the cooking!

Boxing Day dinner was held at the Foxton's and Frank came by to help bring the whole tribe over. Penny had stayed over but there was no crawling into bed with George that night. With two carloads they made a short journey to East Ham in just a few minutes.

Bob Foxton's house was considerably larger than Russell Road but even so with the whole family they had to bring in a few more chairs. Dinner was served and stories were being told and everyone feeling good that they were together. Aunt Ann made a toast to her nephew Frank and thanked him for all he had done in Kenya with the farm and the business and said she now knew that everything would work out very well. Not too many really knew what she was talking about but that left the door open for Frank to announce that everything had been going better than planned and he looked at Nick and said that they should talk, maybe over a glass of sherry after dinner.

It was a little bit like Victorian times as the men, Frank Nick, Bob and Fred all moved in to the front room with a glass in their hand and the women retreated to the kitchen and were left, as with the dirty dishes.
George and Penny weren't quite sure what to do as they retired to the sofa looking at each other. They sat together in silence, being the odd ones out when Penny started to giggle and then just said to George "Maybe we should just go for walk." They both felt a little lout of place so a walk was a very good idea.

In the front room Frank announced once again that things had been going very well and he looked Nick and said, "How would you feel about moving to somewhere like South Ockendon and starting a new career?"

Nick looked more than just a little surprised and wasn't quite sure what to say but before he could answer Frank told him that in two or three months they should be the owners of a new warehouse in South Ockendon and they were going to need a senior manager. They would like Nick to consider taking the position. It wouldn't be for a couple of months or so and there was a plenty of time to explain things in much greater detail.
A meeting had been planned with Mr Morley, the solicitor in a couple of weeks that would clarify everything and there would be even more surprises coming, but Frank held back on saying anything else at the moment.
Nick was quite taken aback and as he stood with a surprised and mystified look on his face Louise entered the room, looked at Frank and said, "Well, have you…?"
Frank smiled and nodded and then Louise looked at Nick and said, "Well dad, you're going to do it aren't you? Please say

yes dad, we have it all planned and you and mum will finally get what you so rightly deserve, plus you can get out of the Docks and have a really good job with a real future for you and mum."

Nick still hadn't said a word when Bob stepped in with a more understandable explanation. He told Nick just what Frank had said that they had an offer accepted on a warehouse they wanted to purchase, plus they were looking at a second one close by as well.

They company needed a manager that they could trust and as Nick had shipping experience as well as being a dock manager for the last few years they wanted him. He explained that the company solicitor was still finalising official documentation but that they expected everything to be completed early in the New Year. Plus there were going to be some radical business changes and Nick was in those plans if he wanted to be.

Nick was feeling a little overwhelmed. "I don't know what to say, there's a lot to think about. I would have to talk it over with Doris and …"

"No worries Dad." Louise was smiling as she said, "Mum's all for it. What do you think us women talk about while we are cleaning up after you men?"

It wasn't as simple as that for Nick and he told them he had to really give it some thought. "What would my duties be, what would you expect of me?

What would.....I think I need a drink!"

Penny and George returned and looked surprised as they could see lots of smiles and a lot of confusion on Nick's face as he stood there scratching his head and mumbling words like but, if, what… " I really don't know what to say."

"Here's that drink, Nick," came Fred's familiar voice as he handed Nick a triple scotch. They were all smiles but Nick was still trying to wrap his thoughts around this Christmas surprise. Eventually he told them that he would sleep on it and talk to Doris and maybe they could get together tomorrow.

"Right now I'm flabbergasted, happy, and getting a little drunk. I think I don't know what I think!" and with that he sat down, gulped his scotch and just said to Fred,"Another one bar keep."

George still didn't know what was going on until Louise explained to him that the family was going up in the world and that Nick was a hopefully going to be a big part of it. Then, sporting a big smile she put her arm around Penny and looked at George. Just like Rose earlier she said, "You had better hold on to this lady George, she's a real keeper."

Penny, just a little embarrassed, smiled and George blushed but this time said "I intend to sis, I intend to."

The next day things seemed a little clearer but Nick was still feeling he had been hit with a surprise quiz and he wasn't sure what the answers were. In such a short time Louise and Frank had made a huge success and the future for them looked better than anyone could have expected just a short time ago. Now Nick was faced with making a decision that could change things for him and Doris too.

He was apprehensive about quitting his job at the docks but at the same time so there was an amazing opportunity that may never present itself again, even if he didn't realise the full extent of that opportunity right now.

The short-term plan was to have Nick take care of the day-to-day management of the warehouse but they hadn't even discussed the long-term plans, which would be decided early in the year when all the legalities were final finished and discussed.

Hey Kid

Bob was already doing a lot of the work but to make things run really well when the warehouse was finalised he needed to be working on the commerce side of the business with Frank. The rest of the plan was to have Nick and Doris to move to South Ockendon where the operation was. He would be close to work and they would be able to get out of their smaller Victorian terraced home and move into a much nicer house in a very nice area that was only a few minutes away from the warehouse

Although it was less than 20 miles from where they were now Nick was concerned that Fred and Rachelle would be too far away from them in their old age. He spoke to Fred about it and was told not to worry and to do what was best for the future.

Doris shared those concerns but her knew her parents would not like to feel that they stood in the way of the family making a better life for themselves.

It was that one major concern that Nick brought up to Louise and Frank. Louise just looked at her dad and said, "Dad, why do you think we are looking at a four bedroomed house to go with the job? Nan and Granddad won't have to stay in that little flat too long and when they're ready you will all be in South Ockendon. no matter what granddad says. Nan's all for it and we know who the real boss is don't we. Plus if granddad puts up a fight about living with you and mum we also have an option on a nice little one bedroom flat as well. We've been doing lots of planning you know."

Then she looked at her dad with the same smile as she looked at him with when she was just a little girl and she knew that she had him just where they wanted him. He wouldn't be able to resist and the deal would be done very soon.

It had been a Boxing Day like none before but Nick's head

was still spinning the next day. Making such a big change at his age was a real leap of faith but that was the one thing he did have, faith in Louise and Frank.

He talked it over with Doris but she had already made her mind up that it was the chance of a lifetime and though she knew there was to be far more detail in the offer she was ready for the move. Nick approached Fred with the concerns he had about being further away from them his argument fell on deaf ears.

"Rachelle and me, well we've been here all our lives and not likely we'll ever move until we leave here feet first." Fred was pretty stubborn when it came to some things and it would be a little difficult to convince him to move any time soon, and he would never stand in the way of Doris and Nick improving their standard of living.

He smiled at Nick and continued, "Maybe when I pop me clogs and Rachelle is on her own, then she may be willing to burden herself on you but until then we still know how to catch the bus and the train and I can even use the telephone kiosk around the corner, so you jump at it Nick, you take that the chance the kids are offering you will find they will be very grateful as well. They need you, Nick and it will be great for the family."

Nick knew Fred was stubborn and also making it difficult to say anything except "yes." He also knew he was right and that he would never convince Fred to move, but maybe in the not too distant future Doris, Rachelle and Louise could!

Rose and Michael came over the next day and before Nick could say anything Rose congratulated him on the new job offer.

"You're going to accept it aren't you dad?" she said in an excited tone that sounded more like an order than a question. He looked a little surprised to say the least. "Bloody Hell, is this a conspiracy, did everyone except me know this was coming?"

They smiled and said nothing but as Nick had already made his mind up to accept it didn't really matter.
Almost immediately after talking with her dad Rose and Penny started to chat and George just sat there with a gloomy look on his face taking second place to his sister once again!

Nick and Michael both smiled as they saw the forlorn look George was now wearing and Nick said, "Come on son, Nan's on her way over so there's going to be too many women cackling in a bit so me and Michael are going to meet granddad at the Trossachs and talk about these conniving women. You've lost your girl for a while, let's go have a pint."
One more night at home and George was off to Penny's until the New Year. He was looking forward to that and some alone time with her and he was hoping her family wouldn't be as intrusive as the Rudge clan!

It had been a Christmas season full of surprises and life changing decisions. No one could have realised what was coming up in the New Year but 1958 was to hold a lot in store for many.

1958

George started back to work along with everyone else as the rainy New Year made its entrance. Penny would start her classes in just a couple of days as well and the routine would start all over again. This year though the whole Rudge family would be making moves like never before.

The second week in January Louise came over with the news that all the paperwork and legalities were finally completed and the solicitor, Mr Morely, wanted to meet with Frank to hand over the approved documentation and future plans.

With Ann also having an interest in the company she had discussed with Frank some of the plans and they wanted everyone who was going to be involved to be present. Ann said, "If this business was to be the success that was being predicted, everyone had to be reading the book on same page and be willing to be part of the progress."

The meeting was arranged for Saturday evening at Bob and Jane Foxton's home. Nick and Doris, Bob and Jane, Frank and Louise, and aunt Ann were all in attendance to hear what the solicitor had to say.

Gilbert Morley was an older gentleman dressed in dark grey pinstripe trousers, a black tie to match his black jacket and he was topped off with a Lock & Company bowler hat. He looked like he was on his way to a stuffy office in the west end more than an Edwardian house in East Ham.

Frank introduced him and said he had been Bert's legal advisor for many years and an exceptional help with the work that had to be done since Bert's passing and leaving Kenya.

He placed his hat and briefcase to the side of the table, pulled out some folders full of papers and wasted no time in delivering the details from the pile of documents in front of him.

He cleared his throat and started in a tone of voice that may have been expected from an Oxford lecturer. " The laws governing different types of business, registrations, international contracts and the like are very complica...."

"Stop right there, you old windbag." Ann's appreciably superior commanding voice was heard from the back of the room. Everyone was surprised, except maybe Bob who now had a wry smile on his face.

She continued, "Gilbert Morley, if you go on one of your long winded, convoluted explanations of what you think we should know and boring us with some tedious, monotonous legal jargon instead of the facts that everyone really need to hear, I swear I will stuff my knickers down your throat and pull them out the other end with a crochet hook. Brevity man, tell these people succinctly and in plain English what they need to know."

There was a tense silence, except for Bob who was going as red in the face as a ripe tomato and trying to hold his laughter in, but everyone else except probably Jane, was wondering what the Hell just happened.
After a long 10 seconds or so that felt like eternity Ann spoke again.

"Just so you all know, Gilbert and I have known each other for many, many years. He was the best man at our wedding and he is a very close and dear friend whom I trust implicitly. He is also the best corporate solicitor in London, if not the country but he is also a windbag that likes the sound of his own voice and I want to get this legal stuff over with so we can all sit and celebrate with a good drink."

Most people would have been totally embarrassed but Gilbert looked on emotionlessly and although he did not look happy he didn't seem offended either. He obviously received Ann's message loud and clear as, with brevity he explained that the laws had changed regarding international agreements and that contracts previously administered and managed by third parties were affected. There were changes in statutes that had a direct effect on the East African Trading Company that was now under Frank's control but they could now be used to the company's benefit.

It only took about 30 minutes more, with Gilbert glancing at Ann several times, to explain the pertinent details and then he went on to discuss the shareholder situation. There were two shareholders, Ann and Frank.

"Frank owns 66.7% of the company and Ann owns 33.3%. It would be possible to operate with two directors but, as I explained in brief, it's not advisable."

He wanted to give more of an explanation as to why it wasn't advisable but looking at Ann and seeing her stern look he quickly retreated from that plan.

"The situation has been remedied by Ann, who has decided to gift the majority of her shares in the company to the family in such a manner that it will facilitate the appropriate amount of directors and still leave the company in the control of Francis Robert Foxton. Should everyone mentioned be agreeable then the following will become effective.

Her shares are to be distributed in the following manner: Robert Francis Foxton, Louise Doris Foxton, and Nicholas Frederick Cumberland Rudge. You will all each receive 10% of shares."

Hey Kid

"Cumberland!" Louise laughingly exclaimed, "Where did that come from, dad?"

Nick was in a state of shock as to what was happening and looking at his daughter he just put his finger to his lips. Louise was quiet but was also fighting back her laughter and doing the tomato imitation that Bob had done earlier.

"That will give the company a very workable Board of five Directors but control will remain in the hands of the Chairman, Francis Robert Foxton. If everyone is agreeable you will sign the documents I have prepared here and they will be duly registered with the government and Minister of Trade on Monday."

Nick and Doris were both experiencing a pleasant state of shock and Nick had questions of how and why but wasn't sure how to word them so he thought it best to stay quite for a while.

Gilbert went on to explain some more legalities and time frames, as well as licencing and trade agreements but they all went over Nick's head as he was still wondering what had just happened and what it all meant.
Within time all of this new information would become general knowledge to him but for now it seemed like every fact in the *Encyclopaedia Britannica.*

Ann explained her reasoning in much simpler terms that Nick actually understood. She had given a lot of thought to what she needed to live her life out in relative comfort and her personal wealth plus her 3.3% share in the company would accommodate all of her needs. Not only would her future be assured but Bob, Jane, Frank, and Louise, and of course Georgina, were her only family now. Along with Louise's family the company would thrive and that is what Bert would have wanted. Even though Louise was one of the three of them who knew what was coming it really hit home when Ann explained it. Thanks to this woman she had only known for a few years her life and the lives of her family would be changed forever. There was no doubt about Nick taking the job now!

With the papers signed and safely in Gilbert's briefcase the evening turned to celebration as Ann produced a couple of bottles of Chateaunauf du Pape, a bottle of Moet champagne, and a bottle of single malt scotch. They raised their glasses and toasted to the future success of the company and Louise made a second giggling toast to my dad, "Sir Cumberland!" which brought a great deal of laughter.

Nick never did tell her the real reason behind his name but it was a family name given to the eldest son, so that meant Fred had it as well but in consideration of his son Nick broke the tradition and didn't pass it on to Joe. For years to come each time Louise brought it up she would hear a different story regarding the reason the name was chosen, each one more absurd than the last.

The meetings between the three "up front workers", Frank, Bob, and Nick started the next week and Nick wasn't finding things the easiest to understand. He could handle workers just fine but by his own admission he was no businessman, just a good hardworking boss. That however, worked just fine and Bob was to be a great help with sharing his experiences as well.

Frank explained to him that the third party contractor was staying on for a year under a new and different contract and that Nick's biggest task would be the warehouse personnel, organisation and distribution.

There would be offices in the new warehouse that would deal with the invoicing, records etc. Frank also explained that as they moved to be closer to work they would all get re-housed, which is where the moving to South Ockendon came in. Frank had wanted give Nick a little more information earlier but Louise said she knew her dad well and said that just a bit at a time would work best, and it did.

The directors would only be paying "ground rent" to the company, which in essence meant free housing. It was something that Gilbert had suggested, as it was legal and tax-free, though Frank, Jane and Ann would stay in East Ham for almost year before they moved.

Things were starting to change and one huge unexpected change was the small Victorian townhouse and the streets of the East End would become a thing of the past as life was changing in a way that none of them could ever have predicted.

It was March and within the next few weeks the big move would start. Nick had given the docks a months notice but Doris quit at the end of the week and now her only job would be to get busy, packing the boxes for the move. Rachelle was a big help and really excited to see them move on. So was Fred, or that's what he would have them believe. He still had a few mates kicking around but he his favourite tradition was the Sunday pint with his son-in-law. He wouldn't let tell anyone but one of the fist things he did was check out the public transport and he had every intention of making as many Sunday trips as they could. He never gave it a thought that Nick or Louise would be coming to pick them up but the future would find a way of maintaining the tradition.

With all the planning and excitement however, George just felt a little in the way. For him the travel time to work would be a little longer but not that great an inconvenience. He would be a lot closer to Brentwood as well but as Penny was still living in Mile End it made very little difference. He was happy for Nick and Doris but he was feeling like everything was moving on and he wasn't really part of the picture.

To make things worse he hadn't been seeing too much of Penny. She was either studying or helping Dorothy plan for her Easter wedding. For the last while their time together had been reduced to just one or two nights a week and the occasional Sunday.

When they were together they made the best of it as they could but George was frustrated. Work had been slow, he wasn't contributing much at home and he wasn't seeing Penny near as much as he wanted to. His only thought was that maybe he would get to be with Penny for longer after Dorothy's wedding.

Easter 1958

Easter arrived and all the planning would now be put to the test as the wedding day was happening.

On Easter Saturday the guests all showed up as expected at St Georges in the East church for the big show. Most of the office staff attended, including Mr Finkelstein and the illusive Messrs Gold, Snodgrass and the rarely seen Snead. George was dressed in his best suit and looking sharp as ever as they all took their place in the church.

A couple of minutes after 1 o'clock the organist stopped the music momentarily and then started up with the Wedding March.

Dorothy looked gorgeous as she walked down the aisle on the arm of her uncle Ed, who George had only met a couple of times before, and then his eyes met Penny's glance and smile. She was one of three bridesmaids but George was totally oblivious to the other two. All he could see was Penny, whose smile and piercing blue eyes was all he could concentrate on.

After the wedding the reception was held at the Mile End Community Hall not far from where Penny lived. George was seated at a table with his work colleagues some distance from the head table. Speeches were made, toasts were given and the food was served. With all that over the party started.
Penny came over to George after the speeches finished and the dancing started. Both she and George blushed as her Uncle Ed looked at them with a big smile and said, "Wow, look at you two. Handsome a pair as ever I've seen. Be your turn next, Penny."

They smiled at each other with an embarrassing silence. Each of them wanted to say something but with them both turning a

deep red colour and having a lump in their throats as big as a
Stonehenge rock they just danced on in silence but he thoughts
going on in their minds were the same.

At about 11 o'clock a very merry Uncle Ed came to Penny and
told her that her mum, Lil had way too much to drink so they
were taking her back to their place and would take care of her.
He told her not to worry and that they would bring her home in
the morning after she slept it off.
Both George and Penny didn't mind that at all as George was
already sleeping over but now they would be alone. They left
the party and went back to the house about 20 minutes later.

The following morning the doorbell rang at about 9.30. Uncle
Ed had brought Penny's mum home. They couldn't find her
keys, which was a good thing as Penny was still in bed with
George!

Penny rushed downstairs and George grabbed some clothes
and headed for Dorothy's room as quickly and quietly as he
could. She opened the door and let them in. She was feeling
very nervous but still managed a smile and asked her mum
how she was feeling. The first thing Penny's mum said was
"I'm okay love. I'm sorry dear I got a bit tipsy. I hope George
didn't mind not being able to stay over."

Penny's heart sank as she shook her head and said it was okay
and then she was horrified as she saw George's shoes by the
front door!
Luckily so did the very understanding Uncle Ed who moved
them unobtrusively with his foot and no one else noticed. The
give away shoes were now residing out of site under the coat
rack.

Ed then said '"C'mon, Lil let's take a weight off and
 I'll make a nice cup of tea." and they went into the kitchen
where they sat round the table and started to re-live old times

and having a laugh just long enough for the scared George to make his escape.

Penny's heart was pounding so fast that the wings on a humming bird wouldn't have matched the speed. She went to run up the stairs but George had been watching and was ready for his escape. He waved at her from the upstairs landing and then tip toed as quickly as he could down the stairs, picked up his shoes and got out of the house without putting them on. All Penny said, in a quick and quite whisper, was "Nan's café." He made his escape hastily and with shoes in hand was around the corner less than five seconds later.

With a huge feeling of relief that they hadn't been caught he put on his shoes, pulled himself together and walked to Nan's café, ordered a tea and waited in silence.

Eventually uncle Ed suggested a bit more rest for Lil would be in order and she went up to bed taking her tea and hangover with her. Ed left and gave Penny a kiss on the forehead and as she went to say something he just winked and put his finger up to his lips, smiled and he was gone.

A few minutes later Penny was at Nan's and told George what had happened then said "He'll be my favourite uncle forever!" They were both relieved as they knew how old fashioned and strict Lil was and had they been caught George could have been castrated with a pair of rusty garden shears!

They decided it would be a lot safer for George to wait an hour or so and the come over to the house. Then they realised that George was still wearing the same clothes as he wore yesterday and that Lil would catch on in no time. They decided it would be best for George just go home and not push their luck any further that day.

Lil would never know a thing about that sleep over and Uncle Ed never said a word about it.

Back at Russell Road Nick and Doris were busy packing the rest of their belongings ready for the removal van to come on

Hey Kid

Monday. Nick was thinking that six months ago he was working steady at a job he thought he would have for life and now everything had changed. The moving van had been arranged for Easter Monday, thanks to Horse Trough Harry who, of course knew someone in the business. Like Fred with his "consumables and other goods contacts" Harry had contacts in all the trades and local businesses and was more than happy to help Nick with a cash deal. Nick had given the docks a month's notice, far more than he needed to, but he wasn't one to burn bridges plus he still had a lot of mates working there and he wanted to keep in touch with them. The East Africa Trading Company may be looking for some good employees in the near future.

George eventually turned up at three o'clock to find just about everything packed and ready to go the next day. Everything that is apart from his room. Doris had given him some boxes days before and now he had just hours to fill them!

On Monday morning the van turned up with Horse Trough with Wally the Wasp in tow to help. George had managed to complete his packing and in two hours from its arrival the van was packed and ready to go.

Fred and Rachelle had walked over to give their blessings to the move on the day and Doris had told them that the new house would be all set up in the next couple of days and they were to come for the weekend. Before Fred could say either yes or give reasons why they couldn't
Nick piped in with "And no arguments. There's two pubs within walking distance and they have to be checked out by professionals."

Fred was all smiles and offered no argument as the van started to pull away. They all took one last look at number 8 in silence but they would never step inside it again. The house would stay empty for about a month before it was sold and someone moved in. Houses were becoming a very saleable commodity in the East End as more and more migrants were looking for their first home in their new country. Doris and Nick were to get £600 for the house and with only having to pay ground rent at the new house they would have more savings than anytime since they had been married.

Their new home was just a few minutes walk away from the train station, surrounded by trees to one side and a field behind them. It was far more spacious than Russell Road and was only three years old. Doris was in her element with four bedrooms, two bathrooms and even an inside toilet downstairs. It was luxury compared to what they had been living in all their lives.

With Horse Trough and company assisting all the furniture was in place in no time. All George had to do was sort his own stuff out and get ready for work the next day. Another good thing was they now had their own telephone, a luxury they thought they would never see.

The Royal Oak was to become the first pub of choice. It was an older pub, built in the early 1800's and not as busy as the Trossachs or Queen Vic but the landlord was friendly and he poured a good pint as well, which were they major requirements before Sunday dinner.

For George the longer trip would mean catching a train to Fenchurch Street at 7.30 and then a short walk to catch the same number 15 Bus he had been travelling on since he started work. The only difference on that ride was it was now only 10 minutes to Shoe Lane.

The Case of Henry Chichester-Brown

Tuesday was a new experience riding on a packed train, seeing so many different faces and finally boarding the number 15 from a stop he had hardly ever noticed before. At work Tuesday was a boring day with almost nothing happening except the sun was shining brightly outside and George was filing old documents inside.

George had been in the office for about two hours when suddenly he heard a babbling raised voice in reception. Miss Allard was covering for Dorothy, who was away on her honeymoon, and it sounded like the Boss lady may be in some distress.

George rushed to assist her but he should have known better as she wasn't in the least perturbed and was slowly but calmly dealing with the loud, almost incoherent panic stricken gentleman.

"I must see Bernhard, it's life or death, you must get him now…"

The short thin man was in a discernable state of overwhelming fear about something and had obviously dressed himself in a hurry as George noticed his one trouser leg was tucked into his sock and his shirt was not completely buttoned up. Something serious was wrong with this strange man and as George appeared Miss Allard discretely signalled him to fetch Mr Finkelstein.

Less than a minute later Finkelstein was there.

"Oscar, what on earth is the problem, man?"
"They've arrested Henry, Bernhard. He's in prison they have him locked up in the police station. There's no telling what they will do to him. He's, he's…."

Hey Kid

Finkelstein looked quite stern and concerned. This man was certainly known to him and within a few seconds he took control of the situation and the visitor calmed down just a little, at least enough to understand what he was saying.

In the calmest of voices he invited Chichester-Brown to his office and as he held the gentlemen gracefully by his arm he looked at Miss Allard and said, "Miss Allard, this is Mr Chichester-Brown, a good and long time friend. Would you kindly do me the favour of making a cup of tea for us and bring it to my office."

It seemed an unusual request, as George had never seen Miss Allard make anyone tea before but she took the request in her stride. She just nodded and the task was considered done.

Finkelstein looked at George and solemnly said, "Give us a few minutes, George then come to my office."

George waited for the tea to be ready, then joined Miss Allard and entered the office with her. Oscar was shaking in the chair as he leaned forward clutching his head in his hands.

George looked on and thought this man must have just murdered his wife or something even worse, but that thought couldn't have been further from the truth.
Miss Allard poured the tea for Oscar and Mr Finkelstein, asked if she could do anything else and with a reply of "No thank you" she simply nodded and left.

"George, Mr Chichester-Brown here needs our assistance urgently and we shall oblige him. Please call for two cars to be at the front of the building in 10 minutes. One is to take my good friend home and you will join me in the other. Bring your notepad, we are going for a ride."

On the way to the police station Finkelstein explained to

Hey Kid

George just a little of what was going on, what George considered "Need to know" at this time.

Chichester-Browns son, Henry, had been arrested the previous evening on a drug related charge and for contravening the homosexual act. He was in Knightsbridge police station where he had been held overnight and, Oscar thought, possibly beaten as well.

Finkelstein said he would visit with Henry and George would wait in the station, observe and also listen to what was being said and inconspicuously take notes.

They soon arrived at the station and Finkelstein ordered the driver to wait for them. Inside the station Finkelstein introduced himself in a very quite, calm and professional manner and informed the duty officer he was there to speak with his client.

The sergeant at the desk looked at Finkelstein and said, "We're busy, you'll have to wait."

George expected Finkelstein to berate the officer and verbalise him to a pulp but in the same quite manner he just said "Very well officer. May I please use your phone?"

The second reply was as blunt and rude as the first.
"No, you may not. There's a public pay phone in the hallway. It's there for the public to use."

His manner was sarcastic and disrespectful to say the least but still Finkelstein didn't react the way George would have expected. Instead he just said "Very well", turned and walked to the public phone. On the way he gave a wry smile and a wink in George's direction.

After a couple of minutes Finkelstein returned and stood there, motionless in front of the Police station counter.

"Now what?" the sergeant muttered but this time Finkelstein said nothing and just kept looking towards the officer. Before anything else was said the phone rang and the sergeant answered.

"Knightsbridge police station, Sergeant Hutchings."

As he listened he went red in the face and his eyes widened enough to be mistaken for hallway mirrors.

"Yes Commissioner, I will sir. Right away sir, yes sir…"

He put the phone down and took an embarrassingly deep breath before turning to Finkelstein and saying "Sorry sir, I didn't realise the case was so urgent. Please wait here and I will arrange for a room immediately for you and your client," and he took off in a hurry.
Finkelstein said nothing but George could tell the old man was pretty pleased with himself!

"This way sir, please follow me." The sergeant's manner was very much changed as Finkelstein followed him behind the counter and through the door, which said "Staff Only" on it.

Inside the room he sat at the single table and Henry was brought to him. As the officer left the room Finkelstein told him he would call him when he had concluded his session with his client and then he also walked across the room and pulled the curtains across the "window," which he was well aware of being a two-way mirror.

He spent close to an hour with Henry, who explained all that happened the previous night. The police had come to his flat and said there had been a complaint so they were investigating.

Hey Kid

Knowing he had done nothing wrong he invited the officers in to listen to what they had to say.
Almost immediately the lead officer, who showed his badge and introduced himself, started to berate him. He said little more before he accused Henry of selling narcotics and then of having unnatural relationships with another man.

Henry denied knowing anything about narcotics and refused to acknowledge his sexuality. Everyone who knew him, including his father and Finkelstein, knew Henry was a queer but Finkelstein immediately knew that there was something about this whole thing was wrong.

The police had searched Henry's flat and one of them found a stash of white powder, which turned out to be cocaine. Henry vehemently denied ever seeing it but they immediately made the arrest and took him to the police station.

Finkelstein questioned Henry further and was satisfied with all the information he got from him. He told Henry that bail would be arranged and he would be out in the next hour or so. With that he banged on the door and the officer outside opened it and let him out.

Returning to the desk he asked the sergeant for the report on the arrest and a copy of the search warrant.
Before the sergeant could answer a voice said "And you are?"

He turned to see a lean looking man who looked to be in his mid to late 30's about 5 feet 10 inches tall wearing a trench coat, a Trilbry hat and smelling of an excess of Old Spice.

"I sir, am the legal counsel for Henry Chichester-Brown and I am about to arrange his bail. And you would be?"

"Detective Inspector Farmer, and the queer ain't going anywhere. I haven't finished questioning him yet."

Hey Kid

George was still waiting for Finkelstein to blow a fuse but once again he remained calm and collected as he looked at the officer, smiled and said   " Oh yes you have Detective Inspector, without me present, you certainly have."

The desk sergeant was desperately trying to catch the attention of his colleague but Farmer wasn't looking. He was about to say something else when Finkelstein turned away and asked the duty officer if he may use the phone again. Farmer looked on in amazement as the officer readily complied. He held his finger to his lips whilst looking at Farmer, who in turn was looking like a fish in a bowl, with his lips moving and no words coming out of his mouth.

After telling the party on the phone that he was finished Finkelstein said thank you and handed the phone to duty officer.

"Yes Commissioner, right away sir."

Ten minutes later Henry was bailed and in Finkelstein's car and they were driving back to the office.

As Henry had allowed the police into his flat it could be taken in law that he had given them permission to search his premises. In court Finkelstein could get all that disallowed in seconds and told Henry not to worry about the narcotics charge at all. As for the homosexuality act there were already a lot of moves underfoot in society and there had only been a few cases even tried in the last couple of years. Finkelstein told him changes in these cases were happening very quickly and he felt that it was very unlikely that the case would even go to court.

George was feeling rather proud of his boss but would soon learn that even Bernhard Finkelstein could be wrong sometimes.

Hey Kid

Later at the office Finkelstein called his friend the Police Commissioner to thank him for his assistance but the news was very disturbing. Only a couple of hours after their conversation his good friend the Police Commissioner had suffered a sudden heart attack and had been transported to the hospital.

Deputy Commissioner Gordon Hatcher was now in charge. Hatcher, as it turned out, was an archenemy of Finkelstein from years ago and now he would have the opportunity to make things difficult for the Barrister who beat him in so many cases early in his police career that Finkelstein once told him that was as insignificant as a pimple on a duck's arse. Hatcher wasn't going to miss out on the chance of beating his old foe.

Finkelstein was furious. He thought the case was done and dusted and all that would be left was some boring paperwork, a 15 minute court appearance at most and a verdict of "Case Dismissed." This time however, it wasn't going to be so easy.

The next day Henry was served with a summons. He was charged with possession and dealing in narcotics and of contravening the homosexuality act. He was taken back to the police station and was bailed all over again when Finkelstein arrived. This time Finkelstein could feel the silent laughter trying to ooze from the grinning corners of the officers mouth's like melting ice running down his back.

Farmer greeted him with a contemptuous grin and said, sarcastically, "Nice to see you again sir."

Finkelstein remained calm and collected but inside Mount Vesuvius was almost at the point of eruption but no one could tell as he smiled and calmly replied "You too, officer."

Back at the office George was called in and asked if he had seen or heard anything when he was in the waiting room.

Hey Kid

George had made notes as instructed. He had learned that
when the boss said to do something then you did it!
The only thing of any significance in his notes referred to a
comment made when one officer said, "I see Farmer nicked
another queer. That's three of them in a year. He'll make
Chief soon."

Finkelstein sat in deep thought for a minute or two then slowly
raising his head he looked at George and stroking his chin
slowly said, as if he had already solved the case, "Methinks
some information on Detective Inspector Farmer would be in
order. I need to know my enemy's weaknesses if I am to
defeat him.

George was told to go and prepare a case file and as he left the
office Finkelstein was already picking up the phone. His
contacts were everywhere and who ever his mysterious
associates were he only ever referred to them by a single name.
The first person he called was Leonard, his contact at the
Department of Motor Vehicles. How many John Farmers
could there be in the London area who had a drivers licence?

There were seven. Four of them ruled out by age and one had
a taxi driver licence. That left two, one who lived in Golders
Green and one in Vauxhall. The first call made was to the
Golders Green and that reached a butchers shop, which left
John Philippe Farmer of number 7 Clover Road, Vauxhall
being the likeliest choice.

George was summoned back into the room and given the
information, including Farmers date of birth from his licence.
He was to go to Somerset House and obtain a birth and a
marriage certificate, if there was one, and the marriage
certificate of his parents, who would be named on the birth
certificate.
Finkelstein then called Ernie, a Private Detective whose
services he often used when he required a more "sensitive"

type information. He requested him to check out Farmer's residence, neighbours and any other relevant information on the man he was about to take on.

By 11 o'clock the following morning he had already amassed a small file on his adversary and he was feeling somewhat pleased at his speedy achievements.

When searching for the birth certificate George had discovered that Farmer was actually a twin. His sister was Danielle Marie Farmer and his parents were listed on the birth certificate as Ronald John Farmer and Marie Sabine Moreau.

Another phone call to his acquaintance Ernie had furnished Finkelstein with the facts that Farmer and his sister were registered on the voting list at the address given and had lived there since 1933.
Farmer drove a Morris Minor, was considered somewhat of a recluse by one of his neighbours. He had no outstanding debts, no pets and he had never been married. He had attended St Paul's Junior School and Lambeth Boarding School and he completed one year of university then enlisted in the Army in late 1940. He completed his service in the Military Police in 1946 and joined the police force later that year later.

There was no more information on his sister except that both he and his sister held British passports, and local Library cards and had both voted in elections.

George stood in amazement at how quickly the information on someone could be obtained, and how much seemingly private information was readily available if you knew the right people.

"Waiting for one more thing, George, then we can paint a picture of our adversary and determine our plan of action"

The "one more thing" was a list of all the arrests that Farmer had been involved in over the last five years. George had no idea how Finkelstein would get his hands on that but by mid-afternoon a large envelope was delivered to the office containing all of the information requested and it was even on Metropolitan Police letterhead!

Reading through the information brought nothing out of the ordinary came to light at first. His rise to Inspector was a little faster than usual but as he served in the Military Police as a sergeant it was understandable. Then Finkelstein started to find some more interesting records.

March 1955 arrests were made at the Arts and Battledress Club on Orange Street in the City. The club was a well-known hang out for society homosexuals. Charges were contravention of the act and lewd behaviour. That was the first.

 Reading on further similar arrests that were made over the years at known places, like the White Horse on Rupert Street and the City of Quebec in Marylebone. All the arrests were very similar, some involving illegal drugs but all involving homosexuals.
Finkelstein had confirmed the link he was looking for.
He had quickly realised that Farmer was a "Queer Basher" but now they had to prove it. He would start by having Ernie get to know Farmer's sister and see what he could find out about him from her.

Two days later Ernie came back dry. The only lead that he had was that his sister spent a lot of time in a family home in Belgium and she didn't seem to have a job. All he had found out about the Belgium residence was that it was less an hour away from Ostend.
He had also located some of Farmer's acquaintances from his Boarding school and the Military Police. His schoolmates said he was very reserved and they nicknamed him "Nobby No Mates." His Army comrades said he was a loner, very

thorough and occasionally a little on the rough side during an arrest or when breaking up a fight but he was diligent and he got results. There was some disappointment reading Ernie's findings, as there was nothing of much value that could be seen in that report.

Finkelstein was frustrated. They had been digging for weeks now and it was almost May. The case would most certainly be tried by the end of June, if not sooner. He had to get more information.

He decided to call Guy de Vent who was a friend and an international Advocate in Ostend and ask him to locate Danielle if she was in Belgium right now and in the meantime he would get Ernie to investigate Farmer's parents and try to find a crumb of something, anything, he could use. Every intuition he had was telling him Farmer had rigged the case but right now verifying his feelings was proving to be extremely difficult.

Ernie was good, very good. The next day he reported that Ronald Farmer died in 1932 when he committed suicide by jumping off Waterloo Bridge. His mother, Marie Farmer was killed in the bombings in October 1940 and Farmer wasn't known to be a member of any club or organisation, that they were aware of and he didn't appear to have any friends outside of work colleagues.

Two days had passed and they were no further ahead. They hadn't located Farmer's sister yet or any other relative or people that knew him during the war with the exception of a Mrs Morris who looked after Farmer's house during the war when he was away. It was like he was invisible in society.

Then Finkelstein received a call from Guy de Vent, which proved to be very enlightening. The Moreau family owned a small farm in Leke, a village some 30 miles south west of

Hey Kid

Ostend. The family had sold most of the farm after WWI and all that remained now was one hectare with the family house that was registered and owned by Danielle and John Farmer.

The title was changed almost two years after the war upon the presentation of the parent's death certificates and the Will of Madame Farmer to the authorities. Until that time it had been in the Moreau family name since it was built.

All that made sense to Finkelstein, as the property would obviously have been left to her children. Then Guy de Vent dropped a bombshell.

"The problem with that, Bernhard is that Mademoiselle Danielle Farmer died in a tragic accident in 1928. It appears there was a fire in a barn and she was burned to death. I have a copy of the Coroners report here that lists accidental death caused by fire."

Finkelstein sat silent trying to get the information straight in his mind. If Danielle was dead then who was the woman with her passport, on the voter's list and who was residing with John Farmer?
As if matters couldn't get any more complicated, George came to Finkelstein the next day and announced he had just received his conscription papers and was to report to Aldershot in two weeks.

"NO, not yet." Finkelstein wore a frustrated, angry look that George had never seen before and he could tell that his boss was at the end of his tether. George was left feeling very uneasy and just a little afraid!

Finkelstein's face turned a deep red, as if he had spent too many hours in the sun and after taking a deep, growling breath he said, "Go away, come back in an hour and say nothing to anyone. Anyone, do you understand?"

George answered with a rather meek "yes sir," then left the office.

Less than an hour later George was summoned back to the office.
"I've had your conscription delayed until this case is done. When we are done you won't be going to Aldershot you will be going to Portsmouth and joining the Marines. Enough of that, we have a case to work on."

George had no idea how his boss had his National Service papers delayed or why he was being drafted into the Marines but he thought it best that he say nothing so he just nodded while he waited for another command. He would just to do as he was told for now.
Finkelstein then barked out some orders to follow.
"Somerset House. Death certificates for John and Marie Farmer. Coroners reports, need those too."

He looked up at George and said, "This case has much more to it than meets the eye, George. I can feel it but cannot put my finger on it. There is something very strange afloat here and we are going to have to work very hard to break down this Detective Inspector Farmer. I can smell a rat and I don't like the taste of vermin one bit. Now go, Somerset House and be quick."

Finkelstein sat back in his chair and gazed up towards the ceiling appearing to have his eyes focused on a far away star as he slipped almost trance like into his innermost thoughts.

Suddenly he came back to reality and called Ernie again. He asked him to find out how many times John or Danielle Farmer had gone to Belgium recently and then he placed a call to Guy de Vent and told him to expect a visit.

He didn't wait for George to return and instead had the driver take him immediately to Somerset House, where he met George coming out of the building.

"I assume you don't have a passport George, is that correct?"
"No, sir, I mean yes sir it's correct, I don't have a passport."

They immediately returned through the revolving doors and re-entering the records office, they obtained a copy of George's birth certificate and returned to the car. They drove straight to the office of the Ministry of Foreign Affairs where Finkelstein had the secretary call the Deputy Minister.

Within an hour and a half George had his photo taken, signed the forms that were thrust in front of him, said almost nothing and was issued with a passport, but he had no idea what was going on. It must have been a record time for a passport to be issued but all George could think was "I'm glad the old man is on my side!"

"We're going to Belgium tomorrow, George. I need a keen pair of eyes and you may have to do some snooping of sorts."

Things were moving so fast that George thought he could probably have a go at Roger Bannister's four-minute mile. He had seen Finkelstein intense before but this time it was like he was possessed, consumed totally and focused in one direction with nothing else occupying his mind.

Somehow George had to get a message to Penny as they were supposed to meet after her class the next day. He called the college from the office but their policy was not to pass messages on to students unless it was an emergency. To George it was an emergency but whoever the old hag on the other end was, she obviously thought otherwise.
Eventually he was able to get a hold of Rose at St Edward's and after giving her a very brief explanation she said she would call someone she knew at the college and let Penny

know what was happening. For George it was a great relief and now he could concentrate on the task at hand.

At nine o'clock sharp the car picked them up and drove them to the ferry terminal at Ramsgate. The drive took almost two hours, which got them to the terminal an hour before the ferry set sail. A four hour crossing, a one hour time difference and getting through customs meant they were in the company of Mr Guy de Vent by 4.30 p.m.

Leke was not that far away from Ostend and by six o'clock they were having a coffee and cake in a small café on the main street in the village.
Finkelstein could speak French adequately but George knew no more than about three words so they conversed in English.

Guy started a conversation with the owner of the café, a short, pudgy balding man wearing a long black half apron that almost touched the floor and was so old he looked like he had been there since the building was erected about 200 years ago. He was the owner and his family had been in Leke for more than eight generations. Guy asked him about the Moreau property and if anyone still lived there, insinuating he had some interest in it.
"Oui, the mademoiselle she visit very often, two or maybe three times a year. She is very quite but she has smile always and she dress very nice."

Guy then asked him about the accident and said he wasn't in the village the week it happened. "I understood the children they play with the lantern in the barn and it catch fire."

The boy, he die in the fire. They bury 'im with the family grave at the church but only the Papa stay and Madame she leave with the other child."

Hey Kid

Now they were all confused. The father, Ronald, had stayed behind and buried the son, John but the mother left with the daughter. But John was living and was a police officer in England. Or was he some imposter who had taken the real John Farmer's identity?

Why did the mother go and not stay for her child's funeral? If it wasn't Danielle that died but some other child and why did they say it was John? So many questions but so few answers.

It was getting dark but Finkelstein wanted to see inside the property where he thought there might just be some answers. They looked around the outside but it was locked tight and unless they broke down a door or smashed a window they weren't getting in.

Guy had an idea and they drove to the local police station. He was well known as an Advocate in Ostend and some of the local police force knew him.

He told them that Finkelstein was the Farmer's legal representative from England and was assisting with some legal issues. He needed some paperwork urgently from the house but he had left the keys in Ostend so the assistance of the local constabulary would be greatly appreciated.

They didn't hesitate and they had a locksmith there with one of them in tow within an hour.

Inside the house there was little that seemed out of the ordinary as they looked through all the draws of the oak desk and the old hand carved bureau that was in the main room. George looked in the wardrobe and saw there were women's clothes hanging there but at one end there was a man's jacket, shirt, and trousers. He quietly pointed that out to Finkelstein who made a mental note of it.

Taking some worthless papers from the bureau he indicated to the officer that he had found what he came for and they were ready to leave.

Hey Kid

George took one last glance around and noticed there was a picture in a frame laying face down on the table. He picked it up and saw it was a picture of the twins only the boy had his face scribbled out.

Guy thanked the police officer for his assistance and then they drove back towards Ostend to a hotel that Guy had arranged for them.

George asked what Finkelstein had made of the picture and he replied that it was strange to say the least and then George, then said, "Did you notice that there were no pictures of other people in the house at all, no family or anything. Just the one face down and the one of the young girl in the bedroom?"

Finkelstein, as sharp has he was, had missed that and he thanked George for his astute observation.

They spent most of the following morning with Guy de Vent and they found out more about the Moreau family from his enquiries. Like many of the inhabitants of Leke they had been there for many years but between the two world wars the family had largely perished and only Marie, her sister Sophia and her brother Sasha had lived to any age to speak of. Sasha died in WWII and Sophia passed away in a nursing home about ten years ago.

Danielle was the only remaining Moreau descendant and now Guy was telling him she was possibly a man. There was something amiss but it wasn't anything obvious and was causing Finkelstein a lot of frustration.

After breakfast Guy took them back to the ferry terminal. Finkelstein thanked his friend as Guy said he would keep looking into things on that side. He wished his English colleague bon chance and bon voyage as they boarded the returning ferry.

Hey Kid

Thoughts were constantly spinning around in Finkelstein's head like children screaming on a merry-go-round, never knowing when to stop. He had a serious look about him that George had never seen the like of before and he would mumble to himself saying, "What is it, what am I missing?"

At six o'clock they disembarked, showed their passports to the officials, walked through the Nothing to Declare lane and marched straight out to the waiting car.
Finkelstein told the driver to go to the office. George's stomach sank as he thought they would be pulling an all night stint but when they got there Finkelstein told the driver to take George home and went to the office alone.

The next day Ernie produced a copy of the Wills and deeds to the house, as well as copies of the Farmer's passports and even how many times both of them had voted in elections, along with their National Insurance numbers and proof that Danielle caught the ferry to Ostend less than four months ago. He also had a second large envelope that was from the Coroners office.

As much as George was in awe at amount of information Ernie was able to obtain, and the speed he could produce it at, he would find out later in life it wasn't just who you knew that was a big help it was also what you knew about them!

Finkelstein read and re-read his notes on the case and gathered an amount of information that looked like it would have filled an encyclopaedia. He wondered if he would ever be ready for court.

George knew that this case had consumed Finkelstein. His boss still had a constant stern look about him and was often deep in thought, conversing only when he had to. He had never seen him so intense before but Finkelstein's determination was something that George thought he would like to rub off on him.

Hey Kid

Finkelstein made several more calls to Guy de Vent and he became very familiar with some of the Belgium laws, but how that could help him remained to be seen.

Finally the notice was given for the trial date. Tuesday June3rd at 10.a.m. in Court 1 of Southwark Crown Court the case would be heard.

On the day of the trial George carried a box of paperwork into court, accompanying Finkelstein who was carrying his head high with a very confident look about him. Something had happened, some thought maybe but George could see the determination and conviction in his boss. Finkelstein was fully armed and ready for the battle that was about to begin.

June 3rd 1958
The Crown v Henry Chichester-Brown

The proceedings started at 10 a.m. as scheduled. The Judge instructed the jury in their role and thanked them in advance for answering the call to duty. He then asked the prosecution and defence if they were ready and as they both answered in the affirmative the Clerk of the Court was instructed to read out the charges against Henry.

When asked for his plea he said "Not Guilty" just as Finkelstein had instructed him.

The Prosecutor was Howard Manning. Finkelstein referred to him as "Magnus Nasus", and with a nose that took up more than its fair share of his face it was easy to guess why. However, his conviction rate was very high and Finkelstein had always treated him with professional respect even though he could not bear the thought of ever losing to him.

Manning called his first witness, Sergeant Paul Butler, the arresting officer. Manning asked him to explain the events of the evening of the arrest and Butler complied in detail.

"At about 5 p.m. we received a tip-off that an illegal narcotics transaction was about to take place at the residence of the accused. I informed my superiors and three of us, myself, Constable Wright and Detective Inspector Farmer were dispatched to check on the incident."
"Upon arriving at the scene the door was answered by the accused who we informed we had reason to believe there were illegal narcotics on the premises. He denied any knowledge and invited us to take a look if we cared to do so. We entered the premises and a couple of minutes later I spotted some white residue on a counter and was sure it was the remnants of

a line of cocaine that had recently been inhaled. When questioned about it he denied having seen it before."

"As I was questioning him Constable Wright came out of the bedroom and he had discovered an envelope containing a white substance, which we believed to be cocaine. At that time we formally arrested the accused and continued our search. We found several magazines relating to perversion and containing pictures of naked men. We also found some photographs of the accused in a semi naked fashion and unnatural pose with another man. We then further arrested him on contravening the Homosexuality act and escorted him to the police station where he was formally charged."

Manning looked rather pleased with himself as the sergeant had given such a clear and concise report and sporting a smug look on his face said "No more questions your honour."

Finkelstein stood up and started his questioning of Butler.

"Sergeant Butler, do you know where this "Tip Off" came from?"

"No sir."
"And Sergeant, did you have a search warrant?"

"No sir, but as the defendant invited us in he waived the right to us having produce one."

"Please just answer the questions without adding information not asked of you and which you are not sufficiently qualified to comment on sergeant."

"Yes Sir"

"We'll let that go for now. Tell me, where was Inspector Farmer when you found your supposed line of Cocaine?"

"I'm not sure exactly where sir but he was present in the dwelling and looking for evidence, as was Constable Wright."

"The officer who found the larger amount of the unknown white substance?"

"Yes sir"

"And the magazines? What did you find and what was their content?"

"We found several copies of "Attitude" that contained stories of unnatural behaviour between men, a book showing naked images of men, and one magazine with an invite to the "Bromley Buggers Ball." All known homosexual material."

"Yes, sergeant Butler, I have seen the material but I shall not ask you again not to add your opinion to the answer."

At that time Finkelstein turned to the jury as he said, "I would like the court to record that the book showing images of naked men was in fact "Michelangelo: A study of sculptures." And the image of the naked man on the cover was that of a somewhat famous statue called "David.""

There were chuckles in the courtroom when the Judge used his gavel to silence the room and told Finkelstein not to bring theatrics into his courtroom.
Finkelstein nodded his head towards the judge and continued his questioning of Butler.

"So, to summarise sergeant Butler, you received an anonymous tip off, you deliberately flouted the law by not bothering to obtain a search warrant, and used deceit to enter the premises. Further you confiscated evidence that was found by individuals without corroborating it was in fact there before you entered the premises and you seized magazines that are available at hundreds, if not thousands, of news outlets, and even museums, across the country. In addition to all that you identified the works of one of the greatest sculptors ever known, as pornography."

Before Butler could answer Finkelstein made his final remark to him and said, "No need to answer sergeant."
Turning then to the judge he simply said, "No more questions M'lord."

"Magnus Nasus" Manning was scowling but he was still feeling confident that he would win his conviction as he called his next witness, DI John Farmer.

He asked the same questions as before and in an almost textbook rehearsed manner the answers were given and when he had finished he sat looking quite pleased with himself. He gave a complacent look in the direction of his opponent as he smugly announced he had no more questions and sat down.

Finkelstein stood up and in a calm monotone voice he started his questioning of Detective Farmer.

"You are John Philippe Farmer are you not?" he asked.

"Yes sir, I am"

"You are a Detective Inspector in the Metropolitan Police Force and you reside in London, I shall not, for obvious reasons, give the full address, and you reside with your sister with your sister Danielle Marie Farmer. Is that correct?"

Farmer looked a little concerned and surprised but he still answered, "Yes sir."

"And you have both resided there for about 25 years, is that correct?"

Farmer was starting to look very uncomfortable but once again he answered, "Yes sir."

Manning stood and objected to the line of questioning as being immaterial to the case. He asked the Judge to instruct Finkelstein to get on with the case and ask appropriate questions.

Finkelstein told the Judge that it was indeed very appropriate and he would now prove his point and was ordered to continue.

"Detective Farmer, you are now on record as saying you have lived and still live with your sister for 25 years at the same address but I have a document here that states otherwise."

Turning to the bench Finkelstein said "M'lord, I would like to enter a copy of the Death Certificate of Danielle Marie Farmer issued by the Belgian authorities in 1928 as exhibit 1 in this case."

Manning was stunned to say the least and there was a surprised silence in the courtroom that was broken by Detective Farmer saying, "No, it's not true. She's alive I tell you, she's alive."

Finkelstein continued, "I also have the autopsy reports of both Ronald and Marie Farmer as well as the police reports from Belgium on a fire in which Danielle Marie Farmer perished. They are in French but I have English translations as well."

Farmer was visibly shaken and Manning asked for a recess so that he may confer with his witness but the Judge thought it more prudent to hear this new evidence so he denied him and asked Finkelstein to continue.
"My Lord, I would like to put before the court the information in a chronological order that will show that the witness is in fact the criminal in this, and other cases, and I shall offer

irrefutable proof to support this accusation."

The Judge allowed Finkelstein to continue, but first asked Farmer, who was now clinging to the bar of the witness stand and had tears starting to roll down his cheeks, if he would care to be seated. He never answered but the Judge ordered a chair for him in which he sat holding his head in his hands and sobbed.

"In the summer of 1928 the Farmer family were visiting the Moreau family residence in Leke, Belgium. Brother and sister John and Daniele were left together to play in the barn. There was a paraffin lamp present and one of them lit the lamp but also dropped it. A fire ensued as a result and one of the children, Danielle, perished."

"The Fire Brigade and Police answered the emergency call and the child's body was removed from the scene and duly delivered to the authorities for the legally required autopsy to be performed."

"Under Belgium law at the time both parents and the other child could all face prosecution for the unfortunate death of the child. Because of this Ronald Farmer insisted that his wife take the surviving child back to England immediately so if there were any legal ramifications that may affect them and there was possibly to be an arrest it would be only him that would be charged. Ronald Farmer was protecting his family, that is why the next day Mrs Farmer boarded a ferry with her son and returned to England."

"The autopsy was quick and the obvious cause of death was severe burn injury. The funeral was arranged and that is where the first lie started. Everyone thought it was the son that had perished because Ronald Farmer, who spoke fluent French, either deliberately misled the priest or there was a remote possibly of a genuine misunderstanding."

You see, the priest's first language was Flemish and when the funeral was arranged it wasn't explained adequately to him which child had died and when the priest said it was John, Ronald made no attempt to correct him. The funeral was held and John Farmer was buried. Only he wasn't. Danielle was."

"Now I must surmise some details which will no doubt be corroborated in the next few minutes. I surmise that Mrs Farmer was overwrought at the loss of her daughter and in an altered or delusional state of mind she thought she could have both children again by dressing her son in her daughters clothes and interchanging the remaining child to take the identity of both."

He looked over towards the witness box at Farmer, head still between his hands and mumbling, "No, no, she's alive."

The court was silent in anticipation of the rest of Finkelstein's explanation and Manning was sitting in stunned silence. Looking at Detective Farmer he continued, "It must have been Hell going to school as a boy and being a girl at home. I will further surmise that this caused unimaginable problems between Ronald and his wife, Marie, which possibly led to the suicide in 1932 of Ronald Farmer. Following that unfortunate death the family moved."

"In 1933 the family relocated and for seven years life as two people continued for John Farmer and his delusional mother, but then a way out presented itself. Marie Farmer died during a bombing raid in October 1940, only it wasn't the Germans that killed her, it was her own child who is present here in the witness box."

"The body of Marie Farmer was found in the rubble of not her own home but in one of the houses behind their residence that were destroyed. The Coroners report stated that she died from a single blow to the head and the pictures show there were no marks on her body whatsoever, not even a bruise."

John Farmer escaped his matriarchal sentence by taking the opportunity of an air raid to murder his mother and plant her body amongst the rubble of the other buildings. He should have at least dressed her in day clothes, as one would have to wonder why she would be in a neighbours house some 80 feet away wearing nothing but a nightgown. The Coroners were so busy during the air raids they missed out on that detail and she became just another war victim."

Farmer looked up with an angry look on his face and with quivering lips he spat out "I didn't. It wasn't like that. She… had to…." And then he stopped.

For the defence, that was on the way to an admission and Finkelstein had truly hit the nail on the head.
"To continue, Mr Farmer joined the Army at the first chance he had after that and he was soon part of the Military Police, a position that helped him gain employment after the war. That's when the next lie started."

"Being back in the house full time his feelings of guilt started to take over and as a way of making things normal again, he started to wear women's clothes around the house. He applied for a passport as Danielle, after all there was no death certificate in England and all the other documents were in order. A library card was easily obtained and voting in the elections made Daniele very real once again.
In a very short time John Farmer had resurrected his sister. He could now also go to Belgium and visit the family home, which he did every year, leaving London as John and arriving in Ostend as Danielle."
"The final lie was born when John was out in public as Danielle and "she" found herself attracted to some of the men

she saw. For John this was wrong, feelings for another man meant he was a homosexual but how could he be, he was also a woman."

"John was now rising through the ranks as a Police officer and he used that opportunity to persecute homosexuals to prove he was in fact a man. Is that not the truth, Detective Farmer?"

All eyes were looking towards the witness box and Farmer was holding his head in his hands when, to the surprise of the court, he stood up, looked towards Finkelstein with a condemning angry look and in a much stronger voice and very different than anyone would have expected said, "Leave my brother alone you bastard, you don't know what she did to us," and then collapsed sobbing and almost unconscious onto the chair.

The courtroom was stunned as jurors and almost everyone else gasped which was followed by a deafening, eerie silence. It was like a shadowy dark cloud had engulfed the courtroom with all those inside trapped in time as they waited to see what would happen next.

The silence and looks of disbelief were broken when the Judge banged his gavel just once and clearing his throat he took charge and addressed the court.

"In view of the new information that has come to light I must first order the Bailiff's to detain John Farmer pending a possible criminal charge. In consideration of his apparent mental condition I am ordering that Mr Farmer be detained and also that a complete medical and psychological examination be performed whilst he is in custody. He is to be held under observation until Her Majesty's Public Prosecutor formulates the Crown's position in this matter and files the appropriate charges."

The judge looked to he jury and continued, "I must now declare this hearing a mistrial and I am directing Her Majesty's Public Prosecutor to make an immediate decision in the matter of the charges pending in the Crown versus Chichester-Brown."

Turning to the prosecutor the Judge put his question forward. "Mr Manning, what say the prosecution in the case before us?"

Manning was defeated and angry at being made to look so inferior. His pride was hurt that he had lost yet another case to Bernhard Finkelstein but to his credit he reacted very professionally and calmly replied to the judge, "The Crown elects not to pursue any of the charges against the accused M'Lord."

Without further ado the Judge thanked and dismissed the jury, banged his gavel for the final time in the case and said, "Case dismissed. Mr Chichester-Brown, you are free to go. This court is now adjourned."

George could hardly get his mind around the whole thing but he knew they won and that was the main thing. Dead children, a fire in Belgium, a man who was a woman who was a man who killed his own mother…Truth really was stranger than fiction!

On the way out of court they passed Acting Commissioner Hatcher who was looking far from happy to say the least. His sarcastic comment to Finkelstein was, "I suppose you're very pleased with your victory today, Finkelstein."

The response came in a quiet but firm and superior tone that carried an unmistakable air of disgust with it and a look of contempt for his advisory. "Victory? Justice was done today sir but there was no victory won. A family's lives were changed forever, even lost because a small boy and girl made the mistake of playing with matches. Victory, Acting

Hey Kid

Commissioner Hatcher, no, I think not."

Hatcher stood there red in the face, embarrassed and speechless like a chastised schoolboy as Finkelstein turned his back on him and walked away.
He despised the man and would not entertain any further conversation from a person he considered one step lower than a fool. He started walking and said, "Come on George, let's get back to the office. I think Mr Farmer may be in need of a good Barrister soon!"

Tomorrow, George thought, was a normal working day, which would probably be very mundane after the trial experience.

At about 10 o'clock the next morning George was summoned into Finkelstein's office.
Finkelstein was looking very relaxed and comfortable sat in his huge chair and after complimenting George on the work he had done on the case he said, "So, you will be off to the Marines very soon."

He didn't wait for George to speak or give a reply but he continued with his dialogue.

"Good thing, serving in the forces. A good experience and I am sure you will do splendid. I obtained your extension until the case was over but Miss Allard has brought to my attention that you still have some holidays due to you. So, here's the plan."
"You shall take tomorrow off but come in Friday for a while, we need you for a short time. Then you can take two weeks off, with pay of course. Maybe you can spend a little time with your young lady."

"You will get a letter with all the details of your conscription next week sometime. We are aware that you are in the midst of moving so I have arranged for the conscription letter to be

delivered here and I will have the driver bring it to you."
"Now, make sure you desk and room is in order and take the
rest of the day off. You deserve it., and George, thank you."

George was surprised but he also felt a little down in the
dumps. Case closed and he wasn't needed now.
He would miss the office and all the interesting people he had
met and spent two and a half years getting to know but then, he
did know the job was temporary when he started.

On Friday he came in as ordered but there was really very little
for him to do. Miss Allard had him check some files and he
also ran a package to an office on Regent Street. When he
came back from his delivery it was 11.30 and the office was
quiet with only Miss Allard talking to Dorothy who was sitting
at the reception desk.

"One more thing, George" Miss Allard said, "We're taking
you for lunch."

George was very surprised but there was nothing to say as he
followed them both to the Folly International restaurant where
Finkelstein, Sebastian, and some of the others were already
sitting at a long table and much to George's delight Penny was
there as well.

"Come on, boy. Sit yourself down next to your young lady
and have a glass of wine." Finkelstein was grinning as he
spoke. He knew this farewell luncheon was a complete
surprise but he had appreciated George's efforts while he was
there and really had a soft spot for the young man.
"Enjoy our send off, to a conscientious employee and a good
friend".

Penny smiled and held his hand under the table for a few
seconds and then she gave him a kiss on the cheek, and
whispered, "I love you."

Hey Kid

After lunch they all returned to the office and Miss Allard presented George with a black leather briefcase engraved with his initials. He tried to make a little bit of a speech but very few words came out and he stopped as he received a few handshakes and a pat or two on the back.

He stood next to Penny and Finkelstein was standing there like the cat that swallowed the canary.

"Thank you George. There's an envelope in the briefcase, a bonus you might say. I also want you to know that when your service in our Armed Forces is over there is a job here for you if you want it. Oh, and by the by we expect a postcard from time to time. Now, go and spend the rest of the day with this beautiful young lady."
Penny had exams coming soon and this was a study day, that she decided was best used in other ways and was more than happy to spend her time with George.

Back home Fred and Rachelle were visiting again and George wanted to talk to Nick. Things had been moving very fast for George and he told Nick that he was in need of some advice. They spoke a little and looked secretive as Doris asked, "What mischief you two up to then, but she was just answered by Nick in the sign language of a smile and drinking a pint of beer. A few minutes later Nick and Fred went of to the pub and George went for a short walk with Penny.

They sat on an old bench not too far from the pub and George held his head a little low and quietly said, " I have to go away soon Penny and I'm really going to miss you."

Penny looked just as sad when he said that and she told him that she would miss him too. "With luck yyou will get some ggood leave and bbe home lots of weekends, George. I really hope they don't ssend you overseas though."

Hey Kid

The thought of not seeing Penny for a while was quite
depressing but there was nothing to be done. For both of them,
two years seemed like forever but time would go by fast, so he
hoped.
"Penny, when my two years is up I have to think about a real
job and I was thinking of taking Mr Finkelstein up on his offer.
It would be a really good opportunity, don't you think?"
Before she could answer he said, "I was thinking something
else as well."
The silence of ten seconds seemed like an eternity as he looked
at Penny and said, "After my two years, when I'm back
permanently, will you marry me?"

Penny's mouth dropped, her blue eyes opened wide and filled
with tears and for a second or two her vocal cords froze. She
was shaking and it was like the butterflies now inhabiting her
stomach were all trying to escape at once.

"Yyyes, George, I will, Yes, Yes, Yes"

She giggled, laughed, hugged and kissed him and shook with
delight.
George was over the moon himself and then he told her he had
actually asked her mum's permission to ask her earlier in the
week and today he talked to his dad as well who gave him his
blessing too.
"My mum doesn't know yet," he said, "Only my dad and your
mum…er, and Dorothy!"
"This is my Nan's ring, Harriet my dad's Mum. My dad gave
me this when she died and he just told me if there was anyone
in the world it would be perfect for, it would be you."
Penny's eyes were full with tears of joy as she said,
"Tthis is the bbest ring ever, George, from the bbest man
I could ever love."
A few more minutes passed as they were both feeling more
than very pleased with themselves and then they walked to the
pub. George poked his head in and gave the thumbs up to

Hey Kid

Nick who instantly slapped Fred on the back and pointed towards George. Fred beamed a big smile. He didn't need telling anything. The old man knew instantly what was going on by the grins on everyone's faces and after the congratulatory hugs and handshakes and obligatory drink they all marched back together to the house.

Doris was more than a little frustrated at the lack of assistance and still busy sorting the kitchen cupboards when they walked noisily in. She was about to say something rude to them for taking so long when Penny said, "Hi Mum."

Doris starred for a second and then noticed Harriet's ring. She dropped the two plates she was holding and hardly noticed as they broke into a thousand pieces, stepping through them to give her daughter-in-law to be and her "little" boy a huge motherly hug and started babbling like a six month old child.

Just like Penny, Doris started to cry and laugh, giggle and smile as well. Rachelle walked in to see what the commotion was all about and Fred just held his hand up and pointed to the ring finger. The party was complete and there was now a third woman with a huge smile and tears!
Nick looked at, George with a smile and shaking his head and said, "Might have been easier to elope!"

On Sunday morning the house was full. The "Rudge Family network information service" had worked wonders and everyone had received the news.

Later in the afternoon back at Penny's house it was no different, with Penny's mum and Dorothy already making the wedding plans more than two years in advance!

George took his two weeks holiday, during which time a letter from the office was hand delivered to him and had taken the time to mentally prepare himself for the next stage of his life.

Hey Kid

Penny settled down after all the excitement and was steadfastly dedicated to her studies and preparing for exams. She would have one more year at Brentwood College and was hoping to be working full time by the time George got demobbed.

George had opened his bonus envelope earlier to find a cheque for £100, almost six months wages.

Finkelstein included a hand written note and thanked George once again for his diligence and his excellent service. Finkelstein had also told Fred that George had a good future and he wanted him to return to the firm when he completed his military service, and that there were lots of opportunities for a man of his qualities.

Louise had told Nick that she had wanted George to be part of the company when he came back from the Marines as well. She was still looking out for her baby brother and George would have some good career choices to make, but not for a couple of years. He could see how bright the future looked but he didn't know what he would do when he returned from National Service, apart from marrying Penny. But now he was a young man who had matured so much since those miserable school days and he was confident that whatever the future held he and Penny would succeed.

The scruffy, troublesome, mischievous kid from the East End who hated school, the prankster and class clown who caused pain and suffering to many of his unsuspecting teachers and who had no idea where he was going in life, had finally grown up.

Hey Kid

About the Author

Stephen Williams was born in the East End of post war London where he spent his childhood. In adult life he has written and delivered academic courses for NGO's around the world and has been an Advocate and Public Speaker on the topics of Burn Rehabilitation and Reintegration for the Disabled at conferences and forums on every continent. Now retired he is pursuing his favourite pastimes, spending time with family and writing.

This story was drawn from his personal East End experiences, stories from his childhood and a vivid imagination. This is Stephen's first novel.

Made in the USA
Columbia, SC
23 December 2017